# THE
# METH
## CONSPIRACY

# THE
# METH
## CONSPIRACY

J.E. HORN

Order this book online at www.trafford.com
or email orders@trafford.com

Most Trafford titles are also available at major online book retailers.

Printed in the United States of America.

ISBN: 978-1-4669-4028-4 (sc)
ISBN: 978-1-4669-4027-7 (e)


*Trafford rev. 09/06/2012*

 www.trafford.com

**North America & international**
toll-free: 1 888 232 4444 (USA & Canada)
phone: 250 383 6864 ♦ fax: 812 355 4082

# DEDICATION

This book is dedicated to those who are currently dealing with the horrors of meth use and meth addiction. Whether you are an addict, a friend or a family member, or in law enforcement please know you are always in my thoughts and prayers. You are not forgotten.

# THANK YOU(S)

First and foremost I must thank my wife Stacy; because she told me too (kidding). She has put up with this writing hobby and fantasy stuff far longer than any sane person should have too. I love you babe.

Second, special thanks to Jason, Lisa, Rich, and Tish who were the first people to read what would eventually become this book. Thanks so much for your words of support and encouragement.

Finally, thank you to my two little helpers: Justin and Morgan. Whenever I was taking myself too seriously you reminded me that there is room in the world for J.R.R. Tolkien, Dora the Explorer, and Sponge Bob.

# In Loving Memory

In loving memory of my mother, who taught me to love books in all their shapes and forms. She showed me the wonderful worlds that could be accessed with a public library card. I miss her every day.

# PROLOGUE

"Sorry, Sir. You need to wait until we can confirm."

To say that Doctor Simms was irritated was an understatement. He held the clipboard in both hands and barely resisted the urge to violate the Hippocratic oath by slamming it into the agents face. Taking a deep breath, he calmed himself.

*My fault I forgot the I.D. Badge.*

"Sir, if you could look into the camera? A little higher? Thank you, Doctor Simms, you may step through."

Giving the agent a terse nod, he stepped through the doors. On the other side, another agent was sitting at the front desk alongside the receptionist. Sally Hughes was a plump brown haired mother of four who always had a smile for anyone who walked through the door of the Severe Trauma section of the hospital.

"Morning, Sally."

"Morning Doctor. All well on the front?"

It had been their private joke for the past three weeks. A bad one, given the circumstances, but humor, even bad humor, could sometimes take the emotional sting out of a horrible situation.

"All is well, private. Carry on."

*Horrible. That is a good word to describe the past few weeks.*

As he walked down the brightly lit corridor to his destination, Simms involuntarily shook his head. It was so hard for the community to come to grips with what had happened. Last year was the shock of a federal investigation that revealed a huge methamphetamine drug ring that was operating just miles from town. Added to that was the revelation that several members of the community, including members of the sheriff's office, knew about it and had been taking bribes to keep things quiet.

Methamphetamine. Crystal Meth. Ice. Crank. It was the drug that had swept America. Such an epidemic that two in ten high schoolers are users. Such a political and social nightmare, that the recently elected president made it her political platform and mission to battle meth with all the resources of the federal government. Her first act as leader of the nation was to enact legislation for the formation of a new federal bureau; the Methamphetamine Control Agency; the MCA. Made up of members from the FBI, CIA, DEA, and a crop of the best young legal prosecutors in the country, it was the spearhead in this new war on drugs.

Even a small town like Hopes End had received funds for a Meth clinic. Currently, there were over twenty individuals receiving treatment; normally that was a large number considering the size of the town. Not so amazing considering the fallout from the Milza brothers being caught and incarcerated. With the two Meth lords behind bars, addicts had begun to come out of the wood works seeking treatment. Many had been runaway teens and sent back to their families. Others had stayed in town to seek comfort and try to get some normalcy back in their lives.

Coming to his destination Simms was surprised to hear voices. With a nod at the MCA agent guarding the entrance, he gave a gentle knock and slowly opened the door. The room was dimly lit and contrasted harshly with the illumination in the hallway.

Old Doc Lotts peered up from his chair next to the bed. The round bulge of his stomach belied the thinness of his limbs. In contrast, Simms himself was slim; almost to the point of being gaunt. An avid runner, he privately disapproved of Doctor Lotts' disregard for his own health; the man was losing days of his life for every minute he let his body go.

However, Lotts was also the hospital chief of staff and could enter any room in the hospital he damn pleased; still, Simm's felt he should have been informed of any discussions occurring with the patient. The conversation stopped as he stepped quietly into the room. The bed's occupant turned a bandaged face away and pretended to look out the window. Out of habit, Simms moved to check the IV bottle; seeing it was almost full, he sighed out loud.

"John, you are supposed to use the morphine for the pain. Just push the damn button."

No response. Grabbing the other chair in the room, Simms joined the strange couple; he could not help feeling as though they were dealing with a stubborn child who refused to take his medicine. Simms took a slow breathe and reminded himself what the man had gone through.

He remembered when Jonathan Champion had first arrived in town. A cocky, self assured federal prosecutor who had swept in and almost immediately zoned in on the most sought after single woman in town; Rebecca Jones. Even Simms had to admit that she was hard to ignore. A dark haired beauty who's racial makeup seemed to be part Caribbean part damn sexy. The only thing that outshone her looks was her cooking. Damn that woman could cook. His own wife had taken her cooking class and Simms was a happier man for it.

In the back of his mind, in the pit of his soul, Simms quietly admitted that he had been somewhat jealous of Champion. The man seemed to be chosen for success by some higher power; the "Golden Boy" the press called him. Before the chosen one's arrival, Simms could reasonably think of himself as the most interesting person in town. His ivy school education seemed to wow and dazzle many of the local yokels; but nothing could compare to the attention the MCA's bright star had brought to the backwater community.

Doctor Lotts cleared his throat; seeing that he had Simms attention, he nodded towards the patient,

"Doctor Simms, John and I were just talking about a few things. He has a request. I told him that as you are his treating physician it would be your call."

Simms leaned back in the chair and folded his arms; waiting. A few ticks of the clock and still the man looked out the window. Keeping his eyes on the back of his head, Simms said,

"Doctor Lotts, since you are serving as official translator today, could you please tell Mr. Champion I would be happy to consider his request on two conditions. One, that he turn around, face me, and ask me himself; second, that he use the morphine at least four times a day. Do those two things and I will consider any request he might have."

Feeling more like a high school principal trying to make two star pupils cooperate than a chief of staff, Lotts simply pleaded,

"John, please."

With a grunt, the man turned toward the doctors. Half his face was completely covered in thick white medical bandages; their edges a bit frayed and red; Simms's made a mental note that he needed to check with the nurses about having them changed. He noticed with barely disguised irritation that the patient had ripped a small hole in the coverings so that the injured eye was discernable; an angry burned thing that had a white film beginning to cover it.

Ignoring the damaged bandage, he pointed a hand at the IV bottle, with elicited another grunt from the patient.

From beneath the blankets the man produced a wireless box resembling a small garage door opener. Pushing the box's red button, he leaned back on the pillows, the effects of the morphine almost immediately working; deadening and relaxing at the same time.

Satisfied, Simms said,

"Now, Mr. Champion, what is it that I can do for you?"

"Take these bandages off."

The voice was raw; and not just from the fire scorched throat. Painful emotions could almost be felt in the air with each forced word. Simms placed his clip board down gently on the bed. As a doctor he recognized that he did not have a very warm and cozy bed side manner and often had to be careful with impulsive remarks. In his most compassionate voice, Simms began,

"John, the damage needs to be covered by the medicated bandages; any exposure, especially to your eye, at this stage could be severe . . . ."

He was interrupted by Doctor Lotts placing a hand on his shoulder. Repressing the urge to shrug it off, Simms turned and said,

"Doctor Lotts, perhaps you can explain to the patient my experience in severe burn trauma? That he could lose all potential functionality in the facial muscles? Not to mention potential infection which may occur regardless of our precautions?"

As he spoke, Doctor Lotts had quietly gotten up from his chair and stood next to the rooms light switch.

"I did all of that, Doctor Simms. However, John indicated that he did have some functionality. John, if you could please close your left eye. I am going to turn off and on the lights. I want you to tell me when they are on and off."

Nodding, John closed his eye.

Off the lights went.

"Off"

On the lights.

"On"

Off the lights.

"Off"

On again.

"On"

Sitting back, Simms was amazed. He had been watching the patients' reactions to the light and it seemed genuine. Ignoring Doctor Lotts as the man returned to his chair, he leaned forward almost reverently, straining to see past the white ripped bandages to the eye beneath.

*He can see with it.*

# CHAPTER ONE

*The gas fumes made the world into a hazy picture. Fire burned flesh to a sticky sweetness; he could feel the bones in one hand give way to the heated pressure. Bones cracked; metal fumed; he could not breathe . . .*

Waking up, the sound of the phone sounded shrill after such a dream. Breathing had slowed, and he swallowed a painful lump down an itchy dry throat. The same dream he had been having for over two years now; every time he closed his eyes, it waited to find him. Lying back in bed, he could feel his body sticking to the sheets after the nightmare. The sweat quickly cooled, causing a shiver of goose bumps as he reached for the annoying phone.

"Hello?"

The voice sounded dry and cracked.

"John? Is that you?"

A mind still muddy from sleep, it took a moment to place the voice.

"Sue?"

A female voice chuckled.

"That's right, pretty boy. Long time, eh?"

The pretty boy comment made him pause. It was an old nickname.

"I'm not interested."

"John, just hear me out. There is this new shit in the schools now. Crazy stuff. We have no idea where it came from. We need . . . ."

"Sue."

He had to stop her before she got really worked up.

"No thanks."

A pause on the other end, then,

"God Damn It, John! You can't just give up! We need you! I . . ."

The click of the phone hanging up sounded loud in the quiet of the morning. Sitting there, he quickly took in the contents of the bed room. Empty liquor bottles vied for supremacy with cheese crusted pizza boxes and old take out menus. The room would be allowed to slowly pile up with waste and debris until it resembled a mini-land fill.

Then he would spend an entire day, cleaning it, vacuuming, and sanitizing the crap out of it; an intentional mess to give him something to do; to give him one day with a purpose. *Pathetic.*

Sue was disappointed. She could only see what he had once been. Not what he had become. Best if she just forgot him. Best if the world would just forget him.

SHE CAME out of the glass door in time to see her son talking with a tall man wearing a trench coat and a dusty cowboy hat. With a sigh mom quickly attempted to intervene and save the poor man from Tommy's cascade of questions. At her voice the man turned his head toward her and for an instant her heart quailed at the sight. Seeing the look on her face, the stranger nodded a farewell, and patted the boy on the head in passing.

The figure moved silently passed her, keeping to the shadowed part of the sidewalk. She waited until the retreating back approached the corner, and then knelt down to look her son in the eyes,

"Did he hurt you?"

Snorting at his mother's constant fear for his safety, which usually kept him from having all sorts of fun, Tommy replied,

"Naw, Mom. I just asked if he was going to a Halloween party. He said his name is John."

"Oh, Tommy." Her tone told him he had done something wrong. Hurriedly he explained,

"But he laughed and said he had been going to the same party for three years now. Can we go to a party this year, Mom? Maybe John would let us come with him? You should have seen his mask, it was really cool."

Jonathan Champion grimaced at the conversation occurring behind his retreating back. He liked the boy. Reminded him of Sam. Of course, most boys did.

He noticed that as people passed those who knew him or of him, most gave a wide berth. Some of them looked like they were afraid to catch the bad luck that his passing might bring. Others looked at him in disgust.

*They should see my bedroom.*

Still others looked upon him with pity. These were the ones that he privately scorned the most. Disgust and fear he could take. It would fuel his anger; give him much needed juice to get through the day. Pity was a weakness that gnawed when it found him; it left him open and vulnerable.

As the walk continued he noticed his reflection in the store front windows, most of them dark and closed for the night. Out of the corner of an eye, he could see that the setting sun and the warped glass showed the blurry image of an almost normal man. A bit on the scrawny side, which made him look taller than his six foot three inches, but a normal man. Unblemished. Unscarred. He always tried to avoid looking at reflections of the right side of his face. Best not to see the damage to dwell on the past.

Watching the startled, frightened or oblivious faces-there were many oblivious faces, though the town was small-that passed around him, he wished he could be sure that the coat collar covered up most of the damage. But the nerves in his face and neck seemed only barely alive, though the doctors had made assurances that some feeling may return in time.

He placed the horror that was now his face between himself and the world. Now, as people who had at one time asked about the criminals he had put away recoiled from him as if he were an infectious leper, he felt a deep pang of loss. Quickly he strangled that, before it could shake his resolve.

He was nearing his destination, the only place where he felt comfortable showing his face besides at home. The building came into view three blocks ahead; RedTree Pharmacy. A scarred and faded sign swung from a rusted pole with the picture of an Indian Chief smoking a pipe still barely discernable. He was walking the three miles from his homestead in order to get more ointment for his scars. Of course, he had asked that it be delivered, but the red man had refused to drive out to the farm.

*Damn, Injun! Who does he think he is?*

*A friend*, said a quiet voice.

The voice quietly reminded him that while John had been receiving treatment from his injuries, Ben had driven out to the house on Tattered Lane twice a week to check on the place. To make sure none of the neighbors were being too neighborly he had explained later. Giving the voice a mental shush, he trudged on.

Now he strode past the courthouse, its gray columns looking straight and proud of the burden of law and justice-the building where he had once been welcomed and honored; where once he had fought with razor sharp words like a well trained gladiator. He had put away some of the most notorious drug dealers and criminals in the country. Hope's End had never had a federal prosecutor to match him.

The "Golden Boy" the local news had called him after the Milza brothers had been found guilty. He had been the toast of the town. The memories were just those now, memories. That life was gone. Gone in a pile of dripping gasoline and flesh burning metal.

John crossed the front of the department store and through the glass he could see a group of young women browsing the cheap jewelry. He could see the curvy outline of their hips and thighs through faded jeans and he felt an involuntary tightening in his throat. Those were curves for other men to caress. While his sexual capacity had not been affected by the accident, he had not been with a woman other than Rebecca for four years; had not wanted another.

A passing car's exhaust fumes bring a chemical smell to the air. Like a bad pipe dream the fumes bring back memories that wash away any thoughts of sex; of a dark den of a lab out of some mad scientist's imagination; a nightmare of rubber tubes, chemical flames, and human misery; and the face of Timothy Dall. Slowing the pace, he sees again in his mind's eye the young teenager's gaunt face, eyes red with exposure to the airborne methamphetamine smoke.

An addict, Tim weighed barely one hundred pounds when Jonathan first met him. The boy's teeth had been corroded black and yellow from meth use, and the local dentist had been forced to pull every one of them. At eighteen, he looked fifty. Tim had been lucky in turning himself in to one of the few county police offices that were not on the Milza brother's payroll.

As the youngest member of the President's new Methamphetamine Control Agency, the MCA, John had been sent to interview the young man. Most of his superiors had thought the lead was a dead end. Just another whacked out teen. And they had sent Jonathan Champion to the rural Kansas town of Hope's End. How wrong they were.

Jonathan Champion, at thirty one, was thought by many to be too young to be applying for a position with the MCA. However, youth and guts is what the fledgling agency was at that time looking for; individuals with prosecution experience to become the hound dogs after meth production. The youngest MCA member to be given full agency prosecutor status, his first assignment was Hopes End, Kansas.

Hopes End. While the county seat of Buckle County it was still a backwater by any city slickers definition of the phrase. The local authorities had in custody a teenage meth user by the name of Timothy Dall. Tim claimed to be a cog in the machine of a huge meth operation. As the youngest prosecutor, with the freshest legs John was given the most likely dead end lead.

Hopes End would be the biggest investigation for the MCA in the first years of its existence. It would propel Jonathan Champion into the glaring lights of fame and gain him the adoration of the public. The investigation led to the arrest of the Milza brothers, Ordoza and Orlando, who were just as Timothy Dall had claimed; operators of the largest meth production facility west of the Mississippi River.

The brothers, exiles from Columbia where they had run afoul of the cocaine lords, had started up shop in Hopes End. Being rural enough to discourage federal attention, yet close enough to highway 37 which led to the west coast, the brothers had over one hundred workers made up mostly of runaway teenagers, illegal immigrants, and drifters.

The Milza's had either cowed or bribed most of the local law enforcement into either looking the other way or cooperating in the operation. Most of the poor souls working the meth lab were addicts themselves and were paid in just enough meth to keep them working to support their habit; but never enough to leave the brothers for long. The Milza's would be placed in federal prison for life; A lesson to all those who marketed meth.

Champion had made his mark. He just had not understood the possible consequences. He had found out how vulnerable he was. And those he loved. Which is why, three years after his time in the sun, Jonathan Champion was walking down the main street of Hopes End, alone in the darkening day. His thoughts switching back to his current situation, he lowered his head and quickened the stride. Blocking out the useless memories of a life gone forever, he concentrated on the matter at hand.

*Ben could have come out to the house. Who does he think he is?*

He fumed again to himself as his boots kicked dusty follicles into the dead air.

*A friend.*

The tiny voice inside said again. Snorting at this, John ignored his quiet conscience and continued making way towards the store. His anger building with each step, he opened the shop door and gritted teeth at the jingling bells which announced his presence. The piece of his mind that he was about to give to the shop's proprietor clicked back into place when he saw Ben had company.

While Benjamin Redelk had never had air conditioning, *didn't believe in it* he would say when asked, the store always seemed a place of cool and quiet. A puddle of safe seclusion; such a place of peace and solitude that John did not consider Ben could have company.

Welcoming door bells faded into the quiet store room air. John found himself facing the wide shouldered Native American and a woman in her late twenties. Sandy blond, she had a light sprinkle of freckles across her nose, and grey blue eyes. Short yet slim, she regarded the tall stranger with a curious look.

Looking up from leaning on the counter, Ben nodded nonchalantly towards his obviously fuming friend. No one intimidated Ben Redelk, not even the dark and shady Jonathan Champion whom most townsfolk whispered had gone mad after the explosion. *How could a man not? They* would often say when the subject would come up.

"John" the big Indian said in greeting.

"Meet Lisa McCall. She is the new county prosecutor; just started today."

Stepping forward, as if on queue, she held out her right hand,

"Mr. Champion, it is a pleasure to meet you. It is nice to finally put a face to the legend."

Unconsciously, he pulled the collar up further over his nose and tucked the right hand closer to his body. Sucking in a painful breathe, he met her friendly stare over the starched collar, then, without a word strode to the back of the shop, quietly shutting the store room door behind. Closing his eyes, he breathed in the smells of floor cleaner and dried foods that filled the small space. *Calm down! She did not mean it. Did not know. Right hand! Face!*

In the days before his marriage, he would have had many words for the pretty attorney. But that was before . . .

*Rebecca . . . Sam . . . .*

He felt himself slowly drowning . . . falling . . . . memories . . . *dangerous . . .*

"John."

A deep, yet quiet voice woke him; A friend's voice.

"John."

Again the voice, this time concerned. Opening his eyes, he saw Ben Redelk's worried expression regarding him from the storeroom doorway.

Looking at his friend, he wanted to be angry, wanted that fury that was his to command just moments before. John wanted to be able to shout and break something. Instead, all he could do was croak out,

"Why?"

Sighing, Ben held the door open and motioned that his friend should come back into the now empty store. Leading him to the old dentist chair, the plainsman set to getting ointments together as John took off his jacket and hat and settled down on worn leather cushions. The smell of pine cones, tree sap, and ben gay filled the little shop. Ben's special ointments were always a mixture of traditional Native American remedies and modern medicine. As he began to apply the cool cream to twisted flesh, Ben finally answered,

"Why did I engineer your meeting with the young Ms. McCall? Why, because she wanted to meet the mysterious Jonathan Champion. She claimed to have read something you wrote in some law journal."

Turning now to look at his friend, John cocked his one remaining eyebrow. Having covered the right side of his friends face with the thick greenish white cream, Ben continued,

"Oh yes, she was quite interested in meeting you."

Grunting in response to the last comment, John laid back further in the chair as strong hands began to rub the cream into his right arm. Brown skin contrasted with red scarred flesh as it relentlessly kneaded feeling back into rough skin. The effect was both painful and relaxing. Closing his eyes, John replied,

"I am damaged goods, Ben; Nothing worth having here."

"Bah, don't try this sorry for yourself shit with me, Johnny boyo."

Grabbing another glob of cream he slapped it on as he continued his ministrations; like a sculptor with a slab of difficult clay.

"You act like you hold a monopoly on grief and loss; the only man to have felt pain. You think Rebecca would have wanted you to be like this? Are your actions making your son proud as he looks down from heaven to see you this way? To see his father wasting the life left to him?"

Only Ben could talk to him this way. Only Ben could mention his wife and Sam and not make him turn cold and distant.

"Now the hand John; Flex your fingers as far as they can go."

Doing as he was told, John looked down on his right hand, still having trouble believing it was his. Two years of treatment rehab and three operations had given back to him its use. While functional, the arm, from the elbow to the remaining tips of his fingers, looked like something out of a science fiction horror film. Warped and scarred flesh seemed to twine up the fore arm like evil vines. Red and white blotches covered the skin, hair would no longer grow on the surface, and half of his nerves were dead and numb. Only two of his four remaining fingers had finger nails and these twisted at odd angles. The doctors had told him to be thankful one of the four was his thumb.

As was his practice, Ben would begin with the face, then turn to the arm, and then back to the face after the ointment had time to soak in. Closing tired eyes, Jonathan could feel the skin on his face loosen a bit as the cream did its work. Continuing on the arm, Ben spoke.

"You have been given life, John; for a purpose; for a reason. You need to spend your time trying to find out what it is, not waste it away out on that empty farm."

Unwillingly, the corners of his mouth twitched in an almost smile. Ben was getting into his lecturing, and it was funny to hear the beefy Indian sound like nothing more than some uptight professor talking ethics.

Seeing the almost smile, the professor said,

"Yes, laugh at me if you want. But as a friend, I must tell you what comes from my heart. Now that I have your attention, Ms. McCall . . . ." and now began Ben's well rehearsed speech on the wonderful qualities of the pretty Ms. McCall.

She was the third woman he had tried on John in the last year since returning from his hospital recovery. With the sound of a friend's voice and the feeling of life being rubbed back into his scarred body, John felt more relaxed and content than he had in quite some time. Closing his eyes for only a moment, he drifted off . . . .

Startling awake, for a moment he did not remember where he was . . . feeling the dentist chair underneath brought him back. Stretching, he rubbed his face which felt better than it had in some time. John noticed that Ben had removed his boots and left a note asking him to lock the store with the key behind the counter. Ending with a good night the note also requested that he bring the key back with him the next morning; another attempt to get him back into town for an accidental meeting with Ms. McCall, no doubt.

Grinning in spite of himself at his friend's unwillingness to give up, John slipped his boots on and stood up. Reaching for the dusty hat and . . . there he was. He had forgotten the large mirror Ben kept behind the dentist chair. Just staring at the reflection . . . what looked back was a nightmare; some creature trying unsuccessfully to pass as human.

The left side of the face showed a ruggedly handsome blond haired man in his mid-thirties with a hazel eye, smooth skin, and a bit of stubble. Moving to the right side, just passed the intact nose, from the cheek to his ear, was just a web of skin gone bad. The fire had made the right side look like a wax mask that had melted but had not quite dripped off his face.

Since he had returned to Hope's End he had removed all of the mirrors at the farm house, even put non-reflective glass in all of the windows to avoid reflective moments like this. What was most startling of all, what the doctors called unexplainable, was the right eye. Almost a pure white, it gazed at him through the mirror like a hard boiled egg with attitude. Against all medical explanations, he could still see clearly out of it. Every now and then one of his doctors would call and try to convince him to participate in a study regarding his eye and its continued use.

*Yeah, I've got that going for me.*

With a final look at the monster in the mirror, acknowledging it with a nod and a tip of his hat, John locked the store and started the three mile hike back home. The air was damp and a brisk wind had taken up. Felt like tornado weather.

TORNADO ALLEY. That part of Kansas that drew the raging killers like bees to honey. In his short time in the dusty town John had seen seven twisters, one even skirting the edges of town. None of those compared to the one that greeted him suddenly as he walked up the creaky porch steps of his home. At least one hundred feet tall, the massive whirlwind filled the yard. Whipping wind tore at his jacket and exposed the damaged arm. Dirt and grass stung his eyes as they were caught in the giant's fury.

He and Rebecca had purchased the three acre homestead just after getting married. It had belonged to an old widower whose family had made the decision to put him in a rest home. To call it a fixer upper was being kind.

Besides a new roof and plumbing, the old barn and equipment shed had to be torn down. These made way for Becky's greenhouse and garden. While a chef by trade, she was determined that her husband, and later both hubby and son, would eat healthy. Healthy meaning vegetables; and still more vegetables.

While nothing edible now grew in the over grown garden, he had kept the green house relatively up to specks. The door worked and the glass was clean enough to see through. Sometimes he thought he could hear Rebecca's voice floating from the greenhouse as she hummed and worked the tomato plants. Memories of his own laughter as he watched Sam try to get small chubby hands on the cultivated greens contrasted sharply with this current predicament. As if it could hear his thoughts, the windy giant moved towards the greenhouse.

"Wait. Stop!"

Not understanding what he was doing and vaguely aware the voice that just yelled was his own, John suddenly found himself standing between the windy terror and the sacred greenhouse. Trembling, and feeling courage hanging by a thread he pleaded.

"Anything. Anything but the greenhouse. Take the house, the garden, but leave the greenhouse."

His words seemed to float before him in the windy evening. As if considering the offer, the twister paused, the wind died a bit, as if reflecting. Knowing he should be alarmed at the things apparent ability to understand his words, John shoved that into the back of his thoughts as he concentrated on saving the greenhouse.

As it continued to pause, John had a chance to study the strange anomaly more closely. Unlike most twisters, which looked like a funnel of badly packed air and debris, this thing was tall and lean, and almost purely white. While its winds did dig up earth and vegetation, no debris marred its surface. It was pure air, tightly compressed. What the hell was it?

As if its decision had been made, the twister continued toward the greenhouse.

*Think. Damn it, think! You used to be quick on your feet!*

"Me! Take Me!"

Waving his arms widely he approached the wind monster. That was the only thing that he could think to name it. Again it stopped, a few feet from the greenhouse; this time seeming to lean towards him. Trying to fight the buffeting winds that threatened to knock him down, John heard a whispery, almost breathless voice.

*You give yourself? Freely?*

Dropping his arms, John looked up at the creature. There are times when a person knows that an important decision, a life altering decision, has snuck up on them at an unexpected moment. Where a few moments before he had been walking up the porch steps, trying to think of a way to avoid going back into town to return Ben's store key, he was now making a deal with a twister; and offering nothing less than himself. Himself, to save the only piece of a world now gone forever.

Some deal. Give up yourself, or lose the greenhouse. Becky's greenhouse. Wrapping trembling arms around himself, he nodded. He must be dreaming, he thought. He must be back at Ben's store still sleeping. Dreaming.

*No dream. You give yourself?*

The words came again. Windy and elusive, but understandable. As if the speaker were constantly out of breath.

Nodding, he said quietly,

"Leave the greenhouse. Take me."

*Freely given, you are taken.*

Gleefully the voice shrieked in delight. He was swept off his feet . . . wind ripping at his clothes. The sensation was odd. Wind whipping all around him, going higher into the air. The last image of the farm was a blur, but he could see that the creature had kept the bargain. The greenhouse still stood.

He truly expected to die then; to be one of the many victims of the unpredictable life of tornado alley; a statistic in the next day's news paper; a blurb in the obituaries. Instead, he was surrounded in wind and darkness. While he could feel the air churn around him, still it was quiet; peaceful. Inexplicably, he felt relaxed. Then, images;

*He saw children playing . . . he was disoriented for a moment . . . one of the kids was himself then . . . his parents watching as he tried to lift a bowling ball . . . His first school memories . . . .* all began pouring out of him. Someone or something was using his brain like a book; flipping his memories like they were so many pages.

*College at Montana State; football; his coach trying to convince him to enter the NFL draft.*

Wind whipped around him, so dark he thought his eyes must be closed, more images;

*Law school, his mother so happy, his father saying he shouldn't become a lawyer, do something honest like the NFL.*

His body was now moving in a circle. Round and round. He thought he could see lights . . . small but dazzling . . .

*His first job with the District Attorney's Office in Chicago . . . . his first trial, cocktail parties, baseball at Wrigley Field . . . .*

New lights, but not as dazzling, he felt that he was falling, but slowly. Gently floating downward. He could see more clearly. Was that land below him? More images . . . .

*Back now in Hopes End. His first assignment with the MCA. His interview with Timothy Dall, the nervous laughter of Sheriff Thomes . . . . later they would learn the Sheriff had been on the Milza brothers payroll . . . .*

He was falling . . . faster now . . . . clouds whipped by him . . . . rain brushed his cheeks . . . . falling . . . .

*Now his first glimpse of Rebecca . . . . she had been a chef at a struggling Italian bistro . . . What can I get you? The waiter had asked. That woman's phone number, he heard his voice respond.*

The images slowed now, as if whomever was invading his mind had finally found something interesting to look at . . .

*His four year marriage to Rebecca passed through his thoughts with heartbreaking detail . . . . each sound of her voice tripping chords of anguish . . . .*

*Stop! No More!* He cried. Or at least he thought he did as the darkness and wind swallowed all sound. Ignoring his pleas, the images continued.

*Sam being born. Coming home from the hospital with Becky and the new arrival. Watching her breast feed for the first time. Dirty diapers, walks in the stroller, the first time he and Becky had made love after the pregnancy . . .*

*No! These are mine! Mine!* He was animalistic now, baring his teeth like fangs. He used his anger, focused it, like a knife, without knowing how to wield it, he struck. For a brief moment he had paused the memories, stopped the slideshow, gained some respite . . . . then without warning, like a mental brick striking his skull, his mind was cracked open again . . . .

*They were leaving the theatre. It was cold; bitter cold. The high school had put on the "Messiah" and Sam had fallen asleep. Rebecca had put him in the child car seat and quickly got in the passenger side. Someone called his name.*

*He turned to talk with one of the clerks from the court house. Out of the corner of his eye, he glimpses a man wearing a trench coat with a strange marking on his face watching intently from under the theater sign. Rebecca yelled for him to get in and turn the heat on. Leaning in through the driver's side, he handed her the keys. Turning back to finish his chat, he heard the cars ignition turn on . . . then he was suddenly engulfed in flames . . . . he flew through the air . . . hit his head . . . and awoke in the hospital days later . . . . his mother sitting by the sick bed . . . her face haggard and drawn . . . his raw voice croaked out,*

*"Becky? Sam?"*

*Her face said it all . . . . his voice now gone . . . he cried silently . . . .*

*ENOUGH! No! NO!*

His anger was like a piece of molten metal flowing through his veins. He let it flood out of him and turned it loose on the power picking at his past pain. He registered shock and surprise from his tormentor, anger, and then withdrawal. Wind whirled through his ears. He thought he could hear birds, smelled something wet and salty, the sea?

Then . . . nothing.

# CHAPTER TWO

Water. Wet and cold. Water was dripping on his lips. Trying to swallow, his throat rebelled, coughing and hacking he tried to sit up, but was too weak. *So tired.* Instead he turned his head to the side and coughed. Hacking sobs ripped through him. His body felt windblown and bruised.

After the hacking subsided, he felt a cool hand at the back of his neck, tilting his head back and then felt water going easily down his throat. This time he drank. So thirsty of a sudden, he guzzled the water greedily. Some of it splashed and made small rivers down his chin.

"Tsk. Let it settle."

A roughly warm voice said. Opening his eyes, John saw a tan and careworn face smiling down at him.

"Listen to Terre. She knows. Been waiting for you. Long time. Long, long, long, . . . ."

The strange creature released her hold and scuttled and hopped away. Rising up on shaky arms, John tried to get a better feel for the surroundings. Cool gray stone made the skin of his hand look pasty white. He was lying on a smooth stone floor. Whether smooth from human hands or from the passage of time and the elements he could not tell.

The rest of the cavern, to big for a cave, was all natures work. Rough rock walls and stalagmites hung from the ceiling, some of them so long that they almost reached the floor. Light was coming from somewhere above, for the place was well lit in a soft yellow glow.

Stone chairs and benches lay scattered and haphazard in a circle. Some were broken while others appeared untouched and whole. In the center of the circle a fire burned in a stone basin. Shaking a still groggy head, he rose groaning to his feet.

"Tsk. Tsk. Air can be a bit ungentle at times; especially when it is excited."

The odd woman grabbed his arm and led him to an unbroken bench close to the fire. As he sat rattled bones on the seat he took the opportunity to observe the strange creature who had suddenly taken charge of him. She was a short squat thing of rags and silks. Bright threads and coarse brown weaves made up a costume of contrasts. One moment her dress, *was it a dress?*, made her look like the filthiest beggar and then a swish of an arm would reveal jewel encrusted fabric which sparkled in the cavern light. Night black hair was tightly braided into a lopsided unorganized heap on her head. Bright blue eyes, free of any other color, peered at him over a wide plump nose.

"You are not the first mage to look at old Terre like that. She has an effect on people. Especially on the first meet." Nodding and humming, she busied herself with the fire.

Closing tired eyes, he tried to figure out what was going on. Either the twister had killed him; he was still asleep in Ben's store and was dreaming; or he was insane.

The smell of something hearty and savory made him open his eyes. Terre stood then smiling knowingly, as if she could read his thoughts. The good smell ended up being a bowl of some kind of soup, which she handed to him.

Suddenly hungry, and seeing no utensils he placed the bowl to his lips. Turning back to the fire with a nod of satisfaction, Terre began humming again. John watched her quietly as he drank. More broth than soup, the mixture refreshed him and seemed to spread warmth through his body. After finishing, and wiping his mouth with a hand, he finally spoke.

"Where am I?"

His voice sounded strained. As if he had yelled for an entire nine innings at a baseball game. Without turning from her fire duties, the woman answered,

"Some call this the cave. Others the meeting place."

"What others?"

Turning around she met his gaze before answering.

"Why, other mages of course."

That was the second time she had called him a mage. The first time he had thought he had heard incorrectly due to his shaky condition. Now there could be no doubt. Stretching his arms and rolling sore neck muscles, he climbed gingerly to his feet.

"I am no mage."

"Oh yes you are my tall friend."

Marching over to him, Terre's voice almost purred.

"Marked by fire you are. Taken by Air. Strong elements you control. What will this world make of you? What will you make of this world?"

Shaking her head and muttering to herself, the odd woman sat down on the stone floor and looked at him expectantly as if waiting for him to answer her rhetorical questions.

Annoyed now, he turned his milky white stare and glared down at her,

"I must be dreaming. Hallucinating, maybe. That twister came through . . . ."

Running his hand through his hair, he noticed for the first time that both face and arm were completely exposed. The trench coat and cowboy hat were long gone, as was most of the right sleeve of his shirt. As if following his thoughts Terre said,

"Yes, fire has marked you strongly. But Air has claimed you as well. Two powerful elements. One so much a part of the other. Powerful."

Her eyes seemed to lose focus for a moment, and then they snapped back to his scarred face.

"Whether you think you are dead or not, Jonathan Champion, yes I saw that thought flitter across your face, you are needed now. Here. I need you. Your people need you."

"My people?"

As if he had not said a word she continued,

"You must go to your people. Or maybe they will come to you. Too much is unclear. All I know is that you are the key. Not just your power, but you."

Putting her hands in her lap, the woman looked up at him as if that had explained everything. Sitting back down and folding his arms across his chest, John jutted out his chin. Rebecca had called it his "stubborn face".

"I am not going anywhere until I wake up or until I understand what is going on here."

Laughing lightly, Terre sprang to her feet and danced over to him. Skipping in circles around the stone bench she almost sang,

"Who understands anything? Even Terre does not *understand.*"

She hummed a wordless tune mockingly while she continued to dance around him laughing and clapping her hands. Suddenly, she stopped and stood directly in front of his brooding form, and stuck a stubby finger inches from his nose.

"Whether you are dreaming or dead, what harm in following me, my Champion? Unless you fear a beautiful woman might lead you astray?" Laughing again, she danced down a passageway that he had not noticed before. Her voice followed back into the cavern,

"Oh Brave Champion, Terre forgot to tell you that the lights follow her in this place."

As if on cue, the yellow glow began to fade. Cursing to himself, he got back on his feet. John did not want to be stuck in the dark, dream or no dream. Unsteady at first, he got trembling legs to work as he followed the fading light of the crazy old woman.

# CHAPTER THREE

*Their humor is as scarred and twisted as they make their bodies.*

These words floated to the front of Grach's thoughts much like the smoke from the pipe drifted over his face. Silently, he gave what for his people was a glare at his tormentor across the campfire flames. Liquid, almost watery, blue eyes regarded him with amusement as they watched as he quietly struggled to come up with a reply that would not cause offense. Thin lips could be seen to just be hiding a sharp toothed smile. Just, that is, as Grach could see the corners of his companions mouth twitch.

"Friend, Tyrell. You know that it would do no good. I simply have no need for that particular . . . sustenance."

Nodding his head vigorously, the other raised a knife across the fire,

"Friend Grach, well do I recall the numerous times you have refused meat with me. And here this whole time I thought it simply because your people were allergic or had a rule against eating the stuff. And yet, my feast brother swears by his own scarred hide that he sat down with a molden herder just a few moons ago and they both partook of a wonderfully bloody hind of *sherki*. Surely, if a herder will eat with such a scoundrel as my feast brother, you, my dear friend, will partake with me?"

The blue man ended his speech with another sharp toothed smile. Feeling somewhat trapped, Grach took a pull on his own skin and considered his companion.

Like most of his kind, Tyrell was tall, slim, and covered in tattoos and scars. Blond hair cut shoulder length that never seemed out of place, contrasted with dark blue skin.

Good looking and fair, like all of his race, Tyrell was not a bad sort.

While most Ferreki, were arrogant in their dealings with other races, Tyrell and his family had always treated fairly with the molden root clans. He even wore suitable clothing so as not to offend his gray skinned companion. The two had been on numerous travels together, as merchants, scouts, and even on the march to the beat of the war drums. If there was one from a race not his own that he would say he could trust it would be Tyrell.

*Would never tell him that, though. His people are . . . difficult to understand.*

They had stopped on their way back from Grach's root holdings to rest for the night. While the news they carried to Tyrell's people was important, it was not so urgent as to require a forced night's travel.

Their current camp site was a spot that they had used numerous times, easily defensible on higher ground and within running distance of a cave if the weather required cover. The night however was fair, if a bit chill in the wind. Nothing too cold that a good dose of drink and a friendly argument could not take care of.

Praying to the Root Mothers to save him from this disgusting moment, Grach leaned forward to take his friends knife with its bloody morsel, when the blue man motioned him to be quiet. Tilting his head, he listened.

"Something is coming our way."

Snatching his hand back, Grach sat still. A moment later the unmistakable sound of a voice drifted towards them. Silently the two companions stood and tried to determine the direction of the disturbance.

Eyes going a bit wide, Tyrell motioned toward the cave mouth. Frowning, Grach unsheathed his stone mace while his taller companion carefully wet the tip of a blow dart pipe. Sounds of feet on stone and a voice could now be distinctly heard. Gripping the weapon hard so that his knuckles turned white, Grach was almost ashamed of his fear; until he noticed the blue man's hand shaking. Unfortunately, knowing that Tyrell was afraid did not bring any humor to the molden as much as it would have any other night. The noise became louder, now. Suddenly, tripping and cursing out of the cave came a Mundane.

"Damn it, Terre! That was not funny!"

Obviously angry, the mund's scarred visage surveyed the clearing with its two inhabitants. Noticing the two companions with weapons drawn, he paused.

*Big one.* Tyrell thought to himself.

While his family owned the services of numerous mundanes, few of them would have reached to their new guest's shoulder. The mund standing before him looked to have the body of a warrior. Tall and broad shouldered, albeit a bit skinny, the weapon masters would still love to get him into the fighting pits.

*The face alone, with that milk white eye, would cause terror in many a weak kneed opponent.*

To be on the safe side, he would keep the blow pipe handy.

"Evening stranger, might we ask what you are doing here?"

While he still had the blow pipe close to his mouth, Tyrell's voice was steady, and had taken on a bit of the patronizing tone that most of his kind did when addressing munds. Standing now with arms folded across his chest, the mund answered,

"You might."

Surprised, Tyrell lowered his pipe.

"You speak Fereki, yes? Are you the house carl or scribe for your lord?"

His face darkening a bit the mund gave another short answer,

"I have no lord."

Turning his head to remark to his shorter companion, Tyrell stopped when he saw his friend's state. Grach had turned a most unhealthy shade of pink, and his lips trembled. Ignoring the strange mund for the moment, he walked over to the molden.

"My friend, are you well?"

Without taking eyes off the mund, Grach answered,

"Heard Fereki, did you? The mund spoke it?"

Confused and concerned for his companion, Tyrell just nodded.

"Well, I hope you have stronger drink with you, because I will be needing it."

Very concerned now, Tyrell bent down close so their words would not carry to the glowering intruder.

"Grach?"

"Molden The lad spoke Molden. He said to you, 'You might.' But it was the Root Mother's, tongue. I swear by the great Root."

Shocked, the blue man turned to regard the strange mund. Feeling a bit uneasy from their stares, the man was now rocking on the balls of his feet. Not realizing that he was thinking out loud, Tyrell said wonderingly,

"A mage. A mundane mage."

STANDING BACK, John could not hear what the two strange looking men were talking about. He frowned, not liking the entire situation. First he gets taken by a twister, then follows a mad woman who leads him on a crazy chase through darkened tunnels, and now he comes upon two strangely dressed, and armed, men who appear to be as shocked to see him as he was when he awoke in the stone cavern.

*One was fucking blue for Christ sake!*

*Add to that that I may be, dreaming, crazy, or dead.*

The two men seemed to now be arguing, with the taller one placing a hand on the shorter one's shoulder. Being outside the tunnels, John's bare feet and arms were exposed to the chill wind. Ignoring the other two, he walked over and knelt down to warm himself by the campfire flames. Seeing the drinking skin, he looked over his shoulder and asked,

"Mind if I have a swig?"

His voice seemed to freeze the mouths of the other two. An answer not forth coming, he shrugged and took a long pull from the skin. Like a cross between wine and brandy, the drink had a small burn before it went down, but then settled easily in his stomach.

Another swig brought a bit of warmth through his body. Leaning back a bit, he looked up as the two companions joined him. Nodding his thanks to the blue man, who had produced a well worn blanket for him, John passed the skin onto the short one.

*Short Bread.*

He thought to himself as he watched as the strange man took a drink. From closer up, Jonathan could see that the small man's skin was a light grey color, and seemed to be covered in uneven bumps. Silence fell over the small company. As an experienced trial lawyer, John knew how powerful a weapon silence could be when used at the right time. So he stared at the flames, waiting for someone to break the nights quiet.

"Where did you get those burns, my tall friend?"

Short Bread asked. Smiling grimly, but not taking his eyes from the flames he answered,

"It was an accident."

"Huh. Some accident. Hope you 'accidentally' took care of the one who caused it." The blue man chimed in.

*Blondie.*

He smiled at the man's new nickname.

"I took care of them before the accident."

Nodding sagely, Blondie said,

"Ahhhhh. Always make sure an enemy is clean dead, friend. Always."

Taking another drink, he tried to pass the skin onto the grey man who ignored him as he gazed thoughtfully at John. Shrugging, Blondie helped himself to another pull and simply stared. Meeting the gaze John commented,

"Where I come from, it is rude to stare."

Blinking as if surprised someone would address him so, Blondie discarded the skin, flowed to his feet and gracefully bowed.

"I apologize. My name is Tyrell Va Tal Lorn, of the Tree'tha. My humble, yet thirsty companion is Grach Chakson, of the stone root valleys."

Sitting back down as gracefully as he had stood, Blondie waited for John to respond.

"Champion, Jonathan Champion."

Leaning across the flames he held out his left hand. After a brief pause, Tyrell and Grach carefully took turns clasping it. Silence again. The fire crackled. Tyrell was the one to break it.

"Jonathon Champion, as you can see, you have surprised us this night. Many times have Grach and I traveled between the stone valleys and the green towers. We have seen many things on our travels, but never have we seen . . . ."

His voice trailed off, seemingly lost for words.

"A what?" John asked as he pulled the blanket tighter around his shoulders.

"A mund mage. That's what you are, by the Root." Though his voice was soft, Grach's words carried through the quiet night.

Closing his eyes, John pulled his knees up and hugged them to his chest.

"That's what she called me."

"Who?" Tyrell leaned forward.

"She called herself Terre. She called me a mage."

"Terre? Is she a mundane goddess?" Blondie leaned forward, his curiosity winning out over his apprehension.

Shrugging, John answered,

"She did not look much like a goddess. Just a strange old woman."

"Sounds like a tale worthy of stronger drink." Blondie pulled from somewhere a tin flask. Taking a pull, he passed it to Grach who waved it off with a wrinkled nose. Taking another pull, he handed it to John. Cautiously putting it up to his nose, John smelled something like bourbon.

"Smells strong."

Saying nothing, Blondie just smiled.

Closing his eyes, a silent prayer, and the flask touched his lips.

*Fire. There is a Fire in my mouth*, he thought. Sitting there with his eyes closed, in the quiet dark night, cradling the flask in his arms as if it were a delicate crystal glass, John waited for the fire to travel through his body. After many moments, the feeling smoldered out. His body felt relaxed. He was comfortable, even in the cool, brisk night air. Opening his eyes he solemnly handed the flask back to the blue man and asked,

"Got anything stronger?"

Scarred man and blue skinned traveler regarded each other for a silent moment, before the quiet night shattered with their laughter.

Leaning back, Grach regarded the laughing duo. Tyrell was on his back now, holding his sides as if they were a cloth sack over filled with saka fruit, and ready to burst. Likewise, the mund's body shuddered with laughter as he gaspingly tried to catch his breathe. Though he was not considered patient by his people's standard, Grach waited quietly, albeit with a foot tapping. Long moments later, with the noise of laughter drifting away into the chill night air, he took the chance to pursue his curiosity.

"Jonathan Champion, you mentioned Terre."

Sitting up again, John wiped a hand across his forehead and nodded.

"That is what she called herself."

"How did you meet her?"

"She said the wind had brought me to her. Wait, not the wind. She said that I had been, 'Taken by Air.'"

Sucking a breathe through brown stained teeth, Grach turned to his blond friend,

"Tyrell, if this is not mages business then I don't know my mace from a butter knife. We should . . ."

"Tell us." The blond held up a hand to his obviously worried companion.

Immediately, barriers went up. The idea that he was either dead or dreaming came to the front of his mind. John was unsure what to do. Looking into the dancing flames he spoke,

"I appear to be far from home. Far from that which I know and those I trust. Perhaps not even in my right mind. Trust is something . . . hard for me to give."

Surging to his feet, his recent trepidation at questioning the mundane forgotten now, Grach brandished his stone mace.

"By the Root Mother's Milk, John'athan Ch'ampion, I am at times a rash warrior. Though I be quick to anger I am quick to forgive." Leaping the flames, he laid the weapon at John's feet and met the sitting man's stare.

"Since you do not know me, I forgive you your mistrust. What you tell me this night is a bond. By my Root Clan's pride, I swear this. I will not reveal your tale lest you permit me."

Eyes wide at this dramatic display, John turned his face to regard the sitting Tyrell who nodded in agreement at his friends oath. Looking back into the flames, he began to speak.

HOURS LATER embers and coals crackled the last of the wood into fiery ash. Daylight slowly approached over the rise. The two companions were silent at the end of his tale. Blondie had a look of abject wonder on his face while short bread's face was nearly impassive. John was exhausted.

His body ached. He was cold regardless of the blanket offered by the traveling pair. His deformed injury was on display for this strange world to view and dissect instead of safe in hiding on his distant farm. Whether this world was his imagination or some strange real twist of events did not matter in one sense; he was still going to have to deal with it.

"Friend Ch'ampion," Grach began,

"I would not be honest with you if I did not say your story stretches my beliefs. My first thought would have been to think you have run away from your master and that my companion and I would be duty bound to return you," lifting a bumpy hand to forestall John's interruption, he continued,

"However, there is the matter of the mode of your arrival to our campsite." He glanced at the cave and went silent.

Following the glance, Champion lifted an eyebrow in question. Blondie gently interrupted,

"What my obscure friend means to say is that he and I have traveled this route many times together. We have camped at this site a number of times. The cave gives good shelter when the weather acts up." Seeing the confused look on their visitor's face, Blondie stood and motioned for John to follow him to the cave entrance.

Standing at the cave mouth, the rising sun gave natural light to the inside. The smell of mold, rock and dirt gave it a familiar earthy smell. Tracing his steps from a few hours before, John entered. The cave walls led back to a small hole in the floor that some past travelers had used for a fire pit; blackened rocks had been placed in a circle around its edge. A short distance back from the fire pit the cave ended in a seemingly solid wall. Placing his hands against the walls rough surface showed him that the seemingly solid wall was exactly that; rock.

There was no evidence of the tunnel that he had followed the strange woman for what had seemed like an endless chase. Closing his eyes, he rested his head against the cold comfort of the rock wall, trying to gage his sanity. Breathing in slowly and slowly out, he took stock of the situation. He did not believe that he was dreaming. Never had a dream been so real.

THE DAY was bright, even for early morning. John's new companions had explained that his arrival at their campsite last night had only slightly disrupted their journey.

They wished to get a few miles out of the way before making camp for an afternoon rest. The strange back pack they had asked him to wear was only slightly uncomfortable as it was made for a shorter person. The sandals likewise were a tight fit but were welcome compared to bare feet on the gravel lined trail.

Blondie and Shortbread were not the type of companions to waste time with constant interrogations. While at times they gave him questioning glances, they were content to allow the day to unfold and keep their thoughts to themselves. In truth, Champion enjoyed the quiet time to settle his thoughts and study his new "travel buddies."

Last night, Grach appeared to be a short squat man with lumpy skin. In the light of day, it was apparent that Grach was not a man, in the human sense, at all. While he had two arms and two legs, that is about where his similarity to the human race ended. With a wide, almost square body, he nearly waddled instead of walked. Stubby fingers gripped a walking staff that would have been too thick for John to get his hand around (his good hand). A long brown robe covered the body from the neck to his ankles but could not hide the fact that a massive form existed underneath. Dark brown eyes matched brown stained teeth, with a nose that appeared much too small for his face.

But, as John noticed last night, the most striking thing about his new companion was the skin. Grey in color, it appeared to be covered with oddly shaped lumps. It made Grach look more like a walking mushroom of some kind.

"What do you think of our chubby warrior?"

In his musings, he had not noticed Blondie appearing next to him. Unlike Grach, who walked a steady pace and kept to the trail, Tyrell seemed to go out of his way to avoid it. One minute walking and chatting, the next he would scamper off into the wooded byways. The man seemed to have so much energy that staying in one place was impossible.

"I would not call him chubby. He has substance, that's for sure."

The blue man's laughter at the answer faded into the tree lined pathway. Tyrell was as different from Grach as a mushroom was to a mountain cat. He did not so much walk as casually stalk his way down the path. He wore a bluish green dyed vest with matching pants that ended at his ankles. The color of the clothing seemed to almost blend into the blue of his skin and the green of the forest. However, John got the feeling that the strange man would be as comfortable without the clothing as not.

The scars that had been noticeable the previous night now almost blazed in the day time. The nature of the patterns that swirled over Tyrell's body made his every movement almost a dizzying exercise to the eyes. Spirals, shapes of animals, and geometric designs all flowed across his arms and chest. He was not as tall as John but his skinny frame made him seem taller. His face, even more fox like in the daylight, was thrown back in laughter. His humor was soon replaced with a serious face.

"We will make camp soon. While Grach and I could continue on we believe that we need to sit with you in moot."

"Moot?"

Raising his hands Blondie floundered a bit,

"Yes moot. To discuss what we must do. To perhaps explain things . . . to plan?"

After John nodded his understanding, Blondie left off his groping attempts to explain with a sigh of relief.

John almost missed the camping spot. One minute he was pondering the up coming "moot" when he realized that he was alone on the path.

Retracing his steps he saw to his left a narrow break in the trees and his two companions settling into a small campsite. Campsite was a bit of a generous description of the spot. Yes there was a shallow bowl of a campfire that Grach was cleaning of debris, and yes there were a couple of fallen trees for seats, but that is where it ended.

Tyrell was putting his packs down and motioned for Champion to do the same. As he unwound the pack he was surprised to see that Grach had produced a fire somehow. Champion suspected his stocky friend hid much more than his girth under the baggy robe. For a few moments the chores of setting camp removed all thought and tension associated with the upcoming moot. However, all good things come to an end, and the three travelers soon found themselves munching in silence on dried fruit that Tyrell had provided.

Surprisingly, it was Grach who broke the silence.

"In three days we will reach River Bend. We need to work something out."

Seeing Champion's confused look, the short man looked to his taller companion for help.

"What Grach means, my new found friend, is that you present a problem for us."

Waving down any objection from Grach he continued on turning towards Champion,

"That you are a mage is no doubt; or something along those lines. Your gift of language is a give away. However, you are also a Mund. A mundane. I fear the sort of . . . . reception you may receive once we get into civilized lands."

The confused look persisted. The blue man took a small piece of worked leather out of his pack and handed it over to Champion. Turning it over in his hands, John could see that it was some sort of collar. A brass buckle was at one end with a latch at the other. A glyph of some kind was worked into the material.

"This is a *bacha*, or service collar. All mundane's who are in service to my clan wear one."

Confusion gave way to anger as comprehension seeped in.

Putting his hands out in a placating gesture, Tyrell continued,

"Please, my friend Champion, please do not rush to judgment. Grach and I are truly thinking of your safety. If you come to River Bend without a *bacha*, things would go badly. Very badly. I know you have questions. Please trust us in this. We have given you our word in friendship. Please, until we can consult with others who are wiser and would do you no harm. Please." Tyrell's eyes pleaded for understanding. Turning his gaze to Grach, the grey man nodded,

"John'athan, it is as Tyrell says. Your safety cannot be assured unless you are seen to be attached to Tyrell's people. The root clans do not deal with mundane's in this fashion. But we cannot return to my clan without our mission completed. We have that duty to both of our peoples. Once we have provided the warning, we can discuss your . . . future options."

The good intentioned brown toothed smile eased Champion's worries more than the stocky man's words. Silently, he attached the collar around his neck and allowed Tyrell to fasten the buckle.

# Chapter Four

Calphan the Merchant would never admit to fear involving the strange mund and his masters. Not fear, unease maybe. The party of three had approached his campfire that evening. He had chosen his camp site with care, in a hollow away from the main road to ensure his fire would not be seen easily. Although there had not been problems between the Mok Empire and the Blue Skins for many years, still he was cautious by nature; but he had no fear of the Ferrekei man. Further, the root brothers were known to not be aggressive and he had experience with the root clans. No not fear . . . but something.

The mund was tall for one. A mute his masters claimed he was, though Calphan was sure the man understood the trade speak that he and the others used. Sitting back, he silently made comparisons between the two munds in his small group and this stranger.

Sipping his camp broth he examined Gret and Breg. Both had been born into service. Both were shorter and had darker complexions. Both went about their duties with no word except to clarify the merchant's wishes. He watched closely as Gret scratched absently at his *bacha* collar and leaned over his evening meal. Then he turned his eyes over to the mund named John.

*Strange name.*

The taller mund sat near the other two. He sat and ate his meal quietly. Yes he was a startling thing to look at with those scars. When Calphan had inquired of the two companions whether the scars had been the result of a rawstone accident they waved it off. It seemed a subject that the two did not want to discuss; or not discuss in front of their mund.

*Why fear saying anything in front of a mund?*

Calphan, like all his people (and most other races) held munds in low regard. A race of non-magic users who could not survive on their own without the superior races to make use of them; who would breed like so many frenzied insects if their population was not controlled; and who in fact were hideously ugly in shape and form. In fact, if other uses had not been developed for them, it was very likely that the whole mund race would have been allowed to go extinct.

He looked over to regard Gret. The mund's hands shook only slightly when he handled the bowl. A week in a rawstone house was a long time for a mund to last but the Empire had needed extra charged stones, so every tradesman in the merchant class had been required to provide a quota. In many cases, such long exposure would make a mund useless for anything else. Bringing Gret on this trip was partly to test his endurance to ensure that Calphan did not need to replace him.

Turning his mind from the annoying contemplation of purchasing a new servant he again pondered the strange mund.

*A gross hairy frog.*

That is was Calphan resembled, John thought to himself as he slowly sipped his broth. Large amphibian eyes stared out of a box shaped face. Catfish like whiskers or hairs protruded from nodules that billowed out of green cheeks. Small suction cups attached to the tips of each finger.

However, the Mok was the first creature that John had met on this strange journey almost as tall as he was. With a large arm span, the Mok would have been very intimidating if he ever stood up. But from the time John and his companions had joined his fire, the Mok had stayed seated and simply given instructions to his two servants.

*A large gross, lazy, hairy frog.*

The cover story that he was a mute did not allow John to communicate with the other two munds. Gret and Breg seemed to ignore him for the most part. Though, at one time it appeared that Breg had been making strange signs with his hands in John's direction. Champion's ignorance or failure to reply seemed to disturb the other mund.

*Humans. We are the three of us, humans. Not Munds.* John thought angrily.

The day before their party had come upon the Mok's campsite, Blondie and Grach had developed a cover story. The story in fact did not fall short of the truth. It was the first time he had been informed that the two companions were bringing word to the southern lands of a *mesk* infestation. Though his two companions did not go into much detail as to what a *mesk* was, it was obvious from their distaste that it was an unwholesome creature. The cover story simply added Champion to the mix with him being in service to Tyrell.

As they approached the campfire of the Mok merchant, Blondie had silently hissed that Mok's could be very perceptive and shrewd. Meaning, Champion was to stick to the story, shut up, and let them do the talking.

"How bad do you judge the *mesk* problem?" Calphan's slurpy voice broke the silence.

Taking a moment to swallow a mouthful, Tyrell answered,

"We do not consider it a problem, at the moment, honored merchant. However, it did infest three settlements of my people and also one of the root clans cave holdings. While it appears to be controlled, we are being cautious and simply sending word to my people in the southern forests with a stop a River's Bend to get the general call out."

Grunting at this, Calphan held his bowl out. Breg sprang to his feet and took the empty container from his masters' hand. Pausing, he also picked up Gret's bowl as well. Gret placed shaking hands in his lap and waited with down turned eyes. John also rose and took the bowls from Tyrell and Grach. Stepping outside of the firelight, he squatted down next to Breg and began silently cleaning.

"What are you playing at?"

The soft question startled him. Glancing over at Breg, the smaller man kept to his task and gave no indication that he had said anything.

"Why didn't you answer my questions?"

This time John had seen the lips move. Stopping in his task, John looked at the other man. Shrugging, Breg continued.

"I asked you if you were being treated well and if you might help me cover for Gret. Don't you know the speech?" Shaking in the negative, he bent back to his task. This time Breg did stop and look at John.

"You are a strange mund. You are mute but do not know the speech? I find that hard to believe. My master is suspicious."

John shrugged again. With a snort Breg stood up,

"Be careful what you . . . . by the cursed one, what is that?"

John stood and followed Breg's pointed arm. Out in the darkness there was movement. Peering, trying to pierce the gloom with his eyes, it appeared as if the forest floor . . . . moved. A strange "hunh-hunh" sound began coming to their ears. Moments later a strange furred animal shuffled into view.

Looking something like a squirrel, but much larger. With a flat narrow tale it shuffled further into the firelight. The sound came from the animal but sounded more like a wheezing as it came closer. It was obvious the creature was sick. Patches of its reddish brown fur had fallen out. The left side of its stomach was bloated and dragged almost on the ground while the right side clearly showed ribs sticking out in stark contrast. Thick white foam bubbled out of its mouth in a slow ooze through small sharp teeth. It fixed the duo with one red rimmed eye, while its other was simply a grisly empty hollow socket.

"*Garesh!*"

And suddenly amber light flooded the night.

*Thousands. There are thousands of them.*

The entire forest floor was covered with the grisly creatures. All marching, wheezing, slowly but inexorably towards the camp site. Turning, John saw that the source of the light was Calphan. The merchant held a staff from which an amber stone had been placed. As the stone burned brightly, smoky tendrils seemed to curl out and away from it. Looking back into the forest, John and Breg were stunned by the grotesque sight and the stench that came with the sickened animals.

John felt someone grab his arm and spin him around.

"We must run before they get our scent!"

Blondie's blue face was inches from his own, and John could see the fear etched there through the flickering amber light. Pushing John along he yelled something at Grach.

Looking over to the other party, John saw Breg lean over and help Gret to his feet. Almost immediately Calphan was at Breg's side and struck him with the back of his hand.

"Fool! If he cannot keep up, he is forest food. Now . . . ."

The Mok never finished his order as he felt himself lifted off the ground. With a *whoosh* the merchant hit the ground and lay there stunned. His staff flew from green hands and with it its amber light. With only the flickering campfire to provide any sort of illumination the Mok grunted to a sitting position.

He saw the scarred mund helping a shocked Breg to his feet. Seeing the Mok struggle to sit up the mund stalked over to him. For the first time in his life, with a face of scarred fury facing him, Calphan admitted in the quiet of his heart that he feared a mund. This mund. Grabbing the offending merchant by the neck John stuck his twisted face into that of the shocked Mok, and the supposedly mute mund hissed,

"If I ever see you hit any human again, *Frog*, I will deep fry your ass. You got that?!"

Dropping him to the ground again, John stomped towards Gret, and quickly led the other mund away. A moment later Breg was at the merchant's side.

"Master, forgive me. Let me help you up. We must leave this place. Now!"

Allowing the fussy servant to help him to his feet, the two began following the others away from the camp site. With the thought of the many tortures, he would inflict on a certain scarred faced mund if they survived this, Calphan fled into the night.

The flight was like a nightmare. Following Tyrell's trail as best as he could, with a shivering Gret behind him, Champion lost track of time as shear terror threatened to overwhelm him. Crashing headlong into bushes and branches, John hardly felt the scratches and abrasions that scored his arms and legs. Twice he had to stop and help a shaking Gret to his feet.

All around them was the wheezing and shuffling of the massive animal horde. Just as panic seemed to overtake them both a flash of light broke through the dark nightmare. Stumbling into a clearing, John and his charge came to a halt at the bottom of a steep rock formation. Waving at them from the top was Blondie. Almost sobbing with relief, he shoved Gret in front of him and began scrambling up the steep formation. The stone was somewhat slippery and hard gravel sprayed as the duo stumbled upwards. Finally reaching the top, Champion flopped to the ground heaving with panic laced exhaustion. Gret slowly sat down and placed his head in shaking hands, rocking back and forth.

After several moments of catching his breath, John took in their surroundings. They were not at the top of the rock formation as he first thought. Instead they were in an open outcropping of rock with the formation continuing upwards several hundred feet. A small tunnel made its way back into the formation and out of sight.

Old boards and half finished logs were strewn across the rocky ground. In one corner the broken haft of what may have been a shovel was half buried. John rose painfully to his feet and walked to where Tyrell stood.

In one hand the blue man held a make shift staff with another of the amber stones that Calphan had used. Peering into the night, his eyes scanned the forest below. With his face close to the stone, John could see the tendrils of smoke slowly swirling into the air along with a familiar scent that his fear struck brain could not recall.

"Mesk"

Before John could ask.

"The mesk have some how made it further to the south than Grach or I realized. I lost track of Calphan and his servant in the forest. Grach and I were laying scent trails to keep the mesk off of us. Grach then was to seek aid."

The worry for his companion was evident even though his voice was calm and unshaken.

"We are safe for the moment. In their current state, the mesk will not attempt the deep incline of the rock, nor do they care about the light. All that consumes their thoughts now is the scent for prey. I am hoping that the scent trails have confused the pack enough that they move on. We need to avoid them going into a frenzy."

Standing next to the blue man, the fumes of the stone continued to bother John. *What was that scent?*

Slowly, it seemed that the seething mass of animal flesh below was calming down. A few creatures had approached the rocky incline but had not made any move to climb it.

John could sense that Tyrell was relaxing a bit when there was a commotion to the left of the horde. Sprinting from between a stand of trees came Calphan and Breg. The frog man came in long loping strides, almost as if he was performing a strange dance maneuver.

Behind him, burdened with both of their packs, Breg struggled to keep up. Like a bee to honey the Mok made for the light of Tyrell's stone. The pair was forced to maneuver around the slow moving mesk, dodging to and fro in an insane dance through the pack. Just as Calphan made it to the bottom of the incline, Breg tumbled to the ground with a cry, the two travel bags falling in front of him. Struggling to his feet, it was obvious that the servant had twisted his ankle as he hobbled forward.

Halfway to the safety of the rock ledge, Calphan looked back at Breg. Skidding to a stop, the Mok turned and headed back towards his hobbling servant. John's esteem for the frog man went up a number of notches. He and Tyrell were both yelling encouragement to the pair as Calphan approached Breg. With a look of astonished relief, Breg held out his hands for help.

Quickly, the Mok pushed past his servant, picked up the fallen travel bags and raced back towards the rock. With a cry of dismay, Breg fell to his knees. With an angry shout, John leaped from the safety of the cave mouth sliding and skidding down the rock. Cursing Frogs and all amphibians, and ignoring the cry from Tyrell, he shouldered past the offensive merchant and raced toward Breg.

On his knees, Breg shied away from the mesk as they slowly circled him. One creature came forward and rubbed its bloated side against the trembling man. Over come with fear, Breg put his head in his hands as other creatures began to circle close. With his chest burning and his legs afire with the effort, John weaved his way through the wheezing mesk's towards Breg.

By the time he had reached him, three creatures were now sniffing and nudging the fallen man. It was apparent that Breg's presence among the *mesk* was doing something to the pack. The animals as a whole began to move quicker, their movements jerky and unusual, and several seemed more agitated.

Reaching Breg, John kicked the closest mesk away from the terror stricken man. Pivoting, he kicked the second animal into the third. The three mesk now were squealing in pain from the attack. Yanking Breg to his feet, the duo began shuffling towards the rocks.

Behind them, the wheezing sounds of the pack were replaced by angry shrill squeals. The mesk still between the pair and the safety of the rock began jumping and running around them. Still, the two kept going; Breg through fear and Champion through stubborn pride.

A few feet in front of them, for no reason that was obvious, one of the mesk attacked its closest neighbor. This sent the rest of the pack into a frenzy as each creature attacked another. Crying out in pain, John saw that a mesk had sunk its fanged mouth into his left calf.

With an angry swat, he sent the horrid thing careening into the frenzied mass. The pain turned his fear into anger. With every pain filled step closer to the rocky incline, John's anger turned into fury. He burned with it.

With the crazed horde now turned into a mass of blood and sharp flashing teeth, it was obvious that the pair was still to far away from the safety of the rock. Mesk now began bumping into their legs causing further stumbles. The rough touch of each animal fueled his anger and John let loose a snarl of rage. There was no room for panic as he roughly dragged the injured Breg behind him.

Kicking any animal that came close felt good but it only increased their frenzy. Finally, one of the creatures launched itself at Breg. Pushing the man to the ground, John caught the offensive animal out of the air. Wrapping it's body around his scarred arm, the mesk sank its teeth into the ropy flesh. Looking at the offensive creature gnawing a bloody mess into his arm, Johm could only think in terms of burning rage.

His rage was like a flame as it coursed through his body; searching for something to ignite. In mere moments, as he watched the mesk make a bloody mess of his arm, the rage found the kindling it had sought. Power. Power buried deep within himself sleeping, waiting.

John could feel the power awake; could feel it ignite and flare up within himself. The power was aware and hungry. Hungry to burn.

*Yes, burnnnnn it all. Yes?*

A raspy voice spoke from the depths of his being; from within the raging flame of power. In his current state of mind John did not even question the existence of the voice as he replied,

"Yes, burn them all."

Holding his arm higher with its unwanted passenger, John's arm began to smoke. The mesk began to writhe in pain as it tried to dislodge itself from the now lethal arm, but it was too late. In a matter of moments, the charred remains of the creature fell to the ground. John looked with a strange detachment at his scarred arm. Coated in bright red flames, the limb seemed to throb with heat. Blood from the mesk bite dripped onto the ground and sizzled where it landed. Looking down at the stunned Breg, he advised,

"Run or burn."

With those simple words, John turned and faced the pack. With fire dripping from his arm, he pointed it at the sickened animals. Flames coursed through his body and exploded from the deformed hand. The voice screamed gleefully through his mind as charred carcasses fell to the ground.

*Yesssss . . . . burn them. Burn them all.*

Fire issued from him in no particular shape or form. Some times fire balls, some times waves, and sometimes indescribable fiery beams flowed from his hand. All resulted in the same charred death. In a matter of moments, the mesk were either dead or fled, but the voice still urged him on as flames crept towards the trees.

Within the voice there was a deep hatred for living things, for animal and forest life alike, and it fed John's rage. Soon bushes and trees burned. John became the fire. His soul was consumed with the purpose of the flames.

*Burn it all.*

Something struck his shoulder. Looking down he saw a fist sized rock rolling to a stop. Without thinking, his fiery anger centered on the offensive stone. In moments, the stone burst from the flame induced pressure. Before he could turn back towards the forest he was struck in the back of the head.

Pain made him dizzy, and his knees wobbled. The fire lost some of its focus and John turned around on shaky legs. Framed against the outline of the rock formation was a man. Taking two uncertain steps towards his attacker, John raised his flame covered arm.

This asshole is going to burn!

*Yesssss . . . burn the asshole . . . . yesssssss.*

Two more steps and John could see the blue skinned man holding another rock. Memory tried to intrude on his flame driven purpose. His steps slowed. The fire in his arm burned a bit lower with uncertainty. Now a few yards from the rock thrower, John could see the man had blond hair and was covered in scars. Lowering his arm, he stared blankly at the strange man.

Stepping towards him, Tyrell spoke as he let the rock slip through his fingers to the ground,

"My friend. Feast Brother. Let the fire go. Jonathan Champion. Please."

The pleading voice struck a nerve. He remembered.

"Blondie?"

The flame sputtered out. The voice went silent. And he fell to his knees. Chills over took him as the angry strength and warmth of the fire fled him.

Feeling himself being helped to his feet, John stumbled where he was led. In moments, he was leaning with his back to the stone wall of the rock formation while Gret covered him with a coarse blanket. The shaking now became stronger and his teeth chattered. He trembled as with a cold fever.

Cold tremors alternated with hot flashes coursed from his arm to the rest of his body.

With chattering teeth, he took in the rest of the companions. Breg sat as far from Calphan as the rock enclosure would allow, alternating between bandaging up his swollen ankle and glaring at the merchant. For his part, the Mok nursed a recently swollen lip; with his other hand he held onto the two travel packs that he had risked everything for. Gret took charge of Champion.

"You need to walk. You have a mage fever. Walking will help get the blood flowing and slow the chills."

"Mage fever. Impossible!"

The Mok's wet voice seemed slurred as he talked around a loose tooth. Shrugging, Gret ignored the merchant and continued to encourage John to walk.

Tyrell was again looking outside of the cave mouth. The early dawn light could be seen creeping slowly into the safety of the cave. He looked down into the burned out clearing that was Champion's handiwork. While he could not see them, he knew the mesk were still there, just out of sight in the forest foliage. His experience with the creatures told him that the pack should have moved on after so many had been killed.

But something kept them here. In a moment, he got his answer. His hissed breathe brought Calphan to stand next to him.

They watched silently as three tall figures appeared out of the woods. Wrapped in some kind of black material, like burial shrouds, the strange figures features were completely hidden from view. A chill ran up Tyrell's spine and his palms began to sweat. There was something strange going on here.

Stopping for a moment, the dark trio craned long necks up to the members of the company in silence. As if in response to some unspoken communication, they stepped forward in unison and spread their hands to the sky.

It was clear to see that those hands were black and clawed. Speaking in a harsh guttural voice, they then pointed toward the cave mouth. With a whooshing sound, black fire erupted from the creature's hands and began making its way up the incline. Sizzling the air with heat, it seemed more liquid than fire. It burned the remaining bodies of the mesk as it traveled its hungry way towards the five waiting in the cave. Tyrell's mouth went dry as more of the harsh words poured forth.

"Back! Back into the tunnel!"

Motioning for Breg and Gret to get John moving, Tyrell spun the shocked Mok from the cave mouth and pushed him toward the tunnel. Already feeling the heat of the unnatural fire on the back of his neck, Tyrell entered the passage. After several feet the narrow tunnel began to widen.

Passing rotten wooden support beams, he heard a loud crackling sound as flames entered the entrance and ignited the ancient wood. Shrugging off his smoking vest, the hairs on the back of his neck began curling from the heat. Suddenly, the whole tunnel groaned and rock began falling from the ceiling. Coughing as bitter dust entered his nose he fell forward and all turned black.

# Chapter Five

He nodded as he walked past the two agents guarding the entrance to the bunker. Inside, more agents prowled the passage, gathering evidence and removing articles from the inside. Still yards away from the entrance to the bunker, the smell of manufactured meth filled the air. Placing a white face mask over nose and mouth, he entered the area that the agents jokingly called the "Lab." It was a bad joke for a situation with little humor.

The place was large and had more of a warehouse feel to it than a room. Large glass and metal apparatuses covered the floor; some rested on tables and stands. Some still bubbled as low flames continued to boil the foul brew. Four of the large glass containers had been broken in the chaos that followed the raid.

Many of those same agents that had participated in the raid had traded guns and bullet proof vests for clip boards and pencils as they took on the huge task of inventorying the evidence. Walking to the back of the Lab, he passed through a large steel door that may have come from an old bank vault. Here another smell intruded.

Intended to be a passageway from the silo to the other larger room, the Milza brothers had converted it into a living quarters of sorts for their, "workers." More like a prison for their slaves. Cots and sleeping bags littered the floor of the long passage. Food wrappers, rotten clothes, and other unsavory tidbits lay in and around the sleeping area. Two spots reeking of human waste showed were the poor souls had been required to live in the same room were they shit.

Pausing, John stopped to pick up a toy truck. The red paint had begun to peel and two wheels were missing, but the toy only confirmed that the Milza's used children as well as adults in their operation. Swallowing down a taste of bile, he continued on to his

*meeting; unhappy with the deal he must make. With the smell
of shit and meth clinging to skin and clothes, he entered the last
room.*

Waking, the smell of meth followed him from the dream. Groaning, John pushed himself off of his rocky pillow. They were in an open enclosure of grey rock. On either side of the merchant, flickering light coming from two of Calphan's stones gave the only illumination. Without the stones, the group would have been swallowed in pitch darkness.

Still nursing his lip, the Mok squatted with Breg as the two looked to be inventorying the contents of the two travel bags. Carefully, Breg placed the contents of the bags into piles by color. Blue, red, and orange. Off to the left was a pile of blackened stones which appeared to have cracks on their surface. Each time Breg removed a cracked stone from the bag, the merchant hissed in annoyance. Breg seemed to have gotten over the fact that his master had left the servant for mesk food a short time ago.

Laying to his left, Gret slept fitfully curled up in his travel cloak. The man's hands did not seem to shake as much in sleep and his coloring was better. Tyrell was standing shirtless examining the entrance to the tunnel the company had fled from. The passage had collapsed and filled with the grey stone of the cavern. The air still smelled of dust and burned wood. The blue man's scars seemed to writhe across his body as the flickering lights danced on blue skin.

Walking over to the Mok, Champion squatted down next to the merchant and for a few moments watched Breg at his chore. With only the click of the stones, the three sat in relative silence. When John spoke, even though his words were softly spoken, the sound echoed through the silence of the cavern.

"Those stones smell like meth." Breg paused in his task to give Champion a questioning look.

"Meth. Methamphetamine. Crank. Meth. The drug?" Grunting, Calphan ignored him and motioned for Breg to continue.

Picking up one the lighted stones, John examined it. The stone was an orange color but gave off an amber light. In the center of the stone a hot white heart seemed to pulse, with orange and amber tendrils of light reaching out to the surface. Where the tendrils touched, small curls of smoke wafted up. A moment later a flash of heat passed through the stone and John cried out in pain and dropped it. With what must have been his idea of a laugh, kind of a wet huffing sound, Calphan produced a leather cloth and used it to pick up the stone. He began to examine the stone for nicks or scrapes due to Champion's rough handling.

"Your kind are all the same. You need to burn before you learn."

Shaking his hand seemed to make the pain lessen. John glared at the merchant. Curbing his anger, he asked.

"What is that thing?"

Continuing his examination, the Mok ignored him.

"It's a rawstone."

John jumped a bit at the voice from behind. He had not noticed that Gret had joined the group.

Shaking his head John gestured,

"A rawstone? But what is it? It smells just like a meth pipe."

Shrugging, Gret explained,

"It's a rawstone. They are used to power lights, cities, and just about anything."

John shook his head again,

"But what the hell is it?"

Interrupting, Calphan said,

"I think scar face here is asking about the properties of the stone. Yes?"

For some reason agreeing with the merchant on anything was irritating. John gave a stiff nod of agreement, and Calphan continued,

"That is a very perceptive question for a mund. The answer is that most of us don't know what goes into making the stones. The mages control all aspects of production and creation of the stones. However, I can tell you that the stones are imbued with power by a method that most munds are very familiar with." He chuckled cruelly. Gret's face paled a bit at the words and even the faithful Breg's hands trembled slightly.

*God, I hate this asshole.*

For the second time that day, John stuck his scarred face into that of the frogs. Grabbing the merchant's shirt with a trembling hand he hissed,

"I am not a fucking mund, you got that? I am a human being. And where I am from we eat frogs like you for breakfast." Calphan brushed John's trembling hand away. Almost falling forward into the merchant's lap, he was saved by Gret's steady grip. Easing him back into a sitting position, John was amazed at how weakened he was after such little effort.

Hearing that annoying laugh again, John looked up to see Calphan absently brushing the shirt where his hand had been as if trying to remove an offensive stain.

"I don't think you are in any condition to make good on any threats, low life. You expended quite a bit of your energy on that mesk pack. I am afraid you are nothing but a pathetic liability for the rest of us. We can't afford to haul you along, here." He motioned for Gret to assist Breg. Though he immediately obeyed, there appeared to be some reluctance in Gret's movements. Apparently Calphan noticed this as well and eyed his servant as he squatted down again to oversee the rawstone count.

A humorous chuckle interrupted the group as Tyrell appeared as if from thin air. His eyes had taken on a cat like yellow hew in the amber light.

"Honored merchant, do you need another sore mouth before you learn respect for my investment here?" Answering the question of who had man handled the Mok earlier, he continued,

"We are all going to stay together. Luckily, from the air currents and scents, I think we will spend no more than a few days underground. This place is Duvwer work, and they never built a tunnel with only one exit. Very practical people, the Duvwer. We will rest here, take stock of our provisions and then set out." Shifting away from the Ferrekei, Calphan did not respond though he did not refute the words of the blue man. Taking John aside, Tyrell helped the taller man to have a seat with his back against the far chamber wall.

Breathing a bit easier as he recovered from the bout of weakness, John shouldered the blanket tighter around his shoulders. Sitting next to him, Blondie handed over the infamous flask of liquid fire. Gratefully, he closed his eyes and took a swig and allowed the liquor to ease the chills from his body. Feeling relaxed and very tired, he pried his eyes open and nodded to the blue man. Nodding back, Blondie said quietly,

"John, Gret was correct. You are showing signs of mage fever. Your actions back there were amazing, and to be honest terrifying. But now we need to spend all of our efforts to get back above ground. What I did not share with the others was that the Duvwer would never abandon a tunnel like this.

It took too much effort to build such a place. They left for a reason, and also . . . ." His voice faded into a hushed whisper,

"I sense something . . . something dangerous. Something that hates. A deep hatred, here. We need to be gone from this place as soon as possible. We will have a moot before we depart."

Nodding again, John closed his eyes, watching as Tyrell walked back over to the Mok and his servants before sleep took him.

A dreamless sleep later, he was gently woken by a shake on the shoulder. Stretching out knotted muscles from sleeping on a stone floor, John was surprised at how good he felt. Seeing that Gret had been the one to rouse him, he allowed the other man to help him up. Though he felt better, he was still shaky on his feet.

Once Gret was assured the taller man would not fall over he handed him a small string of dried meat and some kind of fruit. Looking like a blue strawberry, the taste of a watermelon was a pleasant surprise. His hunger returned as he swallowed and gnawed on the jerky. John began to feel the good effects of the food as he watched the group prepare to head out.

As a surprise, John was handed over a small satchel to carry. Inside was some more of the jerky type meat and a jug with a cork stopper. Gret explained that an agreement had been reached between the two masters and that each party would be given food in case they were separated.

"What kind of agreement?"

With a faint smile Gret answered,

"Your master offered to leave us here *or* we take you along and share the food."

Motioning for him to sit, Tyrell waited until the company gathered around. When he had all their attention, he explained what he and Calphan had witnessed concerning the black figures and the mesk. He stressed that it was of utmost importance that someone from this group reach the outside and get word out concerning the mesk; that Grach may have been prevented from providing the warning.

"What about the dark ones?"

Calphan had appeared bored through Tyrell's little pep talk.

Nodding, Tyrell answered,

"Indeed. Those creatures are beyond my experience. If they seek us for some purpose, I do not know it. We must contact a mage and give it into their hands."

With a grunt, the Mok motioned Tyrell to lead and the small party proceeded further down the tunnel.

Tyrell led the group deeper into the dark and apparently needed no assistance from the two rawstone lights. The dutiful Breg followed the blue man with Master Calphan close behind. Both Breg and Calphan each held a rawstone attached to pieces of shovel shafts that the party had found. John, with Gret's assistance, took up the rear and had to keep a steady pace to stay within the light of the stones.

As the party proceeded, the rough tunnel gave way to smoother stone. Some type of script language began to dot the walls and more bits and pieces of civilization appeared; a broken wheel, a rusted chain, rotted bits of worked leather and cloth.

After what seemed like a dark eternity, Tyrell called the first stop. With a grateful sigh, John laid his bag down and he and Gret sat down next to Breg and the fuming stone. The light revealed that the party had come to a junction of some kind. Three tunnel entrances went off in different directions; Tyrell stood before the left facing entrance and held a quiet discussion with Calphan. Nodding to the Mok, the blue man entered the entrance and disappeared from sight. Walking back, the merchant squatted down far removed from the other three and appeared to be deep in his own thoughts.

"How are you feeling?" Gret asked.

"Good, but tired." He answered.

"That walk should not have taken so much out of me."

Nodding in understanding Gret cautioned,

"That can happen when a mage uses up their energy reserves. You need to be careful. Many mages would need several days in bed to recover from what you did. You seem to recover quickly."

Rubbing a hand over his face, John asked,

"This is all so unreal. Am I dreaming? Am I dead? Is this really happening?"

Seeing the confused looks of the two men, he chuckled ruefully,

"Where I am from, in my worl . . . land, we do not have mages. And frogs don't go around giving orders, and fire does not come out of my hand . . ." lifting his scarred appendage up the two other men flinched as if fire might erupt.

"You must be mad."

It was the first time since entering the tunnels that Breg had spoken to him. He continued,

"Master thinks you are some freak. Some Ferrakei experiment that went wrong. A mund Mage? Nonsense."

For the first time since meeting the man, John saw real anger, real emotion. Shaking off the placating hand that Gret placed on his shoulder, Breg's anger increased,

"You come from some mystical place where there are no mages? Do you know how dangerous such talk is? Do you have any idea how you have endangered us? If master does not sell us to the rawstone guild when, if, we survive this, we should thank the gods, you don't act like a mund who has any training . . . and . . . what by the cursed one is a frog?!"

Although it was evident that Breg's fussy kind of fury was genuine, he sounded like nothing more than a worried mother clucking over her chicks. Able to stare into his red flushed face for only a moment, John suddenly threw his head back and laughed. The tunnel junction echoed with the noise. Sitting further back on his haunches, with tears running down his face John simply could not stop laughing.

The laughter was infectious. Try as he might, Breg could not control his mirth. Whether it was from the fear and stress of their parties' predicament or true humor, he also began to laugh. Gasping for breathe, Gret tried to smother his laughter in his hands which created a noise somewhere in between a snort and a fart. This caused even further laughter. Even the commanding voice of the infuriated merchant was not heard over the din for sometime. Regaining his composure, Breg hopped to his feet and quickly approached his master who instructed him to sit and be quiet.

After the laughter died away, the group waited for Tyrell's return.

It was during John's watch that the Ferrekei arrived back at the resting spot. Gathering up the group, he spoke bluntly.

"All the tunnels appear to go quite some distance. The one on the left has the scent of having a better chance of getting above ground than the others; however, there is a possibility that it may lead us to the Cali Dun Thar."

Calphan sucked his cheeks in and out making an exasperated sound. At John's unresponsive expression, Blondie explained,

"There are strange tales about the Cali Dun Thar, for it is connected to ancient pathways. Not a few Dwuvar have ventured into the old mines, seeking legend and gold, and most have returned. But a few have vanished. And since it is impossible for a dwuvar to lose his way underground, something must have befallen them. I tell you this so that there will be no misunderstandings, but if we keep to the passages dug by the duvwar, we should lessen the risk."

The mood of the group lightened a little, as Tyrell spoke.

Smiling a toothy grin, the blue man motioned for them to follow.

The passages were damp. Every once in a while they would pass a tunnel branching off to one side or the other. John peered down each as he passed, but they were quickly swallowed up in the dark. The stone light sent flickering shadows dancing along the walls, expanding and shrinking as they moved closer or farther from each other, or as the tunnel ceilings rose or fell. At several places, the party had to partially dig with their hands to widen the way as water had eroded sections of the tunnels, but for most of their passage there was ample room. Breg grumbled at times like this for the tools their group had been forced the leave back at the camp site.

John heard Gret, behind him, mutter,

"I'd not want to fall from the path down here; I've lost my direction sense a dozen times."

John said nothing, with the darkness of the tunnels feeling like a physical thing, pushing against him.

While the darkness of the passages and the danger of their circumstances weighed heavily on them, John felt himself bonding with Calphan's two servants. While he had nothing to complain about his time with Grach and Tyrell, being around two other human beings was comforting. At every brief stop the two men would attend to Calphan and then sit with John. Breg nearly laughed to death when John explained what a frog was; and that people really did eat their legs. Receiving a cold glare from the merchant, the three men lapsed into quiet talk until Tyrell called for them to move.

After some time they came to another junction cavern with several tunnels leading out. The company halted here and Tyrell ordered that a watch be posted. The rawstones were wedged into rocks and everyone settled down for a tasteless meal. John stood his turn at watch, and thought that several times shapes moved just out of the stone light. Soon, Breg replaced him and he joined the others who were eating. John asked Tyrell,

"What sort of place is this?"

The blue man paused for a moment before he answered,

"I am not a miner by trade, and my people do not relish the underground, but I believe that this is called a borehole. When the duwvar first mined this part of the mountains, they made many such places. When great veins of silver, iron, or gold would come together, many tunnels would be joined. And as the ore was taken out, caverns like this would be formed. I have been told that there are caverns as large made by natures hand, but have a different look. They have great spikes of stone rising from the floor, and others hanging from the ceilings, unlike this one. We may see these on our journey."

Looking up, John asked,

"How high does it climb?"

Tyrell followed his gaze.

"Can't say exactly. Maybe a hundred feet. Or even two or three times that. While these mountains are still rich with ore, when the duwvar first mined them, the ore was rich beyond imagination. My people enjoyed trade with them for years for the mined precious metals. There are hundreds of tunnels throughout this range, with many levels upward and down from where we stand."

Tyrell swallowed the last of his jerky as he looked on the last of the group finishing their meal.

"Well, we had better be on our way again."

John could not hide a groan,

"I thought we were stopping for the night."

"The sun is yet it the sky, good Champion. We have a good three hours before sunset."

"But it seems . . ."

Tyrell interrupted,

"I know. Time is easy to lose track of, down here in the dark, unless you have the skill of it."

Gathering what little of their gear they had left, the group started off again. After walking a bit they entered a series of twisting, turning passages that seemed to slant down hill. Tyrell explained that the entrance on the west side of the mountains was several feet lower than on the east side, and that they would be moving downward for a good portion of the journey but then would start ascending.

At another time John would have found the needless information the blue man was providing them annoying, but given the circumstances, it was reassuring. Perhaps that was a way for Tyrell to keep the group calm and together.

Later they passed another glory hole, though the ceiling could be seen in this one. Again a number of tunnels led from it in different directions. Blondie picked one with little hesitation and led them through.

Soon, John could hear the sound of water, coming from ahead. Tyrell said, over his shoulder,

"You'll soon see a sight that few living have laid eyes on."

As they walked, the sound of crashing water became louder. They entered another cavern, this one natural and larger than any they had yet seen. The tunnel they came through became a ledge, thirty feet wide, that ran along the left side of the rock wall. Peering over the edge, human eyes could see nothing but darkness stretching away below.

The path rounded a curve in the wall, and as John passed around it, a sight out of a fairy tale greeted them.

*Shit, this whole experience has been a fairy tale.*

A mighty river of water fell over a huge outcropping of stone. Three hundred feet, at least, from where they all stood, the water poured into the cavern, crashing against the rock wall and disappearing into the darkness below.

The waters course caused a colossal sound that made hearing almost impossible. Throughout the running water, colors danced. Gold's, greens, and blues played along the mad rushing waters, painting a colorful picture of light in the darkness.

Tyrell yelled over the sound.

"Millienia ago, this river ran from the Iced Mountains, to the open sea. A great calamity of moving rock opened a fissure under the river bed, and now it runs through the rock, and picks up minerals that give it the colors. This marks the beginning of the Cali Dun Thar. Grach will die of envy when I tell him." Standing quietly, the group stayed still for the moment, marveling at the sight.

Tyrell signaled for the hike to resume, and they moved on. Besides the amazing view, they had been refreshed somewhat by the cool spray of the water. Now their steps led them deeper into the mines, past scores of tunnels and passages.

Sometime later, they came to another cavern, and Tyrell said it was time to rest for the night. The two rawstones looked to be almost used up and their light flickered weakly. Irritated, Calphan exclaimed,

"I hope you know what you are doing, Ferrakei. My profits are going up in smoke as we trudge through this nightmare. If I lose any more stones, I will have to sell myself into servitude to pay my debts."

Chuckling, Tyrell turned,

"And such honest profits, honored merchant. Dozens of rawstones carried in only two leather satchels through the wilderness? Do you have the purchase tablet signed by the rawstone guild? Was the sale sanctioned by a standing mage?"

Calaphan's face turned to chiseled stone. Breg's face flushed and he kept his eyes lowered. Gret lowered his eyes as well but his features had a smug look about them.

Taking a step towards the blue man, the merchant shrilled,

"You dare! I am a merchant of the second order, of highly . . . ."

Suddenly the hairs on John's arms and neck stood up, and a chill touch washed over him, almost making him lose his meager meal.

"Tyrell!" he cried.

"Something is happening!"

Tyrell stood still as a statue, listening. A faint groan echoed down the passageway.

Gret shouted. "I feel it too."

Suddenly, the groaning was heard again, this time closer, a heart stopping sound that chilled the soul.

"By moon and stars!" shouted the blue man.

"A Bane! A Bane is upon us. Quickly, form a circle, or we will be forever lost!"

Tyrell hurriedly instructed the company to make a circle, back to back. From his pack the blue man pulled a stick of wood and quickly applied some sticky substance to the surface which ignited the brand. Other pieces of wood were quickly passed around the company and in moments four torches lit the darkness. Calphan drew a long curved blade from his pack. Tyrell had also produced a blade that now glinted in the torch light. Sweating, John thought the terror that gripped his heart would make it burst.

Hearing a sharp intake of breathe, they looked to the right. Before a warning could be shouted, a figure swooped out of the dark. Almost man shaped, it was darker than the blackness of the cave; twin cold green fires glowed from where its eyes should be. The groan now turned into a shrill, keening sound, as if the creature were in agony.

Tyrell shouted.

"Don't let it touch you, that is how it feeds. Keep close and guard each other. It likes not the feel of iron, or fire!"

It approached them slowly, almost calmly. Stopping the shadow seemed to sniff the air. Then it let out another groan, which grated on the ears, and sounded like despair incarnate. Abruptly, the Mok slashed out, grazing the bane with his blade. A scream that could have shattered glass almost brought them to their knees. With sudden speed, it struck the merchant, sending him down to one knee. Tyrell leapt between the Bane and Calphan, waving his brand. The fire caused the dark creature to back away. The blue man helped the Mok to his feet as he shouted again.

"To me, we must keep the thing at bay. Stand close." Obeying, John stepped closer to the blue man with the others. The Bane drew further back, retreating from the flames.

"We must leave this tunnel." Tyrell shouted over the keening.

"Keep your flames between yourself and the creature. It cannot bear to touch the flames. We must escape now. Hurry!"

Pointing to a tunnel entrance, on the other side of the cavern, Tyrell shouted.

"That way. Quickly."

Keeping a tight formation, the group started toward the tunnel and other unsavory objects came to light. Two ancient corpses lay on the floor. Abandoned torches littered the ground. Following Tyrell's instructions, John and Gret paused to collect a few of the ancient staves as Breg helped his master to the tunnel mouth. Ranging about the edge of the flames, the bane was either unable or unwilling to cross the barrier of fire.

Just as it appeared that the party might make it without incident, Gret stumbled on a broken brand. Falling on his back, the torch flew from his hand and hit the side of the cavern wall, sputtering dark. Shrieking in glee the Bane leapt on the stunned man. Gret screamed as an ice cold hand closed over his arm.

John reacted. Gripping his torch in both hands like a club, he swung the brand straight in between the creatures glowing eyes. He heard the wood make a satisfying thud as it struck the creature. With a groan, the bane released Gret and went into a frenzy of pain, lashing out with ethereal clawed hands. John was struck and thrown across the cavern, his face bouncing off the hard rock hewn wall.

Dizzy, he climbed to his feet to see Tyrell grabbing the injured Gret and dragging him to the small opening of the tunnel where Calphan and Breg held new torches in each hand, creating a small wall of flaming protection. John snaked a hand out to his torch which nearly sputtered out on the ground.

Looking past the creature to the safety of the flames, John's stomach churned as though struck. He was now, behind the bane. He looked helplessly on as the party made their escape.

"John!" screeched Gret.

The party halted for a moment, and Tyrell said,

"We can't stop. The torches are almost spent. We would all perish. We must press on."

Motioning behind him, Breg and Calphan each grabbed an arm of the injured Gret and dragged him further into the safety of the tunnel. John looked and saw the sad face of Tyrell, outlined by the torch flames.

"We must leave him, forest forgive me." said Tyrell to himself, a grim note in his voice.

"John is a feast brother and a friend. He understands."

Fighting uselessly, Gret was dragged further into the tunnel out of sight. The Bane followed the group for a moment, then it stopped and turned to John, as if for the first time seeing the man standing alone with his torch held above his head.

John hesitated for a moment, then spun on his heal and ran to the opposite tunnel. The Bane shrieked and started after him. Tyrell saw the flame of his friends torch flicker in the dark of the other tunnel for an instant, and then darkness.

# Chapter Six

Torch light made shadows dance along the walls as he fled down the passage, heart thudding in his chest. The torch held tightly in one hand as he ran. Looking over his shoulder, John saw two glowing eyes gaining on him. With a grim smile he thought, if that thing catches me, it will only be because I have no life left in my body.

John churned his legs until he was sure they were a blur of movement. He knew if he had to turn and fight the bane, he would die. His fear slowly diminished and he felt the cold certainty and cunning of prey knowing it is hopeless to fight. All his energy was concentrated on fleeing the hunter. He would try any way imaginable to elude the dark death.

Ducking into a side passageway, he hurried down it, checking to see if the bane followed. The glowing eyes appeared at the entrance to the tunnel he had fled down, following. Hunting. The distance between them seemed to have increased. John began to think that many of the creature's victims had died from fear, and not flight. The bane's power lay in the overwhelming terror it caused.

Down another corridor and another sharp turn. Still the eyes followed. Straight ahead was a large cavern and John found himself back to where the party had been attacked. He had circled back around! Racing, he saw the old torch brands lying discarded. Stopping long enough to grab a fresh brand, he transferred the flame from his old torch.

Looking back, he saw the creature closing on him and sped off again. Which tunnel did his companions use? In the terror and panic of the attack, he was all turned around. If he could pick the proper corridor, he had a chance of catching up to the others. Trying to remember Tyrell's words, he picked what he thought was the right one, though in the dim torch light he could not be sure.

The bane let out a scream of rage as he eluded it again. John felt elated as his legs pumped and churned, his long strides eating up the distance of the oncoming tunnel. He almost flew over the stone. Gaining a second wind, he slowed a bit and set a steady pace for himself.

Never could he remember running so fast for so long. Then again, never had life and death depended upon it. In the back of his mind, unnoticed due to the fear coursing through him, a quiet wispy voice chuckled gleefully. It liked this mage.

After what seemed like a lifetime of darkness, he found himself coming towards a series of side tunnels, set close together. Hope died in his chest, because this was not the upward path Tyrell had mentioned. Quickly picking one, John turned as sharply as possible, weaving his way through a sea of passageways. Ducking into another side tunnel, he stopped to catch his breathe. Listening for a moment, John could only hear his own panting. He had been so concentrated on what was before him he was not sure where the bane had gone.

A scream of rage ripped the air, echoing off the walls, but it sounded faint and far away. John leaned against the cool stone wall, and let his body rest. Another scream, and John was sure the bane had lost his scent and was moving away.

A sense of intense relief flooded through him, and he almost wanted to laugh. This was closely followed by the realization of what kind of situation he was in. Standing straight, he took stock. If he could make it back to the rest stop, he could get more torches and maybe a better idea of where his companions went. But, he realized that he had no idea where he was.

Pondering this, suddenly, his energy left him, and he slumped to the ground, chills coursing through his body. His last conscious thoughts were remembering Gret's warning about not pushing himself too hard; then, darkness.

HE FELT water on his face and smelled wood smoke. A strong hand held his head up as water was dribbled into his mouth. Wanting more, he sat up and tried to grab the water source.

An all too familiar chuckle came from near his face and John opened his eyes. Sitting there, nose to nose, holding a water skin tantalizingly out of reach, with a smug smile on her face, was the cause of all of his recent problems.

"Dammit, Terra. Give me that water!"

With another chuckle Terra moved quickly away and tossed the skin over to the ungrateful man and watched him guzzle it. After his thirst was sated, he turned his attention to his nemesis. A nemesis who was completely ignoring him as she was bent brewing something on a newly made fire. Before he made another statement, the smell of brothy stew reached his nose. With his mouth watering, he commented, grudgingly,

"Smells good."

Blue eyes looked up and twinkled at him through the fire light,

"Terra knows her brew, that is for sure; a family secret."

Producing a wooden bowl from out of her strange garments, she poured the precious broth into it and passed it over. Remembering from their first encounter, John took small sips until it cooled and then drank heartily. With a contented sigh, he looked up with a hopeful face.

"That is all I have, my Champion. Be grateful I could reach you here in this place."

Grunting thanks, he hunkered down and stared at the annoying woman. Who annoyingly stared right back at him. Several moments passed as the small fire flickered, until his predicament made him impatient,

"What now?"

Throwing back her head, the woman laughed. It was a wonderful sound that bounced through the darkness. It was infectious and soon John joined her. Hell, why not? He seemed to be laughing a lot lately.

Several moments later, after she had calmed her mirth and used her hands to idly smooth her strange garments, Terra replied,

"Jonathan Champion. The things you say. You are a light in the darkness."

"Huh. An ugly light." He replied,

"Let's agree that you are a striking light and leave it at that, eh?" Getting another smile from John, she continued,

"So you are here, alone except for this lovely woman, who cannot stay by the way, deep below the dark ground. *What are you doing?*"

John ignored that last jibe. Pulling his blanket turned cloak around him he shivered. Seeing that, Terra nodded,

"Ah yes. You used fire for the first time, did you not? I can feel the energy burned from you. You must master fire, or it can consume you. With other elementals you may try other methods, but fire only understands strength."

Glaring at her now, John spat,

"Well, that is great advice now. Why didn't you tell me that before?"

Jumping up, the small woman was now facing him again, with hands on her hips.

"This coming from a boy who thought he was either dead or dreaming? Or, what else did you say? Hallucinating? Ha!

You had to find your own way to your powers, my Champion. Air has always been with you. In fact, it aided in your escape. But fire is different. It will burn you to cinders if you cannot control it . . ."

"Air aided my escape? How?"

His interruption irritated the woman but she answered anyway.

"My Champion, how could you, a human man, have out run a bane unaided? The creature can float through solid stone for cursed sake! You are now scores of miles from the surface. I had to intervene now, at no little cost to myself, to get you back on the path."

Crossing his arms, John jutted his chin at the offensive little woman. Sitting down in resignation, Terra groaned,

"My Champion, your stubbornness is not a virtue here in the cold dark. You need some quick on the job training, as they say in your world."

He gave no sign of giving in and Terra sighed,

"My Champion . . . please?"

He was such a sucker for women when they asked nice. Uncrossing his arms, he nodded.

With a warm smile, she began,

"Call for fire, but this time, gently."


"CALM YOURSELF, dear one. You have done well."

The placating tone annoyed him, but he did not let it show. The old crone annoyed everyone at some point, but it was unwise to be disrespectful to a mage. Piercing blue eyes seemed to peer through his soul, searching for secrets.

The elderly Ferracki mage sat on a chair which forced Tyrell to look upward at her. Colored beads that younger females usually wore were woven throughout white grey hair that flowed to her waist, contrasting with her wrinkled blue arms. Her conceit that she was still a young beauty was legendary. Wearing the red robe that all fire mages seemed to favor, she sat like a queen attending court.

Sipping from a delicate cup, dried old lips drank the bitter smelling tea that most Ferracki preferred. Calling him "Dear one" was a phrase usually reserved for immediate family members, and Tyrell had only seen Gazell on formal occasions. And at those times from a distance, thank the forest! The most powerful mage his people had produced in a millennium, perhaps ever, Gazell spoke with authority like no other clan chief. She seemed lost in thought as he finished his tale.

A throat cleared and he turned his attention to the third individual in the tent. With pale, yellow skin, the red haired Duwvar sat on the floor like Tyrell. Wearing a dark blue shirt and matching trousers, the man looked uncomfortable.

*He most likely would prefer to be underground.* Tyrell thought silently, as he absently ran his hands through the threads of the thick Thur skin rug.

The rug bedecked tent was set not far from the tunnel mouth he had led his party of relieved companions through. Two days ago the small company had arrived in the blessed sunlight. Exhausted, dehydrated and famished, they had spent the first hours foraging the local bushes for berries and nuts. He remembered vividly finding a purple sacha tree, hanging low with unpicked fruit. Even the Mok joined in the excitement and they had spent a blissful time simply eating the watery fruit enjoying the above ground air. The memory brought a smile to his face as the red haired man spoke,

"Do you think you missed something in your recollections?"

"Which part?"

He was being difficult and he knew it. The Duvwar looked beseechingly at the older mage.

"Tisk, Dear one. You know we are talking about this strange mund you and the molden acquired. He sounds fascinating. Did he mention anything of his origins? Who he owed service too? Why, you have not even told us his name or what he looks like." She gave a sunny smile as she sat the cup in her lap.

Gazell and Farg, the duvwar, had arrived at the meager campsite on the second night after the party had exited the tunnels. Two mages and their escorts turned the quiet campsite into a bustling affair with pack animals, tents, and cook fires. Nearly fifty Ferraiki warriors dressed in leather battle harnesses and armed to the teeth had taken custody of the small group.

Later that afternoon Duvwar warriors looking like chitin covered insects in their strange armor arrived with the two mages. All the warriors wore the four sided elemental emblem of the mages, signifying their allegiance. Fire, water, earth, air. The warriors were grim, talked little, and guarded their two charges with deadly seriousness. Tyrell had been immediately separated from Calphan and his servants; he had no doubt they were being questioned as well.

Running a tired hand through his hair, Tyrell could feel exhaustion returning.

"Honored Gazell, if you mean my feast brother, we did not acquire him. He met us under strange circumstances which . . . I am not at liberty to disclose to you. Honor applies."

He had to duck the cup as it flew at his head and shattered into a tent pole. Gazell had regained her composure by the time he turned back to her, wiping ceramic shards from his hair. Her tone did not indicate she had done anything out of the ordinary.

"This is nonsense and you know it, Dear one. Mundanes cannot access their life force, therefore they cannot perform magic. This clan ancient feast brother nonsense might be applied to other magical races, but not a mund. You might as well have named a beast of burden a feast brother!"

He was in a dangerous situation and knew it.

Licking his suddenly dry lips he tried a new approach,

"And does the mesk infestation and these black cloaked creatures not take precedence over the capture of an insignificant mund?"

Sitting back on his haunches the Duvwar's face creased into a scowl,

"The word has gone out concerning the mesk and parties are being gathered to flush them out. These black ones you mentioned, are you sure their garments were not, grey?"

Gazell shifted uncomfortably in her seat. Obviously Farg was treading close to something she found disturbing.

Tyrell shook his head,

"No, honored mage. The cloaks were black, but were wrapped around the creatures and obscured their features; even their feet. The only thing that could be seen was their hands. Clawed like a talon of some large bird or lizard."

Gazell lowered her head, resting her chin on her chest as if in deep contemplation as he spoke. As if reaching a hard decision, her shoulders slumped for a moment, then straightened as she swung her gaze at him. Tyrell barely concealed a shiver.

"We must know everything, dear one. Now!"

The force in her voice made him tremble. He could feel a force pushing at his mind. Shaking his head he tried to move but found himself trapped by the mage's blue gaze. His limbs were frozen to his sides and he could not look away. Gazell's voice sounded soft and alluring.

"Now Dear one, tell us about your new feast brother . . ."

Though he screamed inside his head, Tyrell heard and felt his mouth begin to speak as both mages leaned forward.

# CHAPTER SEVEN

His brain itched. He had never felt this way in his life, but it was the best way John could describe it. With his good hand, he scratched the back of his head amazed at this new situation.

John walked the tunnels in light. Or rather, fire light. It was hard to come to grips with the fact that his arm could shine like a weird human flash light. The first attempts to call fire had met with disaster which burned part of his eyebrow off. His second attempt had lighted Terra's clothing on fire and she had forgiven him only after he had convinced her it was an accident. After the third failure, she had informed him they were going to take a short cut. Before John could react, she had placed both hands on the side of his head. The next thing he remembered was waking up to find he was lying on the ground with Terra peering over him.

After that, things became easier. She recommended that he should call on fire gently, quietly, unless he really needed to burn something. Now, if he concentrated, he could control it; albeit unsteadily.

Air was different. He called for it, and he could sense it, but it was elusive. As if the element thought it was a game. Terra gave up and simply stated that if he needed air, don't count on it yet.

His second talk with Terra had left him as confused as the first. She questioned him at length of his experiences since their first meeting. She was extremely interested in Gret and Breg, spat when he told her of the Mok, and waved her hand vaguely at his story about Blondie.

"The ferrekei can be useful to you. He called you feast brother eh? That should be interesting." But she refused to explain. Of Grach she said nothing, but only rubbed her chin in thought.

Finally, he talked about the rawstones. As he explained their meth smell the small woman's cheerful face became grave.

"My Champion, you will learn more of the rawstones. Seek out your people again, and learn at the right time."

After he had called fire enough times without burning either of them she instructed,

"You must go immediately to Hyberan. Find Mosha the librarian. He has made an interesting discovery. Tell him everything. He can be trusted."

At his attempt to ask questions, she had simply raised her hand for quiet.

"My champion, being here taxes my strength, and I must leave you."

Then with another bowl of broth, and a quick pat on the head, she sent him on his way as she vanished.

So now, he walked.


AFTER AN indefinite period of time, John stopped and looked about the third large cavern he had come upon since fleeing the bane. Like the other two, there was no sight of bodies, food, or wood. Opening his pouch, he grimaced wanly at the empty bottle of water and two pieces of jerky that were his last provisions. Taking a bite of the jerky, which did little for his hunger, he put the food and the bottle away. Setting off again, he tried to find some clue on how to get to the surface. John knew that he had only a limited time before his companions gave him up for dead, but refused to sit in the dark and wait for death to take him.

After long hours, John could hear the sound of water. The water bottle had run dry a few hours ago and thirst began to dominate his thoughts. Hurrying his steps, a dry throat egging him on, he entered a large cavern, the largest he had seen yet. Far away, he could hear the Cali Dun Thar falls, but could not determine their direction. Feeling his heart in his throat, he realized that he had gone even deeper underground.

The passage widened to a perch or landing of some kind and disappeared beneath a huge lake, whose waters lapped against the cavern walls. Falling to his knees, he drank. While the water tasted of iron, it felt sweet and wet on his tongue.

Wiping his mouth and sitting back, he looked about. The ground felt like packed earth and may have been worked by some unknown hand rather than being a natural formation. John thought that perhaps these dwuvar folk had built a landing for boats to cross the lake. With the dim light from his arm, the darkness of the cave and the size of the lake, he could only guess what lay across. To his left he spied a pile of broken timbers, nestled against a recess in the cavern wall.

Walking over to it, he pulled out several pieces and started a small fire. The wood was made up of timber, most likely used to reinforce tunnels. While Terra had told him in time he would be able to control his body temperature, that for now he should wait for further instruction. The idea of burning up from the inside out did not sound appealing.

John began a slow search of the cavern to keep his mind occupied. It was clear that at one time the lake had covered the entire cavern floor as shells and fossils of ancient snails and fish dotted the ground. Looking up from his explorations, John's fire light flickered on what he had first thought was just another part of the cavern wall. Coming closer, he could discern a slab of stone sticking out of the rough rock surface. Other slabs seemed to follow across the entire side of the cavern. Stairs! They were stairs of some kind!

Returning to his fire, John sat and tried to decide what he should do. Either the stairs led some where, or they led nowhere. In any event, it was better than wandering the caverns. Sighing, he felt weariness fall over him like warm water. He needed sleep. After a short rest, he would be able to think with a clear head.

Satisfied that nothing lurked in the shadows, almost too tired to care, John huddle as far as he could in the stone recess. Closing his eyes, he concentrated on quenching the light emitting from his arm. Feeling the element slowly seep from his arm he grunted in satisfaction as the only light that now filled the lake cavern was his campfire. Although he was frightened beyond anything he had experienced in his life, he was exhausted and he soon nodded to sleep. In his dreams, eyes of fire chased him down darkly lit passages. He ran until his lungs burned and his legs felt like lead.

Starting awake, John had no idea how long he had slept, but felt it had been long enough for his legs to feel like walking again. Closing tired eyes, he concentrated on calling fire. Slowly, his arm began to glow and warm light pierced the darkness. Getting to his feet, he saw that the cavern remained unchanged. He knew that the only hope at survival was to keep moving until he found a way out. Coming to the stairs, he took a deep breathe and started up.

GRACH PAUSED by the two ancient corpses, picking up the old torch brands. While he needed no light to travel by, his ancestors had handed down to him senses that defied the darkness; he thought that it would increase the chances of finding John if his friend could see the light. Assuming that Champion still lived, he thought grimly.

He had found Tyrell and his company on the first night they had exited the tunnels. Their happy reunion was darkened by the loss of Champion. Quietly Grach had listened as his friend told him of their terrifying journey, Champion's amazing destruction of the mesk, and of the dark cloaked creatures. From the tone of his voice Grach could sense the fear in his friend as he described the black flames that had nearly engulfed them.

For several minutes after Tyrell had told his story, the two had sat in the quiet of the night, watching as the flames of the small camp fire slowly smoldered away.

Keeping his eye on the sleeping forms of the Mok and his servants, Grach said silently,

"We must help him, somehow, my friend." Nodding, Tyrell answered,

"He is a feast brother, and has saved my life. Honor demands it."

And there, in the dark of the night, the two hatched a plan to try to help their lost friend.

Grach searched for signs of John's passing. The dust was relatively thin, but here and there he could see scuffs in the soil, perhaps made by a sandaled foot. Tracking, the molden made it to passages where the dust was thicker and foot prints could be easily marked. Quickening his pace, he followed them. After several minutes, Grach found himself back in the same cavern and swore. Believing that there was little hope in finding John's tracks again, what with the other marks left by the fight with the Bane, Grach began to examine each passageway leading out of the cavern.

After over an hour, he found a single foot print leading away from the cavern through a passage opposite to the one he had just entered from. Proceeding further, he quickly found several prints, set wide apart, and knew the tall mund must have been running. Hurrying, he saw more tracks, as the dust on the stone floor became thicker.

Grach entered the cavern with the lake and almost lost the trail, until he saw the remains of a fire and the stone stairs on the far side wall. Pulling himself up to the first step, it was obvious to him the ancient stone crafters had little thought for short legged molden in their plans. Climbing up the stairs, he soon came to a stone landing.

Not a landing, he thought, but a path cut into the side of the cavern wall. Before him and disappearing into the darkness of the cavern was a wide stone path. More a road than a path, Grach muttered. Seeing additional tracks, he knew he followed John's trail. The signs showed that he was now journeying at a slower pace. A blackened spot indicated where his friend had built another fire.

Downward the path led him, and the air began to feel heavy. The wind did not stir this deep into the bowels of the mountains and even a molden would find such a place unnerving. After almost a full day of traveling, Grach came to another set of stairs that led off the stone path.

Coming to the bottom, a wide marble street met the molden. With the remains of metal lamp posts on either side, there was no mistaking that at one time this was a major roadway in its day. Grach followed a trail of what seemed to be large straight markings; as though something heavy had dragged its way down here. John's tracks were mixed in with these, and he worried for his friend.

Kneeling down, Grach placed his finger into one of the strange markings; Ground Wyrm. Some said the large creatures were cousins to ancient dragons. Whatever their ancestry, the Wyrms were dangerous. Many a molden settlement had been destroyed by the voracious Wyrms. If John had stumbled onto its lair, then he may be in grave danger. By the looks of the markings, the creature was massive. If John was being hunted by the wyrm, then every moment was critical.

The road way wound downward and soon changed into a hall fashioned from giant stone blocks fitted almost seamlessly together, polished shiny and smooth. Never had Grach seen the like. The road narrowed a bit, and the molden walked silently along. The tracks had vanished for the road was now free of dust. Over head, Grach could see a ceiling and could make out what remained of crystal and diamond chandeliers, hung from chains. To Grach's ears his steady steps echoed loudly off the walls and ceiling. At the far end of the road, large black doors loomed before him, made from black stone. The doors were ajar, and the molden walked cautiously through them.

On the other side a long table ran the length of a huge room. Golden cups and plates lay covered in dust, their owners long since gone. Along the walls, manacles and chains were attached at intervals, making Grach shudder. From the stories of his people he recalled mention of ancient evil that used to live in the dark of the earth. Grach had no doubt the chains were most likely used to imprison poor victims of some long ago bloody practice. Among the plates and cups, the molden now noticed wickedly curved knives and other implements of torture. No doubt, cries of pain once filled the grand place as much as laughter and revelry.

At the end of the hall, he spied another set of doors, these fashioned from wood long turned to stone from age. They were ajar and a light could be seen coming through.

Silently, Grach approached the doors and peered in. Gaping at what he saw, his mace came to his hand on instinct.

Sitting on a pile of silver coins and leaning against a marble statute was John, drinking what looked to be a good flagon of ale. Opposite him, sitting in a throne like chair was a creature out of nightmare.

A head in the shape of a lizard rested on a huge muscled body. Black and red spikes covered the head, and sharp yellowed teeth were caressed by a flickering snake like tongue. A black scaled hand held a crushing grip on a large golden goblet. Leathery wings sprouted from huge shoulders and draped along the back of the throne. If the creature had stood up, it would have measured at least eight feet.

Grach fought down the rare urge to abandon his honor and the mund, for John was sitting, and from his laughter, sharing a drink with a nightmare out of legend; a Dracoth. Stepping forward, Grach's boots disturbed a pile of gold coins.

John turned at the sound, and the Dracoth tilted its head. Alarmingly bright sapphire eyes regarded the stocky warrior. John jumped to his feet at seeing the molden. "Grach!"

Draining his cup, John rushed over to him.

The Dracoth's voice trembled through the hall, sounding very low and un-snake like.

"Welcome, short one. John hast told me that one or more of his friends would be seeking him."

John embraced the molden and then rambled half a dozen questions that Grach barely heard as he could not take his eyes off the seated creature. Behind them, the Dracoth stayed quiet as he observed the reunion. Shaking his head at John's questions, Grach stepped in between his friend and the monster.

"I come alone," he said softly.

"Tyrell tried to dissuade me from searching by myself, but he needed care and our mission was vital."

John nodded.

"I understand."

"What manner of evil is this?" Grach asked.

Chuckling, the Dracoth waved his hand to encompass the entire hall.

"Welcome to my home, warrior. While I do not consider myself evil, I will answer what questions I may."

The molden walked slowly further into the hall, his mace at the ready. Laughing now in full, a rich leathery sound, the Dracoth met Grach's gaze.

"Hold your battle heart but a moment, brave one. I will not harm thee or the human. In fact, your friend has allowed me to allay a centuries old thirst."

Waving his clawed hand towards a far corner of the chamber, Grach saw what appeared to be a barrel of ale, which had been recently opened.

Grach hung his mace on his belt and took out his pipe. Looking around, he saw that they were standing in another vast hall, fashioned from the very rock of the mountain. The walls were covered with faded tapestries that depicted alien dark figures at numerous tasks, many of them bloody.

No race he knew of had fashioned this place. Piles of treasure littered the room; golden cups and bronze shields mixed in with diamond encrusted bowls and rotted silver breast plates. At the far end of the hall, a giant black altar like stone was set on a dais, with high backed chairs set facing it as if for a puppet show.

Sitting down, the molden found himself on top of a lifetime of riches and costly cloth. He settled into the expensive seat, trying to get as comfortable as possible. John sat next to him as the molden refused to take his eyes from the Dracoth and absently began to puff on his pipe.

Watching curiously, the lizard man asked,

"Is that fire you breathe, molden? Have the small ones become dragon kin like my kind?"

Shaking his head, Grach answered,

"My pipe, is all that this is." And he explained its use.

Chuckling again, the Dracoth said,

"Strange has the world become. But your people were always set on doing strange things."

Arching an eyebrow at this, Grach looked to his friend. "John, how and why are you in this place?"

Seemingly unmindful of the Dracoth, John explained,

"I spent what felt like hours and hours wandering the tunnels, trying to find a passage that would lead to the surface. Then I came to the cavern with the lake."

"Yes, I found that as well."

"Following the path around the lake, I stopped to make a fire and rest."

At the molden's nod, he continued on.

"Some sounds woke me up and I found the wide road and tracks that led here."

"I also saw those. I was sore worried you had been taken."

"No, it was a close thing though. It was a huge worm of some kind. God it moved fast for being so fat."

Through his pipe smoke the molden offered,

"Ground Wyrm."

Shrugging, John continued,

"I could tell from the start that it wasn't interested in talking. It was very determined to get where it was going. I thought perhaps it would lead me to the surface. I thought if I could get out of the tunnels, I could have tried to find you or Tyrell."

"A dangerous but brave plan."

John snorted in disgust,

"Yeah, brave until the bugger caught sight of me. I ran fast and swore I felt it breathing down my neck when all of a sudden I was in the hall just outside."

"What happened?"

The Dracoth interrupted,

"I happened, molden. I did not like its company for the creature reminded me of old enemies and older masters. So I dealt with it."

"Dealt with it?"

Doing what must have been the Dracoth's idea of a shrug it answered,

"My powers grow weak with time, but dealing with a mindless slug is not yet beyond me."

Looking to John, the mund just shook his head.

"I don't know what Skurge did, Grach. But whatever it was saved me. And I found him here."

Grach seemed to consider his next words carefully.

"No disrespect is meant from these words, Skurge is it?" at the creatures nod he hurried on.

"But, it is told by our root mothers, wise ones, that the Dracoth have little love in their hearts for others, even their own kind. Why did you save my friend?"

Closing its eyes and slumping back into its throne, Skurge was quiet for a long moment. Then, slowly opened them again and said.

"You are correct, warrior. My kind was ever in search of power and ruler ship over others. Great we were in power, but not so great in wisdom, perhaps."

Taking a last pull on his ale, the creature looked almost sadly on the empty goblet.

"We were rulers of the skies, and only the great fathers could best us. For reasons unknown to us, the great sky fathers gave the dark masters the secret power to control us.

For two millennia we did the bidding of beings lesser than ourselves."

Crushing the goblet in it its clawed hand, it threw the now twisted metal against the wall.

Grach asked,

"Sky fathers? You mean dragons?"

"So your wise ones must call them. Fathers Blood. Mothers Blood. They were our creators and we wished for nothing more than to serve them. When they left the world on some journey beyond time, we became the most powerful beings in all the lands. We ruled the skies and looked down upon the weak dirt bound creatures."

Sitting back, the Dracoth continued his tale.

"But as I said, for some reason the great fathers gave us to the dark masters, and we could do nothing but obey. Obey, or be punished." So saying, Skurge lifted his arms and John and Grach could see tarnished silver manacles around its wrists. Black chains attached to the walls ensured the beasts imprisonment.

"What did you do?" John asked.

Smiling a tooth filled grin, Skurge answered.

"I had lived long under my master's yoke. I grew tired of it. Tired of being used like a beast of burden. So, I struck them down as they feasted in the hall out side, for I knew when the dark ones were deep into their victims, they become easily distracted and vulnerable. For my crime, I was imprisoned here. Constant was my pain as the dark masters made me suffer. I was kept in this hall where their trophies of victory were held. I was but an example to others of my kind of the consequences of disobedience. When the earth's bones shook and my tormentors fled, I was left here, almost forgotten."

Silent for a moment, feeling sorrow for the monster sitting in front of him, Grach said,

"You need us for something."

Nodding, Skurg said,

"Long have I studied the spells placed on the chains that bind me. I cannot break them, for they are attuned to my magic. But, I can be freed."

"How?"

"The Silent One. The sweet darkness. Death can free me."

Silent now, both Grach and John considered the Dracoth's words. Looking at his friend, Grach thoughtfully puffed his pipe. Nodding, John asked,

"Is there no other way?"

Shaking his great head, Skurge answered,

"No, scarred one. I have spent centuries studying my magical prison. The idea of being trapped here for eternity shames me with fear."

Grach looked to John, who bobbed his head in agreement. "Aye, Dracoth, we will do this thing, though it will not gladden my heart."

Smiling sadly, Skurge said,

"My thanks, warrior. Now listen, as I tell you of my life so that I can be remembered in some small way."

The Dracoth then spoke to them of his life, flying the skies of the earth, of far distant lands where men with the heads of dogs lived in tropical cities, and mountains which burned with fire as the earth's blood spattered on their slopes. For long hours, Skurge told tales of the sky fathers and his races sadness at their loss, and his small audience sat silent. Finally, the Dracoth stood. Towering over the two, Skurge spread his wings to their full length and seemed to fill the room, making the hall feel somehow crowded.

"My thanks for attending me in my final hours. Though friendship is something not akin to my kind, I consider you friends just the same."

Pointing with a clawed hand, the creature told John to approach behind the black altar stone. Doing so, John found an ancient brown sack which fell apart when he tried to lift it. Clanging to the floor, was a winged helm made out of a strange grayish metal. A pair of matching gauntlets and a double bladed ax of the same substance rounded out the gift.

Following the Dracoth's instructions, he donned the helm and gauntlets, and reverently picked up the ax. With a black shaft of some kind of dark wood, the weapons twin blades glinted in the torch light. Feeling a bit self conscious, John slowly approached.

The helm had looked a bit big for the skinny mund until he put it on, the molden thought. Now, it seemed to fit him perfectly, as did the gauntlets. Marveling at the ax, Grach could see it was a masterpiece that no molden smith could duplicate. Dressed with his new attire, and his scarred visage, John struck an imposing figure.

The Dracoth took hold of a length of chain and placed it on the stone floor saying,

"Keep these three as gifts, John. They were made by the only race to ever challenge the dark masters, and should be familiar to you. Think kindly on me, and know that not all of my people are incapable of good deeds."

Nodding, John took a firm grip on the weapon's shaft, and with a mighty heave, he cleaved through the chains, sending pieces of silver metal flying against the stone walls. Great cracks were rent into the ancient gray stone and the ground shook. Grabbing Grach's shoulder to steady himself, John saw power radiate from the reptilian figure.

With a roar of triumph, Skurge leapt to perch on the back of his throne and drew himself up to his full height. Looking down on the scarred mund, Grach thought he saw satisfaction in the creature's eyes before black fire engulfed the reptilian body, and the Dracoth was gone. The mountain continued to shake and rumble for several moments as if in tribute to the now freed creature.

# Chapter Eight

The ferocity of the storms the last two days had faded into the grey of the mountains. The sky was clear and calm and the waters of the great Green Lake lay glistening and serene as Nemar rowed his passengers toward their destination. After an uneventful morning of ferrying supplies to the awaiting timber barges that were to make their way to the southern markets, the two passengers had approached him to purchase his services for the rest of the day. Showing a tablet with the mark of the Green Tree Clan, of which he owed service, he had immediately agreed to take the passengers on.

A man was not old until he could no longer work. That simple philosophy had kept Nemar active in the service of his Ferrekei masters for as long as he could remember. Every morning he woke he would greet the day with a warm smile. He would walk to the fountain and draw a drink of water, look at his reflection and say to himself,

"Good to see you Nemar."

Even after he had been offered to retire to his master's green forest estates, a rare tribute, which he had politely declined and requested to be allowed to continue his service until his body gave out. He knew that his life was tied into the slow and steady rhythm of the great lake; its cool waters and temperate weather.

Well, usually temperate. These last storms had an unusual feel to them. At times it felt as if the ground shook alongside the thundering rain and hail. It was out of the ordinary which did not sit well with him. His thoughts of the unusual weather were lost in the ordinary rhythm of the oars slicing through the green waters.

He liked to tell people that at seventy, he was as strong as ever, but it was not true. His arms and shoulders were aching and his heart was thumping as he leaned into the oars. He paused for a moment, and saw the scarred mund speaking to his master.

Strange, he thought, he had never known of a molden to own the services of a mund. Though, his kind did not travel much this far south, in the past Nemar had been genuinely impressed with the way the molden conducted themselves. Though, it was not his place to voice any opinions. A moment later the other mund scooted closer.

"Would you like a break? I have not rowed in quite some time but would be glad to get reacquainted."

Glancing over at the molden who seemed to be starting to doze and paid no attention to the two munds, he shrugged.

"Of course, pretty one. Your master seems to be a mellow sort. But you should ask his permission, nonetheless."

He said the last as if he were scolding an errant child for bad manners. Which in a sense, he was. Grinning, the other mund asked in a respectful voice that bordered on sarcastic,

"Dear Master, may I take a turn at the oars?"

Looking up, the Molden waved his consent and went back to his nap.

Shrugging off his shirt, the tall mund took Nemar's place at the oars. After a few clumsy turns, and with the old man's helpful instructions, the boat began to glide again through the waters. Not as quickly or as smoothly as when he was at the oars, Nemar noted smugly.

"Nasty scars there, son. Are those from a rawstone?"

Grunting with the effort, he replied,

"My name is John, old man. And you are not the first to ask me that."

Strange name. Strange weather. Strange mund with a molden. Very strange.

"Well John, you did not answer my question; and the name is Nemar, not old man."

Sweat now beating down his face and chest, John answered.

"No, it was a fire Nemar. A very bad fire. But not rawstones."

The pair continued in relative silence. It was not often that he had been on the open water, enjoying the breeze through his hair, without the obligation of manning the oars. Nemar found that he was at ease with John the strange mund.

He looked closer at the younger man manning the oars. His blond hair was in need of a proper cut, and it was held back by a strip of leather. Bare-chested, he wore a simple pair of trousers and sandals. His body was lean and almost too skinny, as if he had recently been through some hardship. His bacha collar seemed to fit oddly on him and Nemar just had the sense that he was unused to it. His one good eye was a hazel color and squinted under the sharp afternoon sun; the other was a white like nightmare that he had to be self conscious about.

Nemar had guessed that he had been in the fighting pits at one time since he had the look of a fighter. Also, the clink of metal in the baggage the pair carried was most likely arms of some kind. Nemar was impressed if John was allowed to carry any weapons. Munds were not usually allowed to go anywhere armed, outside of the fighting pits. Especially not in the Mage's city.

Nemar was also enjoying the young man's company. He had three children who were now serving other masters. His two boys worked the great green lake as he did but he did not get to see them often. His daughter had caught the eye of the Sublime Sisters and he had not seen her for years as she served at the great temple. He said a prayer to the un-named gods to look after her every evening before he slept.

"What business does your master have in Hyberan?"

He was pleased to note that when John answered, the effort in his voice had lessened. He was getting more into a rhythm and his body was remembering the oar work.

"His own, mostly. He does not confide much in me."

Nodding, Nemar continued,

"Will your master allow you any free time on your visit?"

"Perhaps, why?"

Glancing back at the still sleeping molden, Nemar leaned forward,

"My daughter serves the Sublime Sisters at their main temple. Could you perhaps get word to her that her father and brothers are well?"

Pausing in his rowing, his scarred face taking on a serious mask, John replied,

"Of course. What is her name?"

Smiling, Nemar said,

"Kitla."

# CHAPTER NINE

The un-named gods moved in times of storms. Little Tia knew this because her mother often had told her stories of the immortal ones; how the spears of the war god could be seen in the lightning and the hammers of the smith god could be heard in the thunder. When the waters grew angry and nothing but the magic of the mages could prevent the waves from washing the city away, it was the sea god's fury.

"Why don't our gods have names, mama?" she had asked one night.

"Because it is dangerous to speak them. Now hush little one, your uncle Yanab is coming over tonight." And with a quick kiss, she had tucked the little girl into her bed and locked the bedroom door.

The eight year old smiled at the memory and quickly doused it as she tried to quell her fear of the storm. She struggled up the muddy slope toward the shrine, her threadbare tunic offering little protection from the howling winds and lashing rain that had hit the city on and off for the past four days. Even her head felt frozen because her mother had shorn away her golden locks three days ago in an attempt to free her of the biting bugs that infected her scalp. Even now, her thin body was littered with sores and bites. Most of them were just mildly itchy, but the rat bite on her foot remained red and swollen. Each step caused pain and the scab was constantly breaking and fresh blood flowing.

But those were matters not worth her attention. They were small discomforts and not worth her concern as she pushed on toward the almost forgotten shrine. When mama had taken sick two days ago, Tia had run to the healer in the center of the slums. Spitefully, he had told her to step back from his door. He did not visit those who could not afford him and had barely listened to her explain that mama would not rise from her bed, that she was hot to the touch and talked to those already dead.

"Go to the Sisters." He said.

Tia had run to the Great Temple and stood in line with others seeking aid. The waiting people all carried offerings for the sisters help. Many had strange and exotic animals in wicker cages; others had precious metals and gifts of food and wine. When she finally made it through the high temple doors, she was met by a boy a little older than herself who asked what offering she had brought. When she tried to explain about mama's sickness he too ordered her away and called out for the next person in line, an old man carrying a wooden cage with two snow white animals that swung from a metal bar with their tails.

Tia did not know what to do and ran back to her home. Mama was awake and spoke to someone that Tia could not see or hear. Mama began to cry. Then Tia began to cry, too.

The storm arrived at dusk and Tia remembered that the gods came with the storms. She decided to speak to them herself.

The shrine of the White Lady was high on a cliff in the hills overlooking the city, close to the sky. Tia thought the gods might hear her if she climbed to it.

She shivered as the night grew colder and was worried that any wild animals roaming the hills would catch the scent of her sores. She stumbled in the dark. Her shin struck a rock and she cried out.

When she was smaller and had hurt herself, she ran to mama, who would hug her, and gently rub away the pain. But that was when they had lived in a much larger house in the country with a flower garden, and all of her uncles had been rich and most were masters. Now they were all munds like mama, old and dirty, and they did not bring rich presents but only a few copper tablets. They no longer stayed and sat and laughed with mama. Mostly they did not speak at all. They would come after dark. Tia would either be sent to her room and told to cover her ears or outside if the weather was nice. They usually left after a short time. Lately, no uncles had come for many days. There were no presents, no copper tablets, and little food.

Tia climbed higher. On top of the cliff she saw the white pillars that surrounded the shrine. Many had fallen down. Few visited the shrine of the White Lady. Mama said the White Lady had once been mortal and had defied the mages to protect the people from their wrath. For her bravery, the gods had made her immortal. Mama said the mages hated the White Lady and therefore let her shrine go into disrepair.

The girl was almost at the end of her strength as she forced her way up the slope and into the pillar circle. She stumbled into the circle, catching herself on a fallen stone. Lightning lit the sky. Tia cried out, for the brilliant light illuminated a figure standing before the White Lady, battling some monster. Tia's legs gave way as she watched the silver helmed giant battle a huge beast, all fur and flashing teeth. The clouds broke just as the god struck the beast down, and the moon shone through the shrine.

Three brown forms lay unmoving at the White Lady's feet. The marble arms of the lady seemed to reach down to her champion and bless him with moonlight. The god then lowered his weapon and turned slowly, rain glistening down his face and arms. The face of the immortal was half beauty, half monster, and Tia knew she viewed a god of war.

Tia stared at him, eyes wide and frightened. Was it a protector god or one of the dark ones? Surely not an evil one, as he had defended the White Lady and she had blessed him. As he stepped towards her, she could see his hair was a sandy color, not made of light like a gods. The face was frightening with its one white eye glaring down at her. Mama never spoke of a god with two faces, but maybe there was one. Tia gazed at him to see if his shoulders sprouted wings like many of mama's stories.

But there were no wings.

The god approached her, and she saw that his other eye was hazel colored, and showed concern.

"What are you doing here?" he asked

"Are you an immortal? A war god of two faces?"

He smiled at her question, and she saw true warmth there.

"No, I am not a god of war. But I guess I do have two faces. I never really thought about it like that."

A wave a dizzy relief washed over her. A god of war would not have healed mama. They only knew how to fight and kill.

"Mama is ill, and I have nothing to offer the Sisters." She said. "But if you heal her, I will work and work, until my fingers and hands bleed, and bring you many offerings. Many gifts. For the rest of my life."

The god turned away and disappeared behind a pillar.

"Please don't leave!" she cried desperately, "Mama is sick!"

He returned with a heavy blanket and a leather pack. Sitting beside her, he wrapped her in the blankets fuzzy warmth. It was the softest thing she had ever felt.

"You came here seeking help for your mother? Has she seen a doctor?"

"What is a doctor? The healer would not come," she told the god, "So I went to the temple, but I had nothing to offer and they sent me away."

"Come, let's go find your mama."

"Thank you." She tried to stand. Her legs gave way, and she fell awkwardly, mud spattering the soft material of the blanket.

"I'm sorry. I'm sorry."

"Don't worry about it." He told her, and lifted her into his arms and began the long walk into the city.

Somewhere during the walk, Tia fell asleep, her head resting on the god's shoulder. The god was speaking to someone. Opening her eyes she saw a strange figure, almost wider than he was tall. She recognized him as one of the plant people. Mama said they were part mushroom. Seeing her awake, the plant man gave her a brown toothed smile.

They walked towards the city walls and the plant man hurried forward to talk to the guards. After a few bronze tablets were exchanged, the small party entered the city and the god asked where she lived. Tia felt embarrassed because they were walking past nice houses, marble walled and roofed with blue tiles. She and mama lived in a shack in the mund quarter of the city. The roof leaked; there were holes in the thin wooden walls through which rats found their way in. The floor was of gritty dirt that stank when it rained and there were no windows.

"I am feeling better now." She said, and the god put her down. Then she led the way home.

As they entered, several rats scurried away from mama.

The god knelt on the floor alongside her and reached out to touch her brow.

"She's alive." He said.

"Grach, stay with her. Can you take me to the healer?" At her nod, the god took Tia by the hand, and together they walked through streets and stopped at the house of the healer.

"He is a very mean and angry man," Tia warned as the god hammered a gauntlet covered fist on the wooden door.

It was flung open, and the healer loomed in the doorway.

"What by the cursed gods . . . ?" he began. Then he saw the two faced god, and Tia saw him change his attitude. He seemed to shrink under that immortal glare.

"Yes? May I . . . h-help you?"

"Gather your medicines and come immediately to . . ." He looked down at Tia, raising his one eyebrow in question,

"The house of Tama, at the corner of red light and grey fountain." She answered.

At the healer's hesitation, the god said,

"You will be well compensated."

The healers face brightened,

"Of course. Immediately."

An hour later, the god, plant man, Tia and the healer all crowded into the small shack. The healer prepared a smelly brew and the god helped mama sit up and drink it. Removing her clothes showed a red swollen belly and bed sores that had broken and scabbed over numerous times. After washing her and dressing the sores, the healer spoke quietly to the god. Tia heard the healer mention the Sublime Sisters as she held mama's hand. Nodding his thanks, the god knelt down next to Tia as the plant man gave a handful of silver tablets to the healer. Bowing his way out the door, he left.

Tia was so happy that mama was sleeping and not talking to people she could not see that she did not hear the god speak, "hmmm?" she asked.

"The healer said that your mother is very ill. And only the Sublime Sisters can heal her."

With tears in her eyes, Tia said,

"But I have nothing to offer."

Looking past her shoulder, the god met the eyes of the plant man, who nodded.

"That is not a problem," the god said, "Come, you must lead us and I will carry your mother."

For the second time that day, Tia found herself before the temple doors. Except this time they were closed. Walking up the steps, the god shifted the sleeping woman into one arm and hammered his metal fist against the ancient wood. Waiting a moment, he did it again. The sound from the blows echoed through the streets and avenues between the nearby buildings.

With a grating sound, one of the doors opened enough to let a small head peek through.

"By the Lady, do you know what time of night it is?" Ignoring this, the god grabbed the open door in his free hand, grunted and flung it wide open. Stumbling back, Tia saw it was the young boy who had sent her away that morning. In a quavering voice, he squeaked,

"You cannot come in here. I will call the guards!"

With mama still in his arms the god leaned down and looked the boy in the face.

"I have a message for Kitla. Do you know her?"

At his nod, the god ordered him off. The boy's bare feet made a slapping sound on the stone as he ran to do the god's bidding. Several moment's later, an older man approached the group and requested that they follow him.

As they followed, two guards dressed in green uniforms appeared on either side of them. While their faces were covered in a kind of green mesh mask so their features could not be discerned, their mannerisms informed the strange company to behave themselves. Tia saw the god tighten his grip on mama.

When they reached their destination, Tia gazed in wonder. It was an immense garden with a high wall surrounding it, and the party walked through an entry way with green pillars on either side. The path through the garden was decorated with shiny green stones, and on the walls were paintings in vivid colors.

Sitting on a stone bench in the middle of the garden, two women waited. Dressed in the green flowing robes of the sisters, with their hair hanging loose as was custom, Tia could see that one sister was a dusky hued Dryan and the other a dark haired mund. Both women were striking and both looked a little annoyed at being up so early. Tia could just see the morning sun light peaking over the garden walls as if to see what was happening.

The god marched them to stand before the women. The mund Sister stood and said,

"I am Kitla. You have a message for me?"

If the Sisters were at all shocked to be talking to a god, they did not show it.

"Yes. From your father, but first this woman needs care."

Frowning, Kitla asked,

"You would hold information from me for treating her?" Her raised eyebrow indicated what she thought of that.

Shrugging his shoulders the god answered, "I get like that sometimes."

Raising a finger to perfectly red lips, the Sister made a pouting face as she thought. Out of the corner of her eye,

Tia could see that two more guards had entered the garden. The air felt tense.

"Has an offering been given?" asked the husky voice of the Dryan Sister.

Still sitting demurely, she looked at the god with obvious interest. Stepping forward slowly, the plant man offered another handful of tablets. Tia ogled as the near morning light glinted off their golden color. She and mama could live for years off that amount.

Making a distasteful grimace, which seemed to mar her lovely features, the Dryan snapped her fingers and called out.

"Rois!"

A few minutes later an older boy walked quickly into the garden, and upon seeing the plant man holding out a gold filled offering, quickly placed himself between the strange party and the sisters. Counting out the tablets, he nodded towards the sisters. With a wave of her hand, the Dryan dismissed him and the guards.

In unison the Sisters turned and ordered them to follow. Hesitantly, Tia followed. She was startled when the plant man took her hand. Seeing his brown smile again gave her courage as they followed mama.

# CHAPTER TEN

John waited with Grach outside the room where the two Sisters had taken Tia and her mother. Some kind of juice had been brought to refresh them and a young robed boy had informed them that Sister Kitla would like to break fast with them that morning. It did not sound like a request.

Leaning his back against a stone wall, he had been offered a chance to take a bath and refresh himself elsewhere but had politely refused. He needed to see this thing through before he felt comfortable.

Taking his gauntlets off, he rubbed sore knuckles. It was lucky that Grach had given him some instruction in how to handle the ax. Though the blades made it different from the molden's mace, it was still a bashers weapon and his friends instructions had ensured he did not cut his own ears off in the fight. Looking over at Grach, he asked,

"What were those things?"

Sitting up, the Molden asnswered,

"They are called Rachers. Though I have never seen them get that large, nor have I ever heard of them being this close to the city. I am sure Tyrell had no idea."

Grunting, John began cleaning off the blood from the nasty creatures. Seeing him at his chore, a young girl brought him a bowl of hot water and some clean rags.

When they had emerged from the tunnels, Grach had explained the plan that he and Tyrell had formed. Describing his visit from Terra, Grach simply shrugged and reasoned that the original plan only called for them to reach the mage city and wait for Tyrell to join them, and searching for this mysterious Mosha person would not add too much difficulty.

Tyrell had instructed the pair to enter the city from the wooded hills to the north of the walls. Very few caravans traveled that way and few would be on the road; further the guards asked few questions. The pair reasoned that the rainy weather would even further hide their arrival. What they did not count on was a nest of those rabid rat dogs that were inhabiting what had first appeared to be a deserted temple or shrine.

As Grach instructed, he had simply hung back from the fight and watched his companion dispose of the three brutes. The beast that Tia had seen him fight had been the first one Grach had dealt with; both had thought it dead. The creature had played possum and then tried to attack Grach from behind; yelling a warning John made a few clumsy swings to get its attention. After that, the injured beast had backed John all the way up to the statute in the center of the shrine. With no where to go, John had to make a stand and had luckily gotten a killing blow on the dying creature.

Looking over at Grach as he inventoried what was left of his funds, Champion cleared his throat.

"Thanks, Grach."

Not looking up, the grey man replied,

"You have a great heart my friend. Helping the little one was the only thing you could do. However, we need to make some choices after things are taken care of here."

Nodding, John went back to cleaning his gear. The gifts from Skurge were amazing. The grey metal was light and hardly impeded him at all. The strange runes that ran along the length of the gauntlets and on the blade of the ax were unreadable to him but for some reason teased at his memory. The helm only had one marking on it; a rune that looked like a flame was emblazoned on the center of the forehead. After finishing his chore, he glanced over to see that Grach had closed his eyes and was snoring softly.

*Good idea.*

With a small grunt, he leaned back against the wall and closed his eyes.

A tapping noise woke him. Opening his eyes he saw a very beautiful sight. Kitla, in her green robe, tapping her foot impatiently against the leg of a chair as she waited for him to wake up.

*My god, she is gorgeous.*

The dark haired woman had a sexual roundness that challenged any man that looked at her. Clear blue eyes looked at him angrily, with those perfect lips that, even though thinned in annoyance at the moment, seemed to cry to be kissed. The robe was cut low at the neckline giving a teasing look at what might lay beneath. Her legs were crossed and one shapely browned calf poked through a tailored slit in the robe. Attached to the calf was a perfectly pedicured foot which was at this time tapping a regular beet.

"Please let me know when you are done ogling me, so we can talk."

Flushing at being so easily read, he sat up too quickly, knocking his armor to the ground. With a curse he gathered up his belongings and put them in his travel bag. This time the blue eyes seemed the laugh.

"I did not know immortals were so clumsy. Especially a two faced god."

Flushing again, he responded,

"The girl was feverish and saw me at that shrine. Is she well? Her mother?"

With a smile that seemed to promise much more, the woman said,

"You first."

*Fair is fair.*

Shrugging, he told her about meeting Nemar on his boat and gave her the short message he had been entrusted. Not satisfied, Kitla then spent the next several minutes interrogating him about her father; how did he look? Did he smell of seaweed ale? Did he mention a woman? Did he say anything else about my brothers?

Finally holding up his hands, John surrendered,

"Hot stuff, you have all that I know. I don't know what seaweed ale is let alone what it smells like. Now please, Tia? Her mother?"

Giving him a piercing look that took his breathe away, she stood and told him to follow. Looking for Grach, Kitla read his mind and answered his unvoiced question,

"We have a molden root garden on the grounds. Your friend will be some time there. Now, if you follow me, you can ogle all you like." And with a dimpled smile, she strode off. Not really a stride, he thought. More like a saunter. And ogle he did.

They passed a number of other green robed women. All seemed exceedingly beautiful. Some smiled prettily as he passed. Most seemed to be busy gardening or cleaning.

*So this is what being Hugh Hefner must be like.*

They passed a group of young girls that were listening attentively to an older green robed woman. One of them was Tia. Seeing him she jumped from her seat on the ground and rushed over. Jumping into his arms, she squealed,

"Two face! I thought you would never wake up! You slept almost all day! Does your neck hurt leaning up against that wall for so long? Grach told me your name was John and that he did not think you were a god. Did you know he really is a plant? Or partially, anyway. Mama is so much better, and look at my new robe . . ."

As the words tumbled out, John smiled, enjoying holding her in his arms; just like Sam. Could that boy talk! A deep sense of contentment filled him. As if a very sore itch that had been on his soul for a very long time was finally being scratched. He realized that with all of the danger and craziness of this new world, or hallucination, he had found a small piece of contentment in Tia. Suddenly lifting her hand to her nose, Tia ended the reflective moment by saying,

"Ew! You stink, John. I think Sister Kilta should take you for a bath."

Laughing, John let her down. Giving him another hug, and getting him to promise to see her soon, she skipped back to the other girls. Turning, he saw Kitla smiling at the scene. Still feeling extremely flustered in her presence, John almost unconsciously rubbed his scarred arm. Understanding seemed to light in those luminous eyes, and Kitla led him to breakfast.

"It's actually almost end day, so this will be most like a snack before night meal."

She had led him to a balcony where a meal of fruit, fresh breads, sliced meats, and stinky cheeses filled a table. Though the fare was simple, his hunger reminded him how long he had not eaten and he fell head long into the meal. After several quiet minutes broken only by the sound of eating, and knowing he could easily eat another helping, he held off and instead leaned back in his chair and sipped at the flavored water provided. While two young girls, both in robes like Tia's, had been present at first to serve, Kitla had shooed them off. Giggling the two had scampered down the hallway.

Rubbing his face, he asked about Tia's mother.

"Tama? She is dong well. Ura, the Sister you met with me early this morning is one of our most skilled healers. Tama had a lesion. What some commonly call a twisted stomach. Ura was able to drain it of the fluids. Both she and Tama are resting now. It is a trying procedure for both healer and patient."

Nodding his thanks, John realized that his whole body ached. The fight with those large rodents at the shrine, coupled with carrying Tia into the city had tired him out; and sleeping against the wall had made his neck sore. Of course, the full stomach was also contributing to making him drowsy. Looking down at his scarred hand, he grimaced as he flexed the stiff fingers. It had been some time since he had been treated by Ben. Thinking of his native friend brought the big Indian's face to mind.

*What would you think of all this, eh Ben? Probably shake your head at your ugly friend's clumsy ways and tell me to try to bed the girl.*

Looking up, he saw Kitla watching as he flexed his hand.

"Does it get stiff at times?"

At his nod, she continued,

"We have many Sisters who treat rawstone injury here. You have to knead the scar tissue to keep it flexible. Have you had this done before?"

God she was beautiful. He nodded again. She rose from her seat and gently took his hand. Rubbing lightly over the damaged skin she nodded. Looking down at him she wrinkled her nose,

"Well, Tia was right. You stink! Now that your belly is full, I think a bath is in order and then I can look at your hand and face. Come with me."

Groaning he got to his feet. Laughing, Kitla exclaimed that Tia's immortal should be able to make it to the baths.

Ogling her all the way, he followed the Sister into a steam filled paradise.

He did not know what he expected, but the baths of the Sublime Sisters were a wonder. Looking something like the pictures of roman bath houses he had seen while still in school, it was huge. Down in the lower levels of the temple, the baths were a labyrinth of marbled columns and cave rock. Kitla walked him past many rooms of different shapes and sizes. He was glad to notice that there were no rawstones, and instead the Sisters relied on what looked to be some type of oil lamp, jutting from the walls at intervals. He could hear the voices of men and women floating down the hallways. Following Kitla around a corner, he distinctly heard the sound of love making and a woman give a wicked laugh. She continued to lead on a curving and round about path and John wondered if she did this to avoid disturbing any of the other bath goers.

Finally, they came to a room which was smaller than the rest. An inviting steaming pool of water sent small tendrils into the dim lighted air. Walking with him to the side of the pool, Kitla indicated the steps which led down into the water and she showed him where a variety of soaps and oils were laid out on a shelf. His clothes needed to be set off to the side and she showed him where numerous towels and white robes were neatly folded on another shelf. With that, she said she would check on him after he had bathed.

While he found Kitla's company pleasant and arousing, he was glad she allowed him privacy. By the dim sounds of it, many of the other bathers were definitely not alone. Undressing, he folded his clothes and stepped in.

Damn, that is hot! Dunking himself helped to accustom his body to the steaming waters. Easing towards the shelf with the soap, he soon learned that the pool had a ledge like seat that allowed him to sit with his head out of the water. Picking through the soaps, he stayed away from the oils, he found one that did not smell as strong as the others and applied it to his hair. With the cold stream baths that he had been forced to have with Grach on their journey, taking a hot bath was a luxury that he had no idea he missed. Soaping down his body, he floated lazily in the steamy heaven. As he floated, he thought over what had happened to him while entering this strange place.

In a matter of a few months, at least he had thought it was a few months, he had nearly died twice. Three times if you count the fight at the shrine. A crazy woman had called him a mage, and not only that, showed him that he might actually be one. He could call fire and air, well not actually call air yet, and now he was floating in a steaming pool after he had been caught ogling the only woman since Rebecca who had aroused him in over four years.

*Rebecca and Sam.*

He searched his feelings. While the memories of them did bring a lump to his throat, the all encompassing depression was not there. The waves of black despair and self pity that had washed over him on an almost daily basis since their deaths seemed like a distant current. He felt the pain and misery of the death of his family soak slowly into regret and sadness. He almost smiled as he conjured up Rebecca's face and what she would think of him wallowing in self pity for so long.

"I'll never forget you, babe. Never." He felt at peace somehow, saying it out loud.

"Well, these waters have had strange affects on the bathers before, but I have never heard of them causing anyone to talk to the thin air."

Startled, John accidentally dunked his face under the water. Coming up for air, coughing and sputtering, he wiped the water from his eyes and caught his breathe.

Kitla was standing above him. Instead of her green dress, she had on one of the white bathing robes. Putting her arms over her head, she stretched her back slightly, making her robe come open.

*My god, that is amazing. Gravity has no effect on this woman's body.*

Seeing that she had his undivided attention, Kitla shrugged the robe off and walked to the side of the pool. Keeping his gaze, she slowing walked down the steps, sinking into the water. Within moments, she was facing him. He could feel the water swirl as she glided past him. Opening her mouth slightly, she reached over and took a bottle of the oils from a nearby shelf.

In the only part of his mind that was not concentrated on the scene in front of him John wondered at the strange sensation of being completely submerged in water from the neck down but having a dry mouth.

Opening the top of the bottle, Kitla gently sniffed its contents. Giving a purr of satisfaction, she faced him again.

"It is best to treat your scar tissue immediately after a hot soak; it makes the skin more attuned to the oils."

Taking him by the hand, she led him from the center of the pool to the shelf. Seating them both, she poured oil on his damaged arm and slowly began to kneed the skin. In a dream like state, he felt her leg touch his own as she worked his arm. Her fingers were stronger than they looked, and he felt the warmth of the water begin to seep into his hand and arm. Leaning back, he continued to watch her through lowered eye lids as she moved closer. He moaned as he felt a firm breast rest on his shoulder.

As if unaware of her affect on him, Kitla began taking each of his four scarred fingers and slowly bending them back and forth, each time a little further until she was satisfied with their flexibility. Turning towards him again, she pressed her body further against his as she slowly massaged his face. The oil on her hands made his face itch at first but then a warmth spread through the rough skin, making it feel loose and relaxed. Closing his eyes, he was in sea of warm, sultry, heaven.

*Eat your heart out Ben*. And in his minds eye his friend smiled, and shook his head.

The heavenly hands moved and brushed against the scruffy stubble on the other side of his face. He had always been fanatical about shaving the half of his face that still grew a beard. He did not want people seeing that he was slovenly as well as deformed.

With a chuckle, the hands moved efficiently as a thicker creamy substance coated his facial hair. From somewhere, she produced a straight razor and proceeded to shave his face. Following her instructions, he closed his eyes as warm water was poured over his head, washing away the shavings and cream.

Smooth and clean, and completely aroused out of his mind, he turned his head toward this goddess. She placed her arms around his neck and he finally got to taste those lips. The kiss was strong and soft and took his breathe away.

Looking her in the eyes, he blurted,

"It's been a while since . . . ."

Nodding she shifted her body slightly and he saw her hand snake below the water. He gasped as she held him firmly, stroking.

Chuckling, she whispered,

"Your body remembers how its done . . . yes?" Reaching for her, he thought,

*That was the sexiest, wickedest, laugh I have ever heard.*

ELDEST SISTER was by far the wisest, smartest, and most formidable woman that Kitla had ever known. She was also a pain in the ass bitch. But of course, Kitla did not let this last thought show on her face.

She sat on a bench in the Eldest Sisters quarters. A stoic room filled with only a sleeping platform, a writing desk, and the benches the women were currently using. Ura sat next to her and had given her a smile of welcoming when she entered. Since that brief respite, she had belonged to Eldest Sister.

Immediately after her time with the strange mund in the baths, a young acolyte had arrived at her door stating that the Eldest Sister needed to speak to her at once. Taking the time to at least put on her green Sister's robe and running a comb through her hair, she hustled to her summons.

To say Kitla was interrogated about the new arrivals was an understatement. Interrogators at times would allow their prisoners time to recover. Eldest Sister had the annoying habit of beginning a follow up question before you got done answering the first. As if by your first few words she gleaned the answer to the first question and impatiently moved on to the next.

"You were there when this mund arrived?"

"Yes, Ura and I . . . ."

"You heard him speak?"

"Well, yes, he said something like . . ."

"Did you hear him say it in the common tongue?"

"Well, er yes, I think so. I understood it so I assumed . . ."

"Did he tell you how he was scarred?"

And on and on it went. By the time it was over, Kitla's mind was in a whirl, she was sweating under the usually comfortable green robe, and her stomach felt like it had been turned upside down. All in all, it was a normal visit with Eldest Sister.

True to form, Eldest sat quietly after the grueling ordeal she had just inflicted. Like Ura, she was a Dryan, and looked much younger than her actual age. With only slight sprinkles of grey at her temples, she was known to serve in the pleasure houses to this day. Some of the temples most prestigious and wealthy patrons were at her beck and call. It was through her efforts for the past one hundred years that hospitals, schools, and orphanages for the betterment of the mistreated mund people had been established and maintained by the Sisterhood.

Ura simply sat with her friend, and squeezed her hand in support.

With a tired sigh, Eldest asked,

"Sister Kitla, you have done well. Is there anything else this interesting mund had to say?"

Shifting in her seat, she removed her hand from Ura's and placed it in her lap. Tilting her head in thought, she answered,

"He did ask about a librarian."

ELDEST SISTER and Ura sat quietly after Kitla had left. Being Dryan in no way gained Ura any special treatment. However, she did understand that the mannerisms of a Dryan female, especially an elder one like Eldest Sister, could be viewed as abrasive by other races. One of Ura's main functions was to be a buffer between the woman and the other sisters.

Though she seethed with impatient questions, Ura kept her peace. Eldest sister lowered her head, resting her chin on her chest and closed her eyes. After several moments, sighing, as if coming to a decision, she looked up and began giving instructions in a quiet level voice to the sitting sister.

# CHAPTER ELEVEN

John sat in the garden waiting for his friend. It was his fourth day in the Great Temple. A small sleeping chamber had been given over for his use. He was grateful for the privacy as it allowed him to practice calling his elementals without temple eyes watching him; he had been trying to get a stronger control of air; the other night he had called air to blow out a candle and instead the unstable thing had blown the bed up against the wall.

Having his own room also allowed for other perks. Kitla had come to his room last night, and the memory produced a scarred half smile. With the succulent Sister's attentions, regular meals, and sleep in a real bed, he felt better than he had since arriving in this strange world.

He had seen Tia often, around the complex performing duties and attending what might have been considered classes of a sort. He had met Tama yesterday, the first time he had seen the woman awake. She was still horribly pale and skinny; but there had been a glow of health in her face. She had simply given him a tear filled thank you and held his hand until Ura had shooed him away to allow her patient to rest. He remembered other episodes in his other life as a prosecutor where victims' families had thanked him. This place was making him feel more complete than he had been since Rebecca and Sam's death. Breathing in a lungful of warm fresh air, he looked around from his bench at the strange garden.

Unlike the other two in the Temple compound, this garden was almost bereft of color. There were no flowers, no trees smartly trimmed into pleasing shapes. Not that it was ugly or uncared for, it was simply strange. Large rocks, big enough to be called boulders, littered the ground. Low orange leafed shrubs dotted the grounds surface. A large awning had been built, so that the garden only had a few hours of exposure to the sun each day. The place felt cool and almost damp even though the sun was high in the sky. Mushrooms of almost every shape or form dotted the rocky surface.

*Kind of like an outdoor cave, if there could be such a thing.*

Thinking back on his recent journey with Grach, he had viewed strange insects and birdlike creatures flying through the air along side the strange plant life; a herd of some kind of giant lizard with fur; bird like monkeys that darted into the water for fish; and others too numerous for his mind to category. He had decided that the creatures that were so foreign to him that he could not mentally classify actually were easier for him to come to grips with. It was the creatures that reminded him of his own world that bothered him; bees should not be blue, but yellow with black stripes; and deer should not have six legs. These creatures were not bees or deer but the resemblance was striking.

Yesterday, he and Tia had made a discovery that reminded him of home. Behind one of the temple kitchens, they had found a kennel full of yapping, tail wagging dogs; four legs, two eyes, and licking tongues. Tia was at first hesitant, but seeing John being licked by two insistent pups had won her over; later she confided in him that dogs in the slum often attacked people. Laughing at their boisterous play, the dogs looked to be a breed much like a Labrador, but being longer of leg, and lighter of build. Their ears were pointed and perked at every sound.

John explained, "I've seen dogs like this before. They are good for hunting and are loyal."

The kennel mistress, a thin droopy lidded woman, named Lil, came over and watched them suspiciously.

"What are you doing here?"

John regarded the dour woman and playfully pulled the muzzle of a rambunctious puppy.

"I haven't seen dogs since I left home. Tia had some free time so we thought we would visit your fine kennel."

At mention of her "fine kennel" the gloomy woman's countenance brightened considerably.

"I try to keep the dogs healthy. We must keep them locked up at times, for they try to harry the temple patrons; some of whom like them not at all."

They both looked up as Tia began to scold a puppy who had soiled her robe. The scolding had lasted all of two seconds as the pup looked up with sorrow filled eyes and Tia had scooped him up for a cuddle.

His recollection was interrupted by a rumbling. Feeling slight tremors under his feet, John stood up thinking that they might be experiencing an earthquake. To his left, the reason for the rumblings showed itself and he watched in slack jawed amazement.

Out of the ground came Grach. Not all at once, but slowly, as if he were just waking from a nap. Stretching his arms over his head, with bits of loose dirt and roots scattering at his arrival, Grach arched his back with a contented groan. Looking about, he spotted Champion and greeted him,

"John, my friend. Are you rested?"

Nodding, John thought it strange to be speaking to someone who was buried waist deep in the ground. Grunting again, Grach surged the rest of the way out of the ground. Motioning for him to sit, John did just that with a thump. Settling next to him, Grach sighed,

"By the root, I needed that. She is a young root mother, and is not yet ready to sprout her own rootlings. And her questions . . . I thought she would never stop asking them; "Where did you go? Who is your clan? When will you be coming back?" Shrugging, the grey man gave a chuckle.

Shaking his head, John replied,

"I have no idea what you are talking about. You just came out of the fucking ground!"

Taking out his pipe, he looked at his taller friend,

"I am a molden, my friend. That is where we start, in the ground, and that is eventually where I will end."

Slapping his confused companion on the back, his face turned a bit serious, through a puff of smoke he said,

"I am worried about Tyrell. He has not attempted to contact us. And while you have been . . . recuperating . . ." he chuckled at John's flush, "I have been going into the city, checking on certain Ferrakei establishments where he has attended in the past. There is no sign of him. No word from him; and I could find none of his family currently in the city."

The pudgy man puffed thoughtfully on his pipe.

"I need to leave Hyberon, and retrace our steps a bit. Try to find out where he could have gone; what may have happened."

Unhappy about the thought of leaving Tia and Kitla, John shrugged his feeling aside and asked,

"When do we leave?"

Smiling his brown smile, Grach replied,

"We were lucky that we did not attract too much attention on our journey my friend. We traveled through mostly uninhabited lands on our way to the city. Your looks, and from what Tyrell tells me of your abilities, could attract some very unwanted attention."

Shaking his head, John said,

"I don't understand."

Chewing on the end of his pipe stem, the grey man nodded,

"I know John. But can you trust me in this? Please?"

Locking gazes with his friend, John was touched by the care and concern for him that he saw there. He had spent the better part of three years backing away from the world; hiding. He finally had found his backbone again; the kind of resolve that had made him one hell of a prosecutor. It was hard for him to back down now; to hide even for a friend. Something was happening here in this world; something that was wrong. His instincts kept telling him that he was missing some important piece to this crazy puzzle.

He kept thinking back to Gret and Breg; the way they talked and acted towards Calphan. The way Breg was threatened by Champion's mere presence and actions. There was something. Something he was missing.

He turned his eyes back to the garden as Grach looked at him appraisingly, as if seeing his inner struggle.

"What should I do while you are gone?"

Smiling, Grach chuckled,

"I have spoken with the Sisters. They are quite open to helping us. Now, about your temper . . ."

# Chapter Twelve

John flew through the air, his arms and legs cart wheeled, trying to find a solid purchase. His face found the ground first as his body followed, skidding across the sandy surface. Spitting grit from his teeth, he slowly rose to his feet rubbing his face. For once he was glad for his numbed scarring. Turning, he faced his tormentor.

Grach had arranged for him to join the Green Guard for a time until he returned. The silent guardians of the temple were very rarely seen but had the ability to appear immediately when trouble arose. The day after his friend had left, John had been summoned by the Captain.

The Captain, John was later to learn was a Gurash; a red skinned people who lived in coastal areas to the south of the city. With a short, sharp nose, that looked smaller due to the large grey eyes and wide mouth, the captains' face was unusually smooth looking. With thin arms that were connected to even thinner shoulders, the Captain resembled some of the kids that John had shoved into lockers while in high school. Below his chest, however, the Captain sported a belly that any beer drinking hick would have been proud of.

*Fat. The guy is fat and soft.*

Therefore, it was a little hard for John to take this guy seriously as he droned on and on about the honor of serving in the Guard; John's attention wandered.

"Do I make myself clear?"

The nasally voice of the Captain suddenly became sharp and John replied,

"Hmm?"

A few moments later, John was eating sand in the practice arena.

*Note to self; Next time this guys says something, listen.*
"Again!"

The order was given, and John walked slowly over to his opponent. Gripping his ax in both hands, he flexed bleeding knuckles as he tried to think of a different strategy.

The Captain stood opposite him, his thin arms crossed, looking as if he were bored with the whole procedure. Breathing heavily, John had numerous cuts and bruises to show for his insolence earlier.

When he had first been ordered to attack the defenseless man, seemingly defenseless, John had balked and only given a half hearted attempt. This resulted in his first soar through the air. The second time he had tried to brain the Captain with the butt of his ax handle; which had resulted in his second trip. Enraged, in John's third attack, he had swung with miss-timed fury right at the Captain's head; only to find that the crafty shit had moved with amazing speed, dodged the blade and sent the taller man flying for a third time.

On his fourth attempt, John moved slower, never taking his eyes off the red skinned man. The object lesson he was getting was very apparent; it also did not help that some of the other guards had come to watch the new guy get broken in. From the corner of his eyes he could see some of the guards taking bets; part of his mind wondered about the points spread. Now a few feet from the Captain, as he moved as if to swing his ax again, he noticed that the Captain's stance changed slightly, leaning a bit more to the left. At the last moment, instead of swinging the blade, he threw it shaft first at his opponent. Immediately, he followed the throw, barreling into the Captain.

Almost effortlessly, the Captain moved from the path of the weapon but John's attack took him by surprise. Both men fell to the sand; John felt a thrill of satisfaction as he heard the breathe whoosh out of the man below him. Jumping clear, he aimed a punch that should have knocked the fat man's head off; if the head had not moved moments before the fist landed. His swing hitting nothing but air, John wobbled off balance towards his opponent. With a grunt, the Captain grabbed his arm and used John's own momentum against him; for the fourth time, he flew through the air. Getting groggily to his feet, he faced the Captain again.

"Enough." The Captain said, approaching John, he handed back his ax.

"Why did you throw the weapon?"

The voice now reminded John of one of his law school professors. Speaking through sand gritty teeth, John answered,

"Attacking you was not working. I am not that good . . . er . . . proficient with the weapon." At the Captain's raised eyebrow, he added,

"Sir."

Nodding in agreement, the Captain added,

"No, you are much less than proficient. You are pathetic. A youngling with a butter knife would have performed better. You definitely do not have the finesse to be anything but a basher; but here in the Guard we can use bashers. Gam!"

From out of the crowd of guards who had been wagering on the contest, a large sour mouthed Gurash walked over. Unlike the captain, this man was all muscle and brawn. Walking up he straightened and clicked his heels as he came to attention,

"Sir."

"This is your new project. You have to get him ready to accompany Sisters into the City. He apparently speaks Gurashi like he was born to it so communicating will be no problem. You may have to break him of his stubbornness, though." With a grim smile, the Captain walked from the arena.

Turning towards Gam, John watched as the big man picked up a practice staff and approached him.

"Well my pretty pup. You just cost me thirty copper tablets with that stupid attack on the Captain. Now, let's see what you can do with that shiny shovel of yours." Sighing, John readied himself for another beating.

THE GREEN GUARD did not have a barracks. Each guard had a room, much like his own. The rooms were spread all over the temple complex. Gam had explained that this was done so that there are Guards located at all areas of the temple at anytime of the day. John had been provided with a green mesh mask and matching uniform. He was to wear the mask everywhere within the temple complex while on duty except his room, the practice area, or the guards' mess hall. Surprisingly, he found that the mask was easy to wear, with tiny holes in the fabric to allow him to breathe and see with little difficulty.

Each night he crawled gratefully into bed, thankful that he was alone and no one could hear his whimpering. There was no thought of practicing calling fire or air; he was too exhausted. Kitla visited every other night to tend to his scarred tissue; or so she claimed. More often than not he fell asleep halfway through her ministrations.

Gam was a fiend. Every morning before the sun rose he had John in the practice arena. He would have him jumping and running; laden down with a back pack full of stones for an hour. After a few minutes to rest they would share a first meal of cold bread and cheeses. Then another hour of training; this time with a heavy practice staff weighed down at one end to simulate his ax. Still with the back pack on.

For this hour Gam would attack him with a whip cord thin wooden rod that left welts when it connected. John was to attempt to block these thrusts and offer a counter attack if he could. All the while Gam called out instructions concerning his stance, his grip, and his emphasis on quickness.

"Bah! Use your weapons' own weight and momentum to help you, pup! If you keep swinging that thing over your head you won't have any strength to block a killing blow."

And for emphasis he smacked the exhausted John on the back of his head.

After a second breakfast the pair would join the rest of the guards for training. This usually involved marching in step, hand to hand fighting, and weapons drills. John was always faced with Gam during weapons practice and it was little more than the morning routine without the rocks.

For weeks Gam was his only companion. He was paired up with the big man for guard duty and learned the pattern the guards followed around the grounds. Even during meals he and the big man sat apart from the other guards. During this time Gam would lecture him on guard protocol and duty. Other than that, the two sat in relative silence. John could not remember a time when he had been too exhausted to venture an opinion of his own. Through it all John held his temper; Grach's last request still fresh in his mind.

Several weeks into this, two Gurash guards joined them for the evening meal. The two might have been brothers, for they had the same sloping foreheads and green speckled eyes. Nodding a greeting, the first to sit said,

"Gam. Introduce us to your latest victim."

"Don't know his name." Turning to John, he asked,

"What's your name, pup?"

"John. Jonathan Champion."

Turning back to the two visitors,

"His name is John."

Both men chuckled at this as Gam went back to his food.

Turning to John, the second one said,

"You must excuse Gam. He lost a large wager . . ."

". . . when you had your initiation with the Captain." The two seemed to finish the other's sentences.

"I am Lorn . . ."

". . . and I am Dorn. We are brothers." Nodding in greetings, John was amazed at their similarities. Without the small brown birth mark on Lorn's left cheek, the two were indistinguishable.

Gam mumbled something that sounded like, "Crazy same births."

Ignoring him, the two brothers turned to John,

"You speak Gurashi very well . . ."

". . . with only a slight accent."

"Did you serve in . . ."

". . . a Gurashi house hold?"

Shaking his head in the negative, his mood suddenly dark, John bent back to his food. An uncomfortable silence reigned for a few moments. Clearing his throat, Lorn, or was it Dorn, broke the quiet,

"It is no shame if you have fled from a vicious master . . ."

". . . we have many munds who are members of the Guard. Many had masters who." The words were interrupted by John slamming his fist down on the table, and he looked up at the startled brothers. Even Gam raised his head and gave the scene an appraising look, though he continued to chew.

"I am in service to no one. I have no master."

Quiet spread to the rest of the mess hall. Guards of all shapes, sizes, and colors stopped to view the strange scene. After a few moments, the two brothers suddenly rediscovered their meal and the hall went back to the steady babble of off duty guards. Taking a moment to calm himself, he said,

"Lorn, Dorn, I apologize. I should not have lost my temper like that. I am sorry."

When Gam spoke, it surprised the others at the table,

"Cursed gods, pup. If I had known it would take two of the biggest talkers in the Guard to get you to show some fire of spirit, I would have handed you over to them long ago. You have put up with my mistreatment far longer than I would have thought. You cost me another thirty tablets."

Sitting in silence, John's eyes bore into Gam's. The big man took his stare calmly, with a slight smirk.

"Are you telling me that you wanted me to get angry? Do something?"

Gam kept chewing and answered through a mouthful,

"Well, I am not the Captain. A Guard needs to follow the code and all that, but he needs to have some spirit. A Guard needs to be a warrior. And warriors know when to call enough, enough. I just didn't think it would take the two talkers over here to bring it out in you."

John sat back in his chair; chagrin, wry humor, and anger all vied for supremacy before he spoke.

"All the extra morning training, the rocks in the pack, that damn stick hitting me over and over, that was just a way too, you just wanted me to . . ." He sputtered to a stop.

There were few people who could render him speechless, but Gam had done just that. Gam's smirk turned into a true grin that spread from ear to ear. His mirth just seemed to fuel the fire that began filling John's belly. Placing his hands on both sides of the table, he stood up and leaned close to Gam.

"If you wanted an ass kicking, you should have just asked me you oversized prick." Without his noticing, the two brothers had exited the table. Standing up himself, Gam's grin turned wolfish,

"Aye, pup that's what I wanted to hear."

". . . THREE BROKEN tables, two chairs, and finally, as if that were not enough, two fellow Guardsmen reported to the infirmary after they tried to separate you two brawlers."

John and Gam stood at attention in the Captain's office. A small cramped space, with barely room for the large desk and chair, the two men nearly touched elbows. John had a need to rub his aching jaw but resisted. In his short time with the Guard, if he had learned one lesson it was not to interrupt the Captain. Ever. Gam stood stoically next to him, giving no hint that the large purple bump over his left eye was troubling him at all.

Feeling the Captain's gaze, John stood a little straighter,

"Guardsman Champion. You have not been a member of the guards long, so I can understand that things may be coming for you slowly. However, wherever it is that you hale from, I can hardly imagine that the scene in the mess hall would be tolerated."

The eyes turned to Gam, the big man shifted uncomfortably in his stance,

"And you Gam. Small wonder you do not have your own unit by now. If I could get you to drop that street brawler mentality, you might be worth something someday. Now, will I have any more trouble from either of you?"

"No, Sir."

"No, Sir."

Leaning back in his chair, the Captain looked them over with a grimace on his face as if he had just caught a whiff of something that smelled bad. Quietly, he said,

"Gentlemen, if I so much as have the slightest difficulty with you, if I even have a dream where you are in any way insubordinate; I will see you both in the practice arena. Understood?"

"Yes, Sir!"

"Yes, Sir!"

Nodding and waving his hand,

"Now get out."

Relieved John turned to go and bumped into Gam, who had not moved. Noticing this as well, the Captain asked,

"Something else, Guardsman?"

"Yes, Sir! Sir, the odds were four to one." And Gam held out his hand.

With a disgusted look, the Captain tossed over a small pouch that clinked when Gam caught it. Gam stood a moment as if gauging its weight.

"Care to count it, Gam?" the Captain asked in an icy tone.

"No, Sir. Thank you Sir." And he turned away towards the door.

The Captain pointed a knobby finger at John and spluttered.

"Damn it, Champion. Couldn't you have lasted one more day? That man is going to be impossible to deal with for weeks. Get out!" Champion quickly followed the other man out the door.

HOURS LATER, in the room of Lorn and Dorn, John had his first taste of alcohol since he had arrived at the temple. A stout ale with a hint of berries went down very easily as he listened to Gam tell the twins about the extra "training" he had John go through the past weeks. The ale and good company seemed to douse any bad feelings that existed in the room.

The twins erupted in laughter when Gam finished with their berating by the captain and the claiming of his gambling winnings. Reaching for another tankard, John enjoyed the simple companionship that permeated the room. Through it all, he could not help but hope that Grach was finding success in tracking down Tyrell.

# Chapter Thirteen

Tyrell no longer had any lasting sense of where he was or of the links between dreams and reality. Voices whispered in his mind, urging him to answer their questions; to give him peace. He ignored them.

Visions swam across his eyes; a two faced man who burned and fought with himself, a woman in a green dress with the face of a skull, black serpents rising up from the earth, grey cloaked figures huddled under a mountain.

Then he saw hundreds of people, munds, standing in a cavern, surrounding a strange old woman with bright blue eyes; one by one they approached the woman and slowly sank into her, their bodies melding. At last, the only one left in the cavern was the old woman, and she began to cry tears of fire.

The voices continued ceaselessly. One sounded like his Father, stern and uncompromising. Another was his mother, pleading with him to join with a woman and stop traveling. He tried to answer her but his lips were cracked, his tongue nothing but a dried stick in his mouth. Then came the voice of his little cousin, who had died the previous summer,

"Come, Cousin. Be with me. It is so lonely here." But below those voices, came the questions.

*Tell us about your friends. You are dying. We wish to help them.*

He felt something touch his body and opened his eyes. A grey cloaked creature held him, forcing him to drink water. The fluid slid like fire down his throat. The figure seemed familiar to him, but he could not place the memory. Suddenly he coughed, and things went black.

"HOW LONG are they going to be in there with him?"

Pacing back and forth, Gazell had not felt this helpless for as long as she could remember. Their efforts at extracting information from the young Ferrakei were a frustrating failure. His mind was locked against them with a stubbornness that defied logic.

She had been among mages for so long she had forgotten about her people's stubbornness; their adherence to honor. Young Tyrell took this to an uncomfortable extreme. She had been ordered to cooperate with their "friends", who were at this time with the poor boy on the other side of a very thick metal door, which Gazell was sure she would break down in one of her infamous impatient outbursts quite soon.

The servants waiting with her stayed quiet, and wisely, simply moved subtly out of her way on each pass down the hallway. She had made Tyrell available on the agreement that he would not be taken from mage custody, that no lasting harm would be done to him, and that all information would be shared. He had been denied food and water for two days, and she was about to step in and put a stop to this business.

Just as she almost called fire, the door swung slowly open. Before it opened all the way she rushed inside, motioning for the servants to follow. Seeing the state of the young Ferrakei, she sucked in an angry breadth.

Tyrell was lying on a stained leather padded table, with only a loincloth to cover his body. His face was gaunt with the lack of sustenance and he looked frail over all. A tall tattooed faced mund was holding him up and having him drink something out of a cup. The place smelled like sweat and suffering.

"Get away from him you filth."

Fire glowed from one finger tip as she focused her anger on the hapless mund. Nodding, the servant gently laid the blue man down and backed away, his palms outstretched.

The healers following her immediately began to tend the helpless Ferrakei. Gazell watched as Tyrell was wrapped in warm blankets and his vital signs were checked; she patently ignored the figure sitting in the corner, with his tattooed servant standing behind the chair.

Two servants entered carrying a stretcher. Carefully, under Gazell's stern gaze, the young Ferrakei was rolled into the stretcher and carried away. As the last servant left, he shut the door behind him. Clasping her hands behind her back, she spoke, her controlled fury chilling the room,

"I would speak with you alone."

Nodding, the figure motioned with his hand and his servant left. When they were alone, Gazell studied the figure in front of her.

There was not much to see. Sitting in the room with her was a figure completely covered in a grey material that was wrapped numerous times around its body. A very expensive grey material, since the silk needed to make it came from only one type of worm located in the far southern deserts. She had been informed that it was a trade agreement with the Mok Empire that kept his people supplied with the stuff. A long body looked somewhat awkward sitting in the chair; its legs, also covered in grey, stuck out like two thin tent poles trying to find canvas. The only things visible were a pair of hands, long and light grey, their fingernails finely manicured, and a pair of dark eyes. Eyes so dark that they looked like two pieces of coal peering at her through a cloud of grey fabric.

"Was that necessary? The boy's mind was obviously mind bound. A very strong binding, I might add. Starving his body would have done nothing to weaken it." Her glare attempted to pierce the figures veiling.

Tilting its head to the side, she was almost surprised to get an answer,

"Your analysis was correct concerning the mind binding. However, we had to ascertain how deep it went and to what levels of his sub consciousness. By refusing him sustenance, or "starving him", we attempted to get a reaction from his mental facilities with the hope it would break or bend the binding."

"Humph. With little success I take it?" Gazell was sure the thing was smiling at her as it answered,

"Correct. Very little success. But, a little success is better than no success. We did learn additional information."

Tapping her foot in irritation, she asked,

"And?"

Placing his hands together, the figure asked,

"First, please tell me what happened with the Mok? The merchant and his munds?"

Gazell quietly ground her teeth. The bastard knew precisely what had happened; it had all been communicated via talk stone from the camp site.

"He apparently had a travel gate. He used it as soon as he and his servants were alone in their tent. The guards did not know for hours that they were no longer in the camp."

The grey head nodded.

"Ahhhhh. Clever. Perhaps this merchant was not so much interested in trade as first thought. Strange for a merchant to have a travel gate; especially while traveling with such a small group. Don't you agree?"

He was rubbing salt into her failure. She assumed the merchant to be just that. There had been no indication that he had a portable travel gate. The things were terribly hard to make and broke down easily often resulting in the death of the user. But, she had made an error and it seemed that she was being required to acknowledge it before they could proceed. With a slight nod, she motioned a hand imploring him to continue.

With a smug smirk that Gazell could not see but was sure was there, he continued.

"There was an indication that Tyrell would be meeting someone here in your city. We were able to discern a small temple of some kind over looking the city. It had a statue of a woman in the middle of pillars of stone. Perhaps a rendezvous point?"

Her foot stopped tapping as she thought,

"What kind of statue?"

Again those coal black eyes regarded her, this time intently. Her pride refused to allow a physical shiver under the alien scrutiny as he answered, but just barely.

"A lady. A white lady."

IT ALWAYS irritated Mosha when he heard himself described as the Madman from Marn. He hated the inaccuracy of the statement. He was not from Marn, but had been born and raised for most of his life in this very city. Simply because the master to which his family owed service had briefly moved his counting house to Marn, to be further away from the regulation of the mages he was sure, Mosha had come to be associated with the backwater, country bumpkin, province. To be called a madman bothered him not at all.

Besides, it was not his birthplace that mattered to his superiors; or his sanity. Nor was it his egomaniac attitude, his disrespect for his fellow librarians, or his bad hygiene. It was his mind that mattered; more specifically, his memory.

Mosha had a colossal memory. In his first two years as a librarian he had completed a complete inventory of the deeds and records for the Marn province. In four years, he had created a new catalog system that was being implemented by most libraries throughout the civilized nations.

His accomplishments were due solely to the fact that he only had to read something once. No referring back to account records, no keeping track of titles and page numbers, no relying on other librarians to help him dig up information. Once he read something, it was with him forever; Or at least until he died.

And it was because of his tremendous achievements, and his huge ego, that the current stagnation of his career was so frustrating.

It was all that woman's fault! That sumptuous tart of a Sublime Sister who had commissioned the library to research a project based on such an insane premise; generously commissioned. And for a madman to call something insane, then it really must be exactly that; who but a madman would know better?

His research had been brilliant; his conclusions, flawless and to be honest, troubling. He had prepared a fully referenced report, followed all of the forms and library protocols, many of which he had refined, and presented his report to the client and a member of the mage counsel. The Sister had seemed fascinated, her Dryan face lit with scholarly interest.

The mage was harder to read. The Ferrakei had listened with quiet patience and had interrupted him half way through the presentation. With a thank you, the mage had only asked if he had made any other copies of his report or kept any record of his research. Assured that there was only the original report, Mosha had been thanked profusely by the client and then dismissed.

Three days later, he had been demoted to an associate librarian and assigned to the lower archives. Now he spent his days in the dankest darkness with only a half filled oil lamp to light his way. For ten years he had spent the daylight hours sifting through water damaged century old documents and taking the orders from a head librarian who was little better than a janitor.

With his demotion also came a reduction in pay. So, instead of having accommodations in the middle city, as most of his colleagues did, he was now reduced to having lodgings above the very table that he consumed his simple fare. A small stuffy room with a mattress filled with straw instead of feathers. Many a night did he drift off in sleep remembering the bright lights and savory foods in the middle city.

But now, his impressive mental capacities had found a puzzle. A mystery. He sat now in one of the dingiest taverns in the city, eating what was most likely two day old stew and pondered this new challenge. Absently, his hand moved to his shirt where he kept the prize hidden. Reassured when his hand brushed the leather binding, he went back to thoughtfully eating his meager meal as his mind mentally chewed on his golden find. Glancing around the one room tavern, he was assured that his only company that night was the owner Rand, a large uneducated lout who often tried to pass street fed chickens for game fowl.

It had been pure chance. Pure luck, oh great gods! He remembered that day of discovery with a smile; ignoring the brown gravy that dripped down his chin onto his rumpled blue librarian's robe.

Agar, the pathetic excuse for a head librarian was on him again. Three damaged bails of documents had recently arrived from a sister library and he had wanted it reviewed in ten days. Ten days! For three bails! The man was a menace and a coward. Mosha recalled that when he had been a fully endowed librarian that Agar had been one of his favorite targets for criticism; but he dismissed that. Surely the man could take a joke now and again.

He had of course been required to stay late for several nights running to meet the insane deadline. One evening, four nights past, he had forgotten to refill his oil lamp; an oil lamp, please! Not even a rawstone light? He wondered if the lamp was just another way for Agar to demean him.

In any event, he began walking down the dimly lit hallway to fill his lamp when he stumbled; and what a stumble! Mosha had fallen head over heels into the stone wall; his impressive rump had been bruised for weeks afterward. The lamp flew from his hands and with it his only light. For a number of moments, he had simply sat there, slumped against the stone wall. With a sob, he rested his head against the flag stones and waited until the dizziness from the fall left him.

With his face plastered against the stone, as his eyesight adjusted to the dark, was when he noticed it. The flagstone directly next to the one that he rested his sweaty head on was a bit taller than all the others. Or rather, it stuck up about an inch higher than all its surrounding counterparts. Leaning back, he scratched his head and pondered the strange stone.

*Are you so bored with your post that you are paying attention to flag stones, Mosha?*

With a self depreciating laugh, he nudged the offensive stone with his foot. Surprisingly, it gave the slightest way. Again he nudged it, and again the stone moved. Licking his lips, he produced his pen knife, the one tool that all librarians carried, and gently began to pry the stone with the blade. The stone, which had moved so easily at first, did not appear interested in cooperating further without encouragement.

Sweating now and breathing heavily, Mosha was about to give up when, with one last jerk, he heard a pop.

Carefully he placed his now dull and chipped pen knife to the side and lifted the stone. Revealed in the darkness was a rectangle case of some kind. Gently, Mosha had eased his discovery out of its hiding place and put it in his lap. The copper case was corroded beyond repair, and small flecks of metal broke off in his lap. Seeing that there were hinges on one side, he carefully opened the lid which screeched in protest. Wrapped in a cloth of purest black nestled a book. Mosha cried in wonderment as he lifted the treasure out of its container. For a treasure it was. To a librarian, what could be worth more than a newly discovered book?

The first night he was too exhausted to even begin to examine his new object. The next morning he had hidden the book in his mattress. Half way to the library, he had turned back, worried beyond any rational explanation. Retrieving the book, he had taken the tongue lashing from Agar for being late with little fuss. From that day on, his discovery stayed with him.

The second night the puzzle deepened. The writing in the book was like none he had ever seen. For hours after he turned into bed he began a long mental catalogue of all the works he had ever read and their script. It was an exhausting list. By the time the sun peeked through the slim window in his room, he was still awake, red eyed from a lack of sleep; but filled with a fire to know; to crack the mystery of the flagstone tome.

His new found excitement translated into his work in the lower archives. He finished Agar's three bails in seven days; impressing the head librarian to the extent that he granted Mosha's request to have a few days to himself. He put those days to good use.

First he read the libraries entire catalogue of works involving language and script. Then, one by one, he read the most ancient of those works trying to find some reference to the script in his book. It was maddening at first; the scope and magnitude of the endeavor before him almost dwarfed his own monumental ego.

The tome's script was almost picture like; elegant in its simplicity. The book itself was a work of art. The cover and binding was of a soft and supple material. While looking initially plain, when opened the script seemed to have a metallic gleam as it caught the light. The lettering changed in style, going from a block kind of type to a more flowing and elegant style in later pages. From this, Mosha concluded that there must have been more than one author; or at least more than one scribe since the text differed to such a degree. Strangely, the book contained no pictures or illustrations of any kind. Only the strange rune like script dominated every page.

Using a piece of almost stale bread to scoop the bowl clean, he thoughtfully chewed the last of his meal. Slowly sipping the remainder of his ale, the bitter brew did not even elicit a grimace of distaste as his mind attempted to put together what he had read earlier in the day. Tomorrow was his last free day. The next would find him back in the library basement, trudging through the boring work that had become his career. There had to be something that he was missing; or some piece that he needed to even have a starting place for his mystery.

Lost in thought he had not noticed he was no longer alone at the table. Jolting him from his thoughtful revelry, he looked into a pair of taunting eyes that he had not seen for ten years. Setting down his tankard, he glowered at the new presence; this intrusion on his joyful reflections.

Glancing over at Rand, he saw the tavern owner speaking quietly with a large man dressed in the uniform of the Green Guard. A moment later, Mosha was alone with the woman and her guardian.

Eldest Sister had not seen the strange librarian for ten years. In fact, it had been a number of days until her contacts could locate the dirty man. She had feared that the mages had swept his body under the rug; literally.

Fortunately he had only been demoted. He had been lucky; the revelations, or questions, that his research had produced was the kind of information that could spark the attention of the mage council. Indeed, the Ferrakei mage in attendance might very well have taken a far more drastic measure than merely having the mund demoted. On reflection, it was always hard for the mages to throw away a valuable resource which most likely played a greater role in his being alive today.

And that Mosha was a valuable resource was unquestionable. His mind was like a sponge sucking up information as if it were water. His presentation ten years ago had been brilliant. His conclusions were amazing and downright ground breaking; and also a political and social nightmare if any of them were remotely true. Then, as now, she had no doubt to the undeniable truth that was presented that day. The problem lay in convincing the rest of the world of it. She also had to admit another truth; she was attracted to intelligent men. She had been downright mesmerized by the obvious intellect of the man ten years ago. Silently, she held the portly librarians gaze and studied him.

The last ten years had not been kind to Mosha. While he had been heavy set when she first met him, Mosha was now grossly overweight. Bloodshot brown eyes indicated that he had not been sleeping well; greasy black hair fell in sluggish waves to the man's shoulders; red flushed cheek's indicated too much ale and not enough exercise. She had no doubt that the demotion had damaged the librarian's huge ego and his health had directly suffered from it.

She was still the most beautiful thing he had ever seen. Only light touches of grey were evident at the temples. He still remembered the day ten years ago when he presented his research. She had seemed to hang on every word, delighted with the knowledge he was uncovering. Almost reflexively, he put his hand into his shirt, his trembling fingers brushing soft leather.

"Don't move. Remove your hand, so I can see it. Slowly. Very slowly."

The voice came from above and behind him. Silently the Green Guardsman had slipped behind Mosha the portly librarian. Mosha stayed still, his eyes wide; looking to the woman, he gave a silent pleading look.

"Guardsman, please step away."

Eldest Sister's voice had taken on the sharp metal of command.

Shaking his green covered head, the man replied,

"With all due respect, Sister. This little get together is not happening one moment longer until pudgy here takes his hand out of his shirt; then he is going to let me see what he was reaching for; if not we are out of here."

The mesh like mask seemed to give the guard a hollow and menacing sounding voice. Shaking slightly, pudgy removed his hand and placed it palm down on the table. With an assurance from Eldest Sister, Mosha nodded.

John had to give the gross little man credit, he seemed to have a backbone. Putting one gauntlet covered hand on the man's shoulder; he used the other to reach into the food stained shirt. Removing the object, he placed it on the table for the Sister to see.

"It's a book." She said,

"Yes, a book. A librarian with a book! How dreadfully dangerous."

With a glare at the Guardsman, Mosha moved to reclaim it. A metal covered hand beat him to it. With his face turning red, Mosha watched as this uneducated thug, of course he was uneducated! Opened his precious find and began to carefully flip the pages. Grinding his teeth, Mosha growled,

"It's not a picture book, you ass. Erotic or otherwise."

John chuckled; pudgy had a sense of humor. No, his interest in the book was real. Ignoring the ass comment he asked,

"What language is this?"

Rolling his eyes, Mosha replied,

"It's a very ancient script that I am working on deciphering. Please give it back, unless of course you can put your vast intellect to work decoding it. I assume you are a genius simply disguised as a mud rutting thug?"

That last comment made John laugh out loud. Carefully closing the tome, he handed it back to the greasy man. He waited until Mosha had the book safely back in his shirt.

"I can't read it. That's for sure. But, I have seen it before."

Mosha made a face and waved his hand dismissively.

"You have seen a book before? Congratulations."

John did not laugh this time.

*This guy was getting downright rude.*

"The writing you little prig. The runes."

Mosha stopped in mid sneer.

"Where?"

The Guardsman did not answer; he simply continued to look down on the little man in silence. Though the green mask covered his features, Mosha had the impression that the big lug was smiling at him. Mosha momentarily mastered his irritation,

"Please?"

Looking over to the Sister, at her nod, the Guardsman slowly pulled back his sleeves, revealing a revelation. On the wrist and forearm of the man's gauntlets, etched in silvery brilliance, were runes. And not just any runes; Mosha's runes. Writing mirroring that of his flagstone tome. Almost without thinking Mosha stood, removed the book and began flipping through its pages, trying to match up the runes gracing the grey metal and the pages in his tome; his mind racing.

Eldest Sister sat back and watched the scene before her. Mosha was completely engrossed in his writing comparison. John simply stood there patiently, allowing the shorter man to peer closely at the writing on the gauntlets. She allowed this to go on for several minutes.

"Mosha, my dear. I am glad to see that your academic lust for knowledge has not burned out completely. Please sit, and talk with me."

Almost reluctantly, he stopped the comparison and the librarian settled down in his chair. With her eyes now completely on the librarian, the Sister had failed to notice the focused intensity that her guardsman was paying to Mosha.

# Chapter Fourteen

An hour later, John stepped out of the doorway to the tavern. Gam appeared near the street light, and gave the all clear sign. Nodding, John motioned for Eldest Sister to proceed. Walking slowly, but steadily down the street, the small group was joined by Lorn and Dorn who had secured the immediate area around the tavern for Eldest Sister's strange meeting.

The unit of four had been working together for two months; escorting the Sisters to and from the city outside the Great Temple. John's time with the three Gurashi had developed a hyper sensitivity to the activities and people around him; the four seemed to mesh and move as one.

John's time in and outside of the Temple had allowed him to observe the city and its inhabitants; behind the safety of the green mask of the guard. While the green collar all mund guardsmen wore identified his race, the mask allowed him to move through the throngs of the city without dealing with the frowns and judgmental looks of the populace.

If he had learned one thing about the city it was this; the place was magical; literally. Everywhere, there was magic. But not the mythical, rabbit out of the hat stuff; this was a true blue power; something that the entire society was based upon.

Kitla had taken him on his first exploit outside the temple walls. It was a culture shock on an amazing scale. He had stopped a few feet from the doors of the temple to watch a juggler entertain the crowd. Large balls of fire were thrown into the air, caught, and then thrown again. From the heat it was obvious that the balls were actually fire; John's scarred arm itched slightly in response. He firmly quieted his elemental who obviously wished to respond in kind to the display.

Magic was everywhere and in everything. Magic allowed wealthy citizens to travel above the heads of the lower classes in air born chariots; it made for fresh water to be pumped and used by the populace; lamps provided heat and light for the night darkened streets; craftsmen used their fine toned magical skills to create marble artworks that surpassed those on earth. Buildings and spires that would have been fantastically impossible in John's world were a normal, everyday architectural sight in the Shinning City. Hyberan. Thousands of city dwellers lived under the protection and rule of the mages.

Technology and sciences were not subjects considered outside of the use of magic. Magic was everything and everywhere. Workshops generated products from forks, spoons, toys and weapons on a scale in comparison to any factory or corporation. All powered by magic. Much of it due to the rawstones.

The stones were everywhere in the city. Lights for seeing, water for drinking, air for breathing, earth for growing; all used the stones to provide the power for everyday life. Everywhere, the scent of the stones left a bad meth filled after taste in his mouth. Although the mages implemented air currents to lessen the acrid smell, still it clung to the shinning city like a dark stain.

In a world where social and political power lay in the use of magic, the munds were simply left out. The munds, or Mundane Race, were therefore all the more pathetic; in the hearts and minds of the magic using races. Munds could not access their life force, Kitla had explained, and therefore could not perform magic. Therefore, their role in society had been delegated to that of an inferior place; one of subjugation and service. The subject was obviously one that weighed heavily on her and John had not pressed for a longer explanation at the time.

He wanted nothing to dampen the time he spent with this exotic beauty who had claimed him. With his training and service with the guard, and her responsibilities of a Sister, their time together was limited. Often he would go days and nights without being with her; a knowing glance across a marble lined hall way; or a quick caress in passing; promising so much more.

However, he tried to put those cold and lonely nights to productive use in practicing with air and fire. Terra's warning about trust had made him hesitant in sharing his secrets. No one but Tyrell and Grach knew of his abilities. And given the fact that the munds, god he hated that word, were not supposed to have magic, he did not want to be singled out. He was unsure of the consequences.

But, the guilt he felt in not sharing this information with his fellow guardsmen and Kitla weighed on him heavily. At some point, he would need to confide in someone. Grach had been gone three months in his search for Tyrell and Champion missed them both. His need to share and talk to someone about his experiences made his head ache. Which was why being chosen to escort Eldest Sister to her somewhat clandestine late night meeting with the librarian had been such a stroke of luck.

Mosha; that greasy, pudgy librarian was Mosha. If he had any reason to doubt the crazy old woman's directions they fled as soon as Eldest Sister had begun trying to woo the portly fellow into helping her; helping her with what, John had no idea. But Mosha was fascinated by the gauntlets. Or rather, the writing on them; and Eldest Sister was happy to use that interest to obtain the librarians help. John had then been instructed to step back from the table as the two began a heated, whispering discussion; ending when Eldest Sister had pointed at John and Mosha had reluctantly nodded agreement.

Lying in bed, John stared up at the ceiling. It was all set up. He was to meet with Mosha tomorrow at the library. The librarian had one more day before he had to return to work. He wanted to spend the time looking at the runes of John's armor and weapon. When his request to have Skurge's gift for a period of time was rejected, Mosha demanded that John be present in person with the objects.

So that was that. He was to meet with the man that Terra had claimed could be trusted. That he was to tell everything. Sighing, John closed his eyes and attempted to clear his thoughts and allow sleep to claim him.

# Chapter Fifteen

He stepped into the room where the two men had been detained. The "room" was actually a suite of rooms that had been constructed at a later time in the bunkers history. Dim light flooded the place; the nicotine smell from the ashtray offset the strong meth smell of the compound somewhat.

That Ordoza and Orlando were brothers was unmistakable. But like many siblings, their facial similarities were offset by their personality differences. Orlando was a brute. Once a South American body builder, the man had let much of his once steroid fueled body run to fat. Belligerent, angry, violent and rude, the man had been the bane of the operations workers. Usually when a word would suffice, Orlando used a kick or a punch to the head to keep the poor devils cowed and submissive.

Watching with blood shot, angry eyes, the fat man had spent most of his short incarceration strapped to the chair, with a mouth gag; as he was now. His first attempt had been to assault a female agent who had returned the favor by crushing one of his knee caps. The brute could not get it through his head that he was no longer in charge; that the game was over. Turning dismissively from Orlando, John fixed his eyes on his true challenge.

Ordoza sat calmly viewing John through watery brown eyes. He leaned slightly back in his chair. Placing a hand carelessly on his brother's shoulder, Orlando visibly relaxed.

Slim verging on gaunt, Ordoza sat like a man in complete control. His hands never shook; his words were carefully chosen. His shoulder length brown hair and large lipped mouth gave him an effeminate appearance. He appeared, even dressed in the orange prison garb to be a man at peace. If anyone had ever come close to unnerving John Champion, it was this man.

Sitting down, John ignored Orlando's attempts to speak through his mouth gag. His face turning an angry red, spittle began to drool down the large man's face; dripping small pools onto the table.

"Orlando."

His brother did not raise his voice; but the effect was almost magical. Orlando stopped sputtering, and leaned back in his chair; greasy sweat making its way down his fat cheeks.

"You know that it bothers my brother when you ignore him, counselor." Ordoza's reprimand would have seemed out of place from any other man.

"I came to talk to you, Ordoza. That's our deal that keeps both of you from a short stay on death row. Simply because you require your brothers presence to ensure your cooperation is of no concern of mine. I need the information you have; you require that he be here as you provide that information. That is enough."

Nodding, with his hand still resting on his brother's shoulder, Ordoza motioned for John to continue.

"We have been able to trace half of the meth you produced to your dealers. However, where did the rest of it go? We find in your books that nearly half, or more, of your product was going to one dealer. One distributor. This person, or persons, is identified in your books as "O". Always in capitals and always written in a grey pen."

Looking up, he could see that the inquiry had shaken both men. Orlando had bowed his head and now quietly sobbed. Ordoza had lost what little color he had in his face; he rubbed his brother's shoulder in a consoling gesture and met John's gaze. Licking dry lips, he answered,

"We never knew who they were, Counselor. We never saw them. They came to us through an eastern European contact. Would meet with them once per year; they would identify how much product they wished, would pay in advance and advise us of the pickup date. It was an odd arrangement; but a profitable one."

"You said you never saw them; but you met with them?"

Nodding, the slim man responded,

"They were always dressed in grey. Sometimes business suits, sometimes in a grey wrap of some kind. Every inch of them was covered. Gloves, socks, sometimes ski masks. Except their eyes; black things; dark."

Gripping his brother a bit tighter he continued,

"Orlando made the mistake of getting into an argument with them, for the third shipment, was it?"

The fat man nodded, his sobbing got louder, sighing, Ordoza continued,

"Well, they did something to poor Orlando. Something that had him writhing in pain on the floor." Shrugging he continued,

"They left us that day, and I thought we would never see them again. Poor Orlando recovered, though he was never the same. However, the next year they contacted us and our business continued with them until your raid."

Waking, John sat up, wiping the sleep from his eyes. Strange that he dreamed about the brothers. Their conversations were never very productive; mostly confirming what John and his team had already learned dismantling their operation. Shaking his head, he headed to the mess hall for an early breakfast.

THE MAGE gave her minion an icy eyed stare that most would have shriveled under. However, being cowed, even in the presence of his employer, was not something Maer would allow. His profession demanded fearlessness; even in the face of a mages fury. So he sat relaxed, attentive of course, but relaxed. The silence in the small chamber was tense; even dangerous. He buried the urge to smile.

Gazell did not like the Seran. They were a sneaky, clever people who were too handy at killing. However, they were also extremely talented at finding lost items; especially if those items happened to be people. Maer had handled sensitive matters for the council before. At least he stayed bought once purchased.

"So you found the Mok and his munds?"

"Yes honored Mage."

She gritted her teeth. The word "honored" always seemed to be in a mocking tone from Maer's mouth.

"And?"

"The merchant is not what he seems. He is holed up at the Mok embassy. He pretends to sit quietly in the background, but it is obvious that he is running the place. I was not allowed to speak directly with him. However, I was assured that he and his servants would be willing to provide us with whatever information concerning his journey with Tyrell."

Pondering this, the mage began to tap her foot. Her mother had thought it an un-lady like habit and had tried to disabuse her daughter of it by tying her foot to a chair leg every time she sat down. However, once she had been tested as a mage, she had been allowed this one vice.

"I am assuming the Mok's want something in return?"

Giving her a sharp toothed smile, Maer nodded in acknowledgement. Snorting in disgust, she said,

"You have two more days to search the city. Then, set up a meeting with this so called merchant. I need to meet him face to face before I can convince the counsel."

With a wave of her hand, she dismissed him. Alone with her thoughts, Gazell's worry over this mysterious mund increased. Absently, she waved her hand through the air; she hated the smell of dog.

TIA LOOKED for a place off the path to dump her basket. The acolytes of the temple had been working since mid morning cleaning the site of the shrine. When they had first arrived, she had been a bit confused.

Her memories of the shrine were off key with what she saw before her. Where she had firmly believed that the statue was white, in reality it was a brown color due to the lichen that had attached to the stone. Once the girls had begun to remove the vile fungus, it revealed to the light of day a white marble veined with green throughout.

Long delicate arms reached out from the statue as if blessing the world. On that stormy night she was convinced that the lady was blessing John; whom she thought at the time was a two faced war god. Blushing a bit at her childish foolishness, she continued down the path.

The shrine of the White Lady was surely a holy place. Looking over Hyberon, the lady seemed a beacon of safety and refuge for the cities inhabitants. The Sisters taught that the White Lady had been the only Sister to also practice magic as a mage. She had believed that magic was a great responsibility and that mages should use their powers to guide and protect people; not rule. She had argued, and later fought, against the other mages. She had been overwhelmed. The story goes that a group of mund artisans built the shrine shortly after her death out of love and respect. For the White Lady believed in serving and protecting all people; including munds.

The acolytes had carefully removed all of the birds' nests, doing their best to place them into nearby trees. Some of the older girls used small scythes to cut down the long grasses and small bushes that had grown between the pillars. Other acolytes were white washing the columns and the place already seemed to get brighter from their work.

Tia waved at Sister Ura, who was overseeing the cleaning. One Green Guard followed silently behind the Sister, while the other three had stationed themselves around the shrine. While there was no evidence of any rashers, except the three bodies that the guards had removed, Eldest Sister had insisted that a guard unit accompany the group.

As Tia continued her way down the path, she reminisced about the change in her fortunes. She had found in the Sisterhood a place of safety for her mother and herself. Not only that, she had been delighted when the Sisters insisted that she learn to read and write. Music was also encouraged, although with her first attempts at singing she had been gently advised that her voice should be used for her own personal enjoyment and not that of others.

She was learning to be a Sister and could think of no better life for a mund girl. It was true that she was scared of one day serving in the pleasure houses; but her mother assured her that the Sisters took care of their own and to give pleasure for the support of the temple was a true blessing. Tama, her mother, had absolutely bloomed while living in the temple; literally.

At first she had been asked to assist with the tending of the temple gardens. Tia had been afraid of her mother's still fragile health, but Sister Ura had assured her that being outdoors in the fresh air would do Tama good. The head gardener soon found in Tama a kindred spirit in the love of growing things. In a short time, Tama was constantly consulted on everything from rose petals to onions. She had fretted about not accompanying Tia out of the temple today but Ura had assured her that the Guards could handle any trouble. The only other person who Tama would adhere to so readily was John.

Tia smiled as the image of the ugly man came to mind. She did not mind thinking of him as ugly, and in truth John often referred to himself as the ugly guardsman; though Gam sometimes called him the cute puppy. When this happened, John would get a gleam in his good eye and the two would head off towards the training circle and "Play" as John called it. Tia silently believed that any playing with the large Gam would involve a bit more than chasing each other and pulling pony tails.

John would have dinner with Tia and her mother as often as he could. Sometimes Sister Kitla would join them; sometimes not. While Tia had no hard feelings towards the beautiful sister, she did enjoy having John to herself during these dinner moments. Even Tama had stopped being so shy and quiet around the big man. Their last dinner had resulted in John spilling some ale on Tia's robe and Tama had scolded him for being so careless. She recalled the sound of John trying to apologize through his own laughter. Smiling, she found a spot to dump her basket and began walking back up the path.

"What a beautiful smile, my pretty one. Such a pretty smile for a pretty girl."

The voice froze Tia in mid step. The words themselves did not send a shiver down her spine; but something about the tone of voice made her quiver. From behind one of the fallen pillars stepped a Seren. Short and compact, like all his race, this Seren was missing an ear. Dark black fur and cruel eyes looked at her from a face that could have been cute and puppy cuddly, if it did not sport a vicious smile accompanied by canine fangs.

One Ear gave a short low bark and six more seren appeared behind him. All sported red trousers and a red sash that crossed their chests. The four sided insignia of the mages was emblazoned on the center of each sash. Seven pairs of eyes viewed her with cruel promise; red tongues darting through their sharp teeth made soft panting sounds.

Taking a slow step, Tia tried to back away; keeping the basket between herself and the dangerous creatures. With a swift swipe of his clawed hand, the one eared leader knocked the basket from her terrified fingers and gripped her wrist. Twisting it painfully, his grin widened at her gasp. Tia thought,

*He is going to eat me.*

Leaning close, the seren sniffed her hand. Nodding, he growled something at his pack and she found herself surrounded. A fur covered hand stopped her scream. She bit down hard on the hand and tasted blood. What must have been a seren chuckle came to her ears, but the hand stayed clamped over her mouth. Slowly they began dragging her down the path, away from the shrine.

"Hold!"

Tia almost fainted in relief. A Guardsman stood at the bottom of the path. Another appeared to either side and a fourth in front. All four guards had drawn weapons; three blades and an ax now faced the pack. Handing her over to another seren, one ear stepped forward, his hands out stretched.

"We are on official business of the counsel, Greenie. This girl has the scent of one we seek. Stand down."

Sighing in feigned disappointment, the ax wielder stepped forward,

"I would gladly follow the will of the counsel, if this girl was not the province of the Sisters of the Sublime. Taking her into custody is unacceptable. Any such request to speak to her must be made to the Eldest of the order. I wish it could be otherwise my fine friend. You could have saved yourself a jog from the city."

With a low snarl from One-Ear, the pack closed tighter around her. Tia felt smothered by the dark fur and strong smell of canine that assaulted her nostrils. She could feel the danger in the air.

Grimly, Gam silently cursed to himself. The damn dogs had the girl well hemmed in. He couldn't go in there and start bashing doggy brains in without taking the chance of harming the girl. He gave the three other guards a slight hand signal, and placed his weapon on the ground. Moving towards the pack, he kept his eyes on the leader.

Coming to within a few feet of the seren, Gam stood with his arms crossed. Looking the creature up and down, taking note of the mage emblem, he asked in a quiet voice,

"What now, pack leader? We cannot let you go, unless you give us the girl. You cannot go, unless you have the girl. How do we get out of this mess?"

Shrugging in agreement, Maer answered,

"My instructions are explicit; as are the punishments for failure. The girl must come with me."

Nodding in understanding, Gam answered,

"Then I will come with you as well. My fellows here will escort the women at the shrine back to the temple. No one touches the girl but me. We go to your masters and await the Eldest Sister. Agreed?"

# CHAPTER SIXTEEN

Mosha was giddy with excitement. His mind raced with the possibilities. The precious book safely within the folds of his blue librarian's robe, he hummed an off key tune to himself. John followed the pudgy man with a half smile on his masked face. He looked forward to being able to sit down and explain to this annoying little man what he had gone through since coming to this strange world. When he mentioned to Mosha that this was his first visit to the Mages Tower, or Citadel, the librarian went into a well rehearsed spiel about the history of the City.

The Great Temple of the Sisters was actually in the oldest part of Hyberan; and the City was not really one City, but several merged together over time. Each sub-city catered to a different race or group. For instance, the gurashi's city was located near the port and dockyards, since they were a people tied to the sea; the Sisters and the mund ghetto occupied the old city grounds; other groups and races dominated certain sections of Hyberan. But at the center of it all, was the Citadel. Like the hub of a wheel, the Mages Tower jutted out from the center of the City like so many silver threaded needles. Hundreds of towers dominated a floating island of stone and marble.

Four "bridges" allowed access to the tower. Waiting their turn, Mosha explained that the bridges were actually large stone barges that were operated by air and earth mages working in concert. The earth mages enabled the stone to become much lighter in weight but maintain its strength; this allowed the air mages to guide the barges back and forth between the Citadel and the City. Each barge could carry hundreds of people at a time.

John was struck by the enormity of building such a vehicle; let alone having it float off the ground. The barges themselves were of fairly simple construction. A long flat rectangle piece of smoothed marble slab, with poles driven at intervals around the outside of the stone. In between the poles, heavy cords or braided rope allowed people to hold on while seated on stone benches that circled the inside of the strange vessel. A bored looking guard demanded their business and papers. Handing over the freshly signed letter from Eldest Sister, the guard spent a few seconds reading then motioned for both of them to find a seat.

At the front of the barge sat two mages, with their hands resting in their laps. One mage was a gurashi, with a green robe indicating he was an earth mage; the other mage, presumably the air mage, looked every inch like a large dark furred dog in a white robe. Mosha nudged Champion in the ribs and told him not to stare at the seren as they often had bad temperaments.

Once the barge was filled, the earth mage knelt on the stone floor of the barge, placing his bare hands on the stone. A moment later, he nodded to the air mage, who then stood, and raised his arms. Slowly, gently, the stone slab rose into the air. It was an amazing experience; much stranger than flying in an airplane and more like riding a very slow moving rollercoaster.

Up, and up, the barge rose; several hundred feet into the air. John was thankful for the guard mask as he was sure his mouth was hanging open in slack jawed amazement. The lower floors of the citadel were made of a black colored stone. Gradually, as the barge moved higher, the stone became lighter, until it blazed with a pristine white. Birds and low flying clouds drifted close to the barge. Mosha cursed as one of the birds left a messy deposit on his shoulder.

Finally, the barge crested the lower walls of the citadel, and gently floated down to a stone cobbled space that looked like nothing so much as this world's form of a landing strip. Upon touching the ground, with a slight jolt, another guard hurried to the barge and instructed everyone to exit the vessel, from the opposite side of the sitting mages. John glanced over at the two mages who seemed to be having a quiet conversation with each other, and ignoring the rabble that was disembarking.

Following the guard, Mosha and John were ushered into a hallway where they were again asked their business and John again produced the letter. This time the guard took the letter and placed it into a numbered locker type box. Handing John a copper tablet stamped with a corresponding number, the guard explained that the letter would be returned when John left the tower grounds and provided the tablet.

Then the guard demanded that John hand over his gauntlets and ax. After a few moments of Mosha sputtering protests that his vital research would be detrimentally harmed without access to the writing, the guard threw up his hands in surrender, requiring only that John keep the weapon strapped to his back. Nodding in satisfaction, Mosha motioned John to follow.

Mosha was elated. Soon, he would have an entire day to examine and compare the runes from the book to that of the Guard's armor and weapons. Further, he would hear the story of how the man came to possess such historic pieces of hardware. Humming to himself, it was not until he was halfway up the second flight of stairs that he realized he was alone.

Giving an exasperated snort, he turned his pudgy frame around and climbed back down the stairs only to see the Guard disappear around a corner. Cursing at the time he was wasting because of the stupid lout, he tucked up his librarian's robe in both hands and ran or waddled as fast as he could after the errant Guard.

JOHN WAS focused. He could see the tall skinny man now; he had walked between two pillars and disappeared. Coming to the pillars, he saw a narrow door. Pushing through the opening, he came immediately to a set of stairs, spiraling down into dimly lit darkness. Without a second thought, he descended two steps at a time.

As he went lower and lower, his mind drifted back to that last horrific night. Of the car explosion; his family burning to death amidst smoldering metal and flaming gasoline. And a figure dressed in a trench coat; a man with a tattooed face, watching it all.

When he had recovered enough from the explosion to speak, he had called nearly every law enforcement agency in the country; he had thought that the tattoo was a gang sign of some sort. After weeks of research, he had turned to the idea that it was a cultural tattoo mark; some aboriginal marking or body paint. It took him almost a year to finally abandon the search for an answer to the strange tattoo. One of his early therapists had gently questioned whether the man even existed; that it may have been part of a post traumatic hallucination.

*Hallucination my ass, the fucker is somewhere at the bottom of these stairs.*

John lengthened his stride, his hand barely gripping the railing as he plunged downward. Soon the railing gave way to a rock wall. With a jolt he found himself at the bottom of the stairs. Dark rock walls were dimly lit by rawstone lamps, that jutted from the walls at intervals; a hallway led away from the stairs.

Slowing, he followed the passage, as it wound around and down. Just ahead was an opening of some kind. Peering around the corner, John could see that he was just inside of a stone balcony of some kind. Another set of stairs led down to a large open space. Glancing over the rail, he could see stretchers or beds of some kind, spaced evenly on the floor below; hundreds of them. Tattoo faced men walked down the rows; occasionally bending down to the beds. Barely discernable, figures could be seen lying on the stretchers; unmoving and silent. The smell of meth hung in the air like a heavy fog; almost suffocating.

From the shadows of the balcony he did not think he would be detected. But the darkened safety would not allow him to see what was going on down there; he needed a private one on one with one of the paint faced boys. For several moments, he watched as each bed ridden figure was checked. After what seemed an eternity, the tattooed men had moved on and were out of his sight. With a low cursed prayer, he exited the balcony and hurried down the stairs. Hitting the bottom, he skidded behind the shadowy presence of the stairwell.

*Thank god these fella's like it dark down here.*

Light came from somewhere above; a steady dim orange that blanketed the room. From his hiding place, John could see no sign of movement. Slowly, he stepped towards the nearest stretcher and looked down. A woman, between thirty and forty lay strapped to a bed. Leather constraints on her wrists and ankles insured she stayed put. A metal mask of some kind covered her face and was fused to the bed restricting any head movement; a small glass vial bubbled on the forehead of the mask; metal tubes attached to the vial reached into her nostrils and mouth. Reaching his hand into the mask, he carefully peeled back her lips. She did not move an eyelash. Corrosion and tooth decay had made the teeth black and yellow. The sickly sweet smell of rotting gums nearly made him gag. Blue bloodshot eyes stared off into nothing; her mind seemingly trapped. Placing his face next to the bubbling vial, he lifted his green mask over his nose. Meth. Someone was pumping her with meth.

John felt something gritty on his finger tips. Looking down at his hand, he noticed a fine red powder on his skin where he had touched the woman's lips. Raising his hand to his nose he grimaced at the bitter scent.

Wiping his hand clean on his shirt, he leaned down to examine the mask. Towards the top of the metal mask, something glowed. Leaning over the poor creature, he could see a stone that was secured into the metal; a rawstone. The stone pulsated slowly, getting slightly brighter each moment. As John watched, he thought the pulsing coincided with the poor woman's breathing.

On first glance, it appeared that the metal construct actually rested on her face; but on further examination he could see that there was a thick rubbery material that was placed between the metal and skin. Curious, John tried to touch the rubbery stuff and accidentally grazed the metal. Damn, that's hot. Rubbing his now red finger, the need to ensure the mask did not touch the victim's skin became obvious. It also became apparent why many people had attributed his burns to the rawstones.

Standing straight again, he felt wetness on his cheeks. Reaching up to his face, he felt his own tears streaking down. He could not help it. Lying before him was a nightmare, a monstrosity that he never could have imagined. Somehow, these people were being force fed meth; but for what purpose? How did the rawstones play into this?

The answer was close; he could almost feel it; smell it alongside the stuffy meth fumes. Looking up, he saw that the beds went on for as far as the dim light would let him see; and beyond. Hundreds; no, thousands of human beings were laying here; their bodies being polluted with meth; trapped with no hope. He thought back to Calphan's cruel chuckle in the caverns that seemed like a life time ago. Pieces of a puzzle, that he did not even know he had been putting together, clicked into place.

"What are you doing here?"

John reached up and pulled his own mask down and turned. Walking towards him was a younger version of the man he had followed down the stairs. Tall and skinny, the boys face was dominated by a now familiar spiral shaped tattoo. With short spiky hair, he looked like a fork with a toothpick for a handle. A grey tunic of some kind with matching trousers allowed him to fade in and out of the dim light as he approached. Coming to stand before John, he asked again,

"What are you doing here?"

Flexing his metal covered fists, John responded,

"I have some questions for you."

A confused look momentarily passed over the boy's face, to be replaced with a serene mask of attentiveness, making the spiral ripple.

"Of course Master. Forgive me; I did not recognize you in your . . . costume? How may I assist you?"

Shrugging, John motioned his hand towards the stairs and balcony beyond,

"I need you to come with me, up the stairs."

Nodding immediately, the boy replied,

"Of course, Master. With your permission, let me first advise the overseer."

"NO!"

The boy stopped in mid turn, surprised by the outburst.

"No." John said, quieter this time,

"It will only take a moment. Please follow me."

Now the kid's mask of quiet respect cracked and confusion showed through again. He was obviously struggling with what John was asking him. Coming to a decision, he answered,

"Of course, Master. I am at your service."

Nodding, John led the way back up the stairs, hoping that the boy was following. He was reassured when footsteps echoed behind him.

MOSHA WAS a mess. Sweat flooded down red flushed cheeks. His librarian's robe was a rumpled heap. He had been up and down the stair wells seven times. He had asked anyone he passed if they had seen the Green Guardsman. Most had simply said no; one, a fellow librarian had claimed, in a straight face, to have seen the said guardsman in the lavatory on the fourth level. Thanking him profusely, Mosha had spent half an hour combing the lavatory and the entire fourth level when he realized that he had been duped; in fact, he thought the man was one of Agar's lackeys and was more than likely having a good laugh about it.

The entire morning had been lost because the stupid lout could not follow him up a simple flight of stairs. His vision of studying the runes at leisure, and drilling the guardsman about his amazing armor was shattered. Even if the big green fool popped up this very second he would have only a few hours of time left to study the runes. The library closed early every other ten day; which was today!

So lost was Mosha in his own frustration that when he was grabbed from behind he made hardly a sound. For a fat man, it was always very disconcerting when he left his feet; so when he was picked up, his legs kept walking in mid air for a moment, as if he still strode on the good solid earth. At the last minute, Mosha tried to scream for help, when a handful of iron tasting metal was thrust in his mouth. He felt himself being dragged backward, into the dark.

A door swung shut.

"Mosha. Stop fighting."

The familiar voice brought an instant flood of relief; then fury.

"You small brained fool! Let go of me! Where have you . . ." Mosha's tirade stopped in mid sentence as his feet touched the floor. Which was really unfair since he was really good at yelling at people and had been mentally practicing what he was going to say to the missing man since his second flight of stairs. But, the sight before him was almost incomprehensible and shut him up in mid tirade.

They were inside what looked to be a large, old closet, given the jackets and moth eaten hats in evidence. On the floor was a young mund with a spiral tattoo; a boy; obviously unconscious. Leaning down next to him, the missing Guardsman was dabbing at the poor boy's mouth with what looked to be part of a ripped jacket. Quietly, the unconscious boy groaned.

"What happened? Did the boy fall?"

Shaking his head, the Guardsman answered,

"I hit him too hard. He started to see through my ruse. Smart kid. Sometimes, I forget that I have this hardware covering my fists."

Staring at the large man, Mosha repeated,

"You hit him." It was not a question.

"Yeah, genius. I hit the guy. Now, where can we go where no one can find us?"

A silent moment. Then,

"You bloody, lug brained idiot! You can't go off and start knocking people out. In the Mages Tower! We could . . . I could . . . get expelled from the library. We could be sold in service to the Mok's! We have to get this boy medical attention and then think up some way . . . ."

Suddenly, there was light. A bright light. A fire to be more precise. Not that fire was by itself very earth shattering. In fact, Mosha much preferred the light provided by a rawstone lamp. No, this fire was interesting because it was coming from the Guardsman's hand; his entire arm to be precise. The smell of burning fabric filled the room as the big man's green sleeve burned away. Stepping back, Mosha listened in stunned silence,

"Mosha, I was told by someone I could trust you. That means something to me in my book. That said, if you open your mouth, and anything except, 'Ok, John, I know just the place where we can hide out', comes out, I am going to make your fat ass into so much cooked bacon. Got that?"

Ten minutes later, the trio was in the back of a stockroom, filled with shelves of ancient documents. Sunshine flooded through the only window in the room, giving much needed light to its current occupants. At least sunlight could not be used to make bacon. Mosha had still not gotten over what he had witnessed. He watched silently as the Guardsman had carefully sat the semi-unconscious boy in the corner, propped up against the back wall of the room. Sitting down, the big man rubbed his shoulder,

"For a skinny guy, he got heavy pretty quick."

John was grateful for the guard training he had gone through the past months. Still, his body ached from the recent flight from the nightmare basement, or whatever that place was at the bottom of the stairs. He looked over at Mosha, who watched him in silence. Sighing, John knelt down next to his, prisoner? *I guess*, and shook him gently by the shoulder.

Slowly the boy opened his eyes, and blinked several times. Lowering his head, he vomited violently in between his legs. John grimaced and stood away from the mess as the boy's stomach emptied onto the floor. Crossing his arms, he watched until the retching subsided. After it passed, the boy wearily leaned his head against the wall, looking over at John and Mosha. Memory came back suddenly, and he tried to stand up too quickly. Groaning, he fell back against the wall, holding his head. After several moments, he looked up at the tall Guardsman.

"Why, Master? What happened? Did you hit me?"

Shrugging, John answered,

"Yeah. Sorry about that, kid. You were about to start asking me some questions, I could not answer. I just need to talk with you."

Pushing himself from the wall, he sat up a little straighter,

"I don't understand, master. Why are you masked? Why are you with this unmarked mund? I would never dare to question you, but if I am to be of assistance, perhaps a little information? Unless this is a test? I did not think my testing was to advance until next year."

The boy brightened a bit at the last sentence.

John looked down at him for a moment and then slowly nodded.

"Yes, it is a test. This is how it works, I am going to ask you some questions, and no matter how strange they sound, you are to answer. Understand?"

Nodding in the affirmative, the boy looked like nothing more than an eager puppy willing to please. John felt a pang of guilt about taking advantage of such innocence.

"What is your name?"

"I am Remi, Master."

"Good. Remi, I have seen your face before; or rather that mark on your face. What does it signify?"

"It is my service mark, Master."

"In service to whom?"

The boy chuckled as if he and John shared a private Joke.

"To you Master. To the Orda."

"And who or what are the Orda?"

Now the boy looked confused, he took a moment to think, his answer was a bit unsure.

"You are Orda, Master. The Orda are the Masters. I serve the Orda."

John sighed. He had been afraid of that kind of response.

"What were you doing when I found you?"

"I was tending the sleepers, Master. That is my duty."

He sat up a bit straighter, any discomfort associated with his recent meeting with John's fist seemed to be lessening.

"Sleepers? Are they really asleep?"

"Yes and no, Master. The body sleeps but the mind is active. It is the only way."

"The only way to what?"

"Why, to feed the rawstones, Master."

John silently mulled this over. Things began to make sense. The munds, or humans; the rawstones.

"What is it that you feed to the sleepers? What makes them sleep?"

"The red sand Master."

"The red powder?"

"Yes, Master."

"And what is in the vial on the sleepers mask?"

"The White Tar, Master." The boy made a look of distaste.

"Why do you give them the White Tar?"

"To feed the rawstones."

They were going in a bit of a circle.

"I take it you did not like the answer?"

Mosha had been quietly watching the conversation before him. Though he could not understand it, or rather, he could not understand the boy, he could tell that the Guardsman was not having much luck.

Looking over at him, John shrugged,

"Not really. I am a bit out of practice in obtaining information this way."

Nodding, Mosha, said,

"Tell me what he said. I could understand your questions, but not the answers."

John spent a moment explaining the information that the boy had provided.

"Hmmmmm . . . well, it is common knowledge that munds are used to fuel the rawstones and the effect that has on us; it is what makes us useful to the magic born. Some say it is the only real reason we have not been wiped out as a race. I did not know of such a large facility in the mages tower; but it makes sense. I don't know who these Orda are; I have never read about them in any of the Histories, and I have read most of them. The common belief is that the mages create the rawstones."

Remi had hesitantly raised his hand. Feeling very much like a teacher in a high school class John asked,

"Yes, Remi?"

"Master, how is it that this unmarked mund understands Orda? He is not one of the Marked. He understands but does not speak it?"

John sensed that he was heading towards turbulent waters here.

"Remi, your test is done. You did very well."

John nearly winced at the bright smile that lit the boys face. John had to continue with the charade for just a little longer.

"Remi, this is what I need you to do . . ."

# CHAPTER SEVENTEEN

"And now I am here. I am hallucinating, dreaming, or I am really on another world."

Mosha and John were sitting in his tiny room above the Inn. Mosha sat on his sorry excuse for a bed; a straw mattress that had seen better days. John sat on the floor, his back against the wall, staring at a point just above Mosha's head.

Next to Mosha on the bed were John's gauntlets and ax; they lay untouched as the librarian had been so mesmerized by the story unfolded to him. Mosha watched as the big man rubbed his scarred face; the green guards mask lay off to the side.

Mosha had seen munds who were horribly scarred from rawstone fires before. And John did have a horrible set of scars; but not from rawstones; not from his account.

On any other day he would have dismissed the story as the ramblings of a mad man. But he had seen the fire burn from the man's hand. Had witnessed him speak to the boy, Remi. Clearing his throat, he said,

"So, the boy, Remi, heard you speak this Orda, language. While I heard you speak the common tongue?"

Nodding, John said,

"That is how it usually works."

Snorting, Mosha let go of his breadth that he did not realize he was holding. John had instructed the boy to wait until the sun had gone down to leave the shelter of the stockroom. He refused to consider permanently silencing the boy; killing kids was not an option. Plus, Remi's innocence had touched him.

"Well, yes, that is how it works for a mage. A mage! Not a mund."

Spreading his hands wide, John shrugged,

"How do you explain it? Terra called me a mage. Tyrell said I was a mage. I am sure that some of the Sisters and Guards are suspicious if they have not figured it out. I am sorry I threatened to turn you into bacon, though."

Mosha rolled his eyes at the apology. Trying to take his mind off the immediate conversation, he picked up one of the gauntlets.

"Your sleeve burned off."

Looking down, John grimaced at the scarred arm sticking out from what was left of his sleeve. Flexing the fingers, he said,

"I will just get it repaired. Several of the Sisters are seamstresses."

Mosha shook his head; obviously magical ability did not lead to intelligence. Holding up the gauntlet, he said,

"Yes, I am sure that the Sisters could repair your sleeve just fine. The point, my dense friend, is that while your sleeve is gone, this did not burn." And he tossed the gauntlet across the room.

Catching the metal glove, John looked it over. There was not a blemish on the grey metal. Not a mark to show that he had encased the metal in fire.

He smiled,

"Skurge."

At Mosha's questioning look he went on,

"Skurge. The Dracoth that saved me in the caverns."

"I remember that part of your story. In fact, I remember your entire story. And?"

"He said that I would appreciate the gift; the armor. Maybe he knew it had certain properties; qualities that would allow me to use magic while wearing the stuff."

Mosha bit back a bitter reply; the lug might be right. This creature, this Dracoth, may indeed have known. He had so much to think over; so much to ponder. He had one of the greatest mysteries sitting in his room; a mund mage. A Mundane Mage!

OUT OF sight, a tall dark shape used a shielding magic that the world had not seen in a millennia. People walked past it, oblivious to the terror that was standing among them. Its attention was focused solely on the small window above the simple Inn.

The trap had been set. It only had to follow and make sure the mage took the bait. When dark came, it would find its brethren. Then the mage would be dealt with. It was their way.

AS NIGHT deepened, Calphan the Merchant waited. At least, Calphan was the name and persona that he was using currently. He really did not like being Calphan. The merchant embodied all of the most disagreeable aspects of the Mok people; and little of their virtues. Calphan was greedy, pompous, impossible to reason with, and disdainful of anyone who was not a Mok. In fact, with these characteristics, Calphan was not a very good merchant at all. However, being Calphan allowed him to travel in certain circles of civilization that would otherwise be closed to him. Therefore, keeping Calphan alive and in the world was an advantage that he could not deny.

Night air was cooling, and he suppressed a shiver. He did not like being out here, in the open like this. Not that he feared being caught. Nor did he fear his two servants waking to find him gone; a generous dose of Laka Root would ensure the two munds slept soundly until morning. No, he felt vulnerable because of who he was waiting to meet.

He had survived this long by following a very simple principle; if someone tries to kill you, kill them; if you can't kill them, avoid them. Now, he waited to meet a creature who had recently tried to send him to a burning grave. He shifted his stance slightly, watching as the shadows lengthened.

The place for the meeting was a little used warehouse in the tanning district of the Mok sub-city of Hyberan. The materials used by the tanning guild were pungent and filled the air with a dry chemical smell. He had chosen the place to avoid his guests being discovered; or rather smelled. And they did smell; he grimaced in distaste. You could almost taste the strong reptilian scent in your mouth when they were present. He also had concerns about pursuit after the seren from the Mage Council had visited the embassy. With the strong smells of the tanning district, even a seren would have difficulty identifying his scent; or that of his guests.

He waited in the shadows of a building across the street from the warehouse. This angle gave him a view of anyone entering or leaving the building. He had been told to wait for a full glass. In half that time, he noticed movement at the far end of the street.

Slowly, two shadows detached themselves from the darkness. Approaching the warehouse, the pair brought with them a sinister air of alien malice. Gliding sinuously across the cobbled stones, the two stopped in front of the warehouse door. For several moments, they waited. Calphan studied the pair with a practiced eye.

Nothing of the creature's features could be seen. Both were dressed from head to toe in a ragged black material. After several moments, one of the figures turned suddenly and peered at Calphan's hiding place. Although he could not see the creature's eyes, he felt them boring into him. After a moment, the two disappeared into the warehouse. Taking a deep breath, he followed.

The warehouse smelled of wet wool. He passed through bales of the stuff as he silently stepped through the open spaced aisles of the building. He paused, and craned his neck to make a careful survey of a large open space of floor in the center of the warehouse. An opening in the ceiling allowed moonlight to illuminate the place with a dim glow. He smelled the pair seconds before they appeared.

Silently, evolving from the shadows the creatures considered him from an impressive height. There were few races that could look down on a fully grown Mok adult, and the merchant named Calphan found the experience disconcerting. The three conspirators regarded each other in heavy silence. Calphan calmly surveyed the two before him; waiting was something he could do. Finally, they broke the silence,

*"The Mages know of the mesk infestation. They are now working together with the Ferrekei and the plant men to control any spreading of the creatures. It is unfortunate."*

It was impossible to tell which of the pair was talking. The voices sounded like words spoken from the grave. It almost made him shudder; almost.

"Unfortunate. That is a kind word to use to describe what happened. Our plans for the north lands are in ruins; the mages will not be preoccupied with a full mesk outbreak. Also, you lost control of the mesk; and then you nearly killed me."

Giving what might have been a shrug, the voices replied,

"It was not our intention. The mage who destroyed the mesk swarm was powerful. We could not let his act go unanswered. It is not our way."

He ground his teeth in frustration. He was under strict orders to give these "friends" of the Empress every courtesy and assistance. In truth, their power was impressive; he had not known of their destructive abilities.

"There were three of you in the north. Where is your companion?"

The pair began to sway their necks slightly in unison,

"We felt the mage use his power in the city. We have gone to search for him. He must be dealt with. It is our way."

So, Champion has resurfaced. He was impressed. He had had agents scouring every nook and cranny of the city for months searching for the mund with mage like powers. Such a freak of nature could be very valuable to the Empire.

"Where is he now?"

"In the Mages Sanctuary. The Tower."

Almost he lost his composure; almost. He closed his eyes for a moment; reigned in his anger. Opening them, he said,

"You went in to the Mages Tower? The Citadel?"

A strange hissing noise came from the pair. It took a moment to realize that they were laughing.

"Hsss . . . Hhssss. No, Mok. We are not yet ready to venture into the Mages Sanctuary. We are not ready. Yet. We wait. We watch. We will find the powerful mage and destroy him. It is our way."

Staring at the pair for a moment, he shook his head.

"There are other matters we need to address. I must advise the Empress."

THE HALL of Mages was impressive. Eldest Sister had to admit that; grudgingly. She had been in the great room a number of times and it still impressed her. Vaulted marble arches raced upwards to a brilliant star studded canvas of light on the ceiling. Any astrologer could tell you that the ceiling was a perfect replica of the celestial heavens; heroes, gods and goddesses, villains and martyrs; all alive in the constellations. How the jeweled stars blazed so brightly was unknown; even by the mages. The Citadel had been built as a haven for the mages during the Great Dark; a time of chaos and upheaval that was hard for the mind to conceive of today.

The Hall was said to be a sanctuary to all mages; a place of protection given to them by some forgotten race of magic users. Every few years a historian or artisan tried to solve the riddle of the hall; more hypotheses' were birthed but little to no true answers. Plus, it added to the mystery of the mages, which sat fine with the council, Eldest Sister was sure.

Other than the ceiling, the hall was bare. No tapestries on the stone walls; no colorful designs anywhere. The mages have kept the place like it was for centuries; bare and stoic.

Boring, thought Eldest Sister.

She and her group waited patiently; quietly.

They had not arrived quietly. Upon entering the hall she had raised her voice to such an extent, and made it quite clear that she would see her Guardsman and the acolyte Tia immediately. Only after numerous orders for silence, which she ignored and which only succeeded in having her increase the volume of her voice, were her two charges led into the hall.

Now Gam and Tia both stood on the other side of the hall where they could be seen; on either side of them stood two young mages; both fire by their sashes. She had been informed that the pair had been taken into custody by one of the many seren packs that the mage counsel used for tracking down troublesome citizens. Both Tia and Gam looked well alleviating her fears that they had been interrogated harshly. Silently she fumed and waited; silently.

*Stupid tart*, Gazell thought to herself as she studied the Eldest Sister and her party.

Standing behind the concealment curtain, she could not be seen by the petitioners in the hall. A wonderfully crafted magic, the curtain was a binding of air and fire that created the illusion of invisibility. It was a very convenient creation that allowed the counsel to take stock of any situation developing in the great hall before entering. She had not had a chance to speak to the girl or the guardsman before they were escorted to the hall. But it was of little matter.

Maer had found the strange mund's scent and informed her that a trap was waiting to be sprung. She allowed herself a hard smile; this mund mage business would be taken care of shortly. The grey man would have no cause to doubt the understanding his people had with the counsel. Still, she began tapping her foot to a nervous beat.

*Tap, Tap, Tap.*

*Nothings done until it's done.* Her mother's voice reminded her from the back of her mind.

*True*, Gazell thought, *too true*.

*Tap-tap-tap.*

# Chapter Eighteen

Calphan looked at the two before him. They gathered in the same warehouse where he had met the dark ones the night before. He thought he could still smell their stench in the bales of wool surrounding the meeting. It had been some time that he had taken counsel with such high member's of Mok society; let alone a member of the Imperial Court. He cleared his throat,

"Are there any more questions that I may answer?"

"Just this, spymaster, how are we to trust these . . . creatures to do what needs to be done?"

Mage Archen was a high ranking member of the Imperial Court. On top of that, he was one of the most powerful mages that the Empire had ever produced; he was also a member of the Mages High Counsel. Like all Mok's with magical ability, he was trained here in Hyberan. However, unlike some Mok Mages his allegiance was to the Empire first and foremost. The idea of mage unity through their magic was an illusion that both the rulers of Hyberan and the Empire fostered. The Treaty of Seven Fires guaranteed the Empire training of all of its magic users by the standards of the Mages Counsel. That this had benefitted the Empire was beyond doubt; however, the humiliation of a treaty three hundred years old still haunted the Empress. If not for the power of the mages, this part of the continent would be under the Empire's rule.

Giving the mage a deferential nod, Calphan answered,

"I understand your reluctance, Honored Mage. However, the Empress has given her "friends" the benefit of her trust. Her orders are specific and explicit; we follow her plan to the letter or face bitter imperial reprisal."

Archen snorted. He was small for a Mok. Almost delicate in his dark blue mages robe. If not for his magical ability he would most likely have been cast out by his brood kin. But that delicate frame belied an ability to craft water magic few other mages could match. He was not someone to offend carelessly.

Looking to his left, Archen asked the only other member of their small conspiracy,

"And what does the Master of the Armada have to say? I see Bruda did not have the courage to come himself."

The third Mok stiffened slightly at the slur against his commanding officer. Like Archen, Commander Furk did not have a size typical of a Mok; his frame went in the other direction. The commander was huge; check that, enormous. Standing nearly half again as tall as Calphan, the brute outweighed the spymaster by a hundred pounds; Pounds of muscle. Even squatting down, as he was now, the commander filled up the warehouse with his sheer size. The green scaled armor he sported gave him a girth and immensity that he did not really need. The voice was surprisingly high for a warrior of such size,

"The Armada is ready. Concealed of course. Once the signal is sent, we will do our duty. As we always do."

He glowered down on the small mage. Archen ignored the commanders clumsy reprimand. The mage spoke directly to Calphan,

"Yes, I am sure when there is any brutalizing of unarmed civilians, Bruda and his brood can be relied upon. But my brethren and I will be inside the Citadel, surrounded by soon to be enemy mages. We will be in dire straits if this plan does not go smoothly."

Calphan silently agreed. The Empress was putting too much faith in the dark ones. An ally that had already failed once with the northern mesk infestations; an ally who fails to deliver on promises is not much of an ally. However, his duty was clear, so he kept his thoughts to himself and said instead,

"The Empress is secure in her faith of the dark ones. She would not risk so much of the Empire's interests unless success and glory were certain. We have only to play our parts."

Archen chewed his lower lips in thought,

"And what is your part to play, spymaster? I do not see you risking anything in this venture."

Smiling, he really did like the small mage, he answered,

"The Empress has impressed upon me to take care of a small matter. A personal matter. Fear not, honored mage, you will see my handiwork before this matter is closed."

Archen grimaced,

"You have no idea how non-comforting that makes me feel, spymaster. No idea at all."

Calphan simply smiled and bowed. He really did like the little fellow.

GRACH SILENTLY watched his friend rest against the side of the skiff as the vessel glided smoothly through the waters of the harbor. It had been months since he had left Hyberan to search for Tyrell. The molden had traveled back to the entrance of the caverns, followed the almost cold trail back to Hyberan; then to Tyrell's clan lands where he had found his friend in the care of his family.

The story was that Tyrell had been returned to his home by the warriors sworn to the Mages Council. That he had been found wandering by the road; lost and near dead. The great mage Gazell herself had cared for him; what an honor it had been for the family! Gazell herself had promised to come to their humble lands to look in on the hapless wanderer on her return from Hyberan.

The family of course had questions for Grach; where had he been? When did he and Tyrell become separated? Was he injured at all? Did he know about the mesk infestation?

He gave vague answers to most of the questions. It was clear that the story portrayed to Tyrell's kin held shards of the truth but was far from the whole stone. As he listened to the account provided to the family by the mage, he made eye contact with Tyrell. While skinny and weakened from his ordeal, the fire in the blue man's eyes belied his body's condition. As soon as Tyrell convinced his family that he was well enough to travel, and on the pretense that he wished to thank Gazell in person for her assistance, the pair had taken leave of the clan.

Due to Tyrell's weakened state, they had traveled at a leisurely pace. Though his friend wanted to push for the city, Grach would not allow it. Grach knew Tyrell was eaten away with guilt. Tyrell could not recall how long he was under the control of the mages; nor could he recall if he had divulged anything about Jonathan Champion. The Ferrakei's honor demanded that he try to assist the mund in any way he could.

Though somewhat mollified that John had found sanctuary with the Sisters, Tyrell still felt driven to assure his safety. A safety that Grach could not in all honesty provide assurance; he had left the city months ago.

As Grach watched his friend, he noticed the slight shaking of the blue man's hands. His mouth firmed in an unhappy line. When they arrived at the temple, Grach would request that Ura look at Tyrell. He prayed silently to the Root Mothers that all was well.

He felt apprehensive; the night had a strange smell to it.

URA WASHED the remaining blood from the man's neck. Half of his face was a ghastly mess; she had done what she could but he still might lose the eye. The arms would set properly, assuming he stayed in bed for several days. She was more worried by the method used to hurt the mund.

Obviously he owed service to a master. From the color of his bacha collar she believed that it was a Mok, though it was hard to determine due to the blood caked all over the thing. He spoke a language she believed to be Mokai, though no one here in the Temple could verify; the Sisters had little if anything to do with the Empire.

Neither party believed the other should exist and that made relations difficult. There were horror stories of traveling Sisters attempting to establish charter houses in the Mok homeland; the houses lasted as long as it took the Mok's to burn them to the ground; the Sister's usually lasted a few minutes longer depending how imaginative the Mok's were.

No, this mund had been beaten for a purpose. His tormentors obviously had the opportunity to kill him; the damage done to his face told that story alone. But they did not do much harm to his legs; in fact his legs were suspiciously absent of any damage at all.

The acolyte manning the main doors had come running into the garden where she was taking her night meal with a few other sisters. When she had arrived, two of the Guardsmen had lifted the man to a sitting position; blood had trickled down the white marble steps; so much blood. In fact, Ura was surprised that the man had not fainted from blood loss alone before he stumbled up the steps.

The only thing that the injured man had been able to say with any clarity had been a whisper in broken common,

"Take me to the mage . . . the mund mage."

Ura was one of three Sisters who knew of Jonathan Champion's potential. While he had never demonstrated anything approaching magic that she had witnessed, that he had the mage ability for language was undeniable. She had been there the first day he had marched brashly into the temple and asked for Kitla. His Dryan had been perfect; which was why Ura was shocked when Kitla had answered him in the common; shaken to her core as a matter of fact.

So now she waited by the injured man's bedside. She had given instructions to be immediately notified if Champion, Kitla or Eldest Sister returned to the temple. She hummed a quiet Dryan lullaby that usually calmed her nerves; usually.

JOHN KNEW he had disappointed Mosha. The librarian had wanted to keep one of the gauntlets for the evening but John had quietly refused. When Mosha had become belligerent in his request, waving his arms around and claiming John was an ignorant bystander who had simply lucked his way into finding a piece of a great mystery, the refusal had been more firm. He had promised to allow the pudgy man to see them the next evening if he came to the Great Temple after the work day.

While Mosha could be irritating, that was an understatement, John walked back down the darkened streets with a feeling of relief; finding Mosha had been a lucky thing. Hopefully the two of them could put together some answers; why he was here, for instance. With this thought fixed firmly in his mind, John walked on as the rawstone lamps just began to glow brighter in the darkening day.

THE CREATURE followed the mage; quietly shielded. Its blood called for it to kill; destroy. But it reined in the hunters call. Its kind had learned a level of patience; of caution. They would not make the same mistakes. So, cautiously, it watched the mage walk up the steps of the temple. Watched as he questioned the acolytes cleaning the blood off the stone steps. Watched as he then ran up the remaining steps, two at a time into the Great Temple. It smiled, knowing the anger and pain that the mage would soon experience.

JOHN ENTERED the room at a run; and nearly knocked over Ura in the process. After he gave her a quick apology she waived him off and motioned to the corner of the room. Sitting next to a figure on a bed was a blue skinned man. Skinny and sickly John almost did not recognize him. Tyrell looked over his shoulder and gave his friend a warm smile. Standing up on shaky legs, he embraced the taller man. John was shocked at how brittle his friend felt; like the man was made of bird bones.

After Tyrell had released him, a hard slap on the back nearly took his breath away. He had not noticed Grach upon entering the room. Grasping the plant man's arm in friendship he felt the warmth of their companionship wash over him. It was amazing how much he had missed the odd couple. Before they could begin to reminisce, Tyrell motioned towards the bed.

At first John did not recognize the wretched man laid out before him. Someone had taken a definite dislike to one side of the guys face; the eye was completely closed by puffy bruised skin and white bone could be seen protruding from over the eyebrow. Both arms were now in casts; the chemical smell of a recent casting settled in the air. At Tyrell's urging, he sat in the chair next to the bed. Grach leaned down near the man and said quietly just above his ear,

"Gret, John is here. Can you speak with him?"

John could not keep the horror from his eyes as the man slowly turned his face to look at him. Gret looked up at him, his mouth edged in pain. Licking dry lips, the abused man said,

"John. Thank . . . cursed gods. You're here."

He tried to move one of his arms, but grimaced in pain. John placed his hand gently on the man's cast.

"I'm here Gret. What happened to you?"

Gret began a weak laugh, that ended in a bubbling cough. The three companion's watched helplessly as Gret's body convulsed. After it subsided he, said,

"Too much to tell now, John. Too much. My body hurts. Where am I?"

John had tears in his eyes. He could not help it. Gret, solid common sense Gret, lay before his eyes; in pain. Terrible pain.

"Your in the Great Temple, Gret. The Sisters will look after you."

Shaking his head, Gret nearly coughed again.

"No time. No time. Breg. Help Breg."

Gret then closed his eyes and settled back into the hospital bed. His breathing was regular but shallow; as if the air raked his throat with each lungful.

John looked up as Tyrell put a hand on his shoulder. Sitting down in a chair next to him, the Ferrekei spoke,

"We were here when Gret arrived. He was almost unconscious with his injuries. But through the pain he was able to tell us that Calphan is here in the city. Involved in some plot. Gret had few details. All he knew was that Breg had begun to speak to other people about you; other munds.

Telling them that he had seen a mund mage. Calphan learned of it."

"So what?"

Grach spoke up,

"Champion, the Mok's often treat their mund's badly. They are considered little more than chattel. The news of a mund mage could create problems; insurrection. Calphan would have responded harshly."

Looking down on the shattered face of Gret, John again felt the fury building in him. He felt fire gleefully wrap its hot fingers around the anger and fan it, gently at first, then with a wind of flame. Not a wind of flame. Air. Air had joined in. Fickle and feckless air had joined the mad parade.

John stood, his body rigid. He could taste the fire on his lips; feel the air sensuously stroke his hair. He gently touched Gret's damaged face with his finger tips. Then, turning towards Grach, his voice little more than a growl, he asked,

"Where?"

# CHAPTER NINETEEN

Gazell watched from concealment as Eldest Sister made her arguments to the counsel. She demanded the release of her guardsman and acolyte. When told that the pair were part of an investigation, she demanded to know the source and reason for the investigation. This was information she would never receive. One, because only the three eldest mages on the counsel knew of the mund mage; certainly the judicial representative that was dealing with the irate Sister now had no knowledge. Second, if they did inform her of the nature of the investigation, the true nature, she and her companions would not be allowed to leave the Hall.

Killing Sublime Sisters was never a good idea; they held a special place in the hearts of the simple populace. Riots and chaos was something that the counsel tried to avoid at all costs. Plus, other members of the counsel would then demand to know the nature of the investigation as well. What a mess that would be.

Her attention was taken from the proceedings by a slight warmth on her arm. Smiling, she placed her hands over the hidden rawstone. Maer was to contact her as soon as the mund was close to being taken. Giving the Eldest Sister a glare the woman could not appreciate, Gazell left the Hall using the entrance reserved for council members. If she had stayed but a few moments longer she would have observed the large group of Mok mages that entered the hall; seeming to chat quietly among themselves, as they slowly spread throughout the hall.

MAER COULD not believe his luck. He and his pack had followed the mund's scent to the steps of the Great

Temple. Since the darkening day had begun to end, he feared that they had a cold sleepless night ahead of them watching the now darkened building. Just as he had settled the pack in regular shifts for the night, the crazy man came storming out. Behind him waddled a molden trying to keep up with the larger man's long strides.

Signaling his pack brothers, Maer smiled a canine grin. The mage would be pleased. He quickly flicked a claw against a rawstone hidden in his sash and waited until he felt it spring to life. Once he felt the warm throbbing of the stone, he moved swiftly in the wake of his prey.

JOHN SLOWED his pace, allowing Grach to catch up. As soon as the molden came a breast with him he growled,

"Where?"

Following his friends pointed arm, they turned down a dimly lit street.

The pair were headed towards a warehouse in the Mok section of the city. To say that Grach had second thoughts as to whether this was a good idea was an understatement. Tyrell had gone further and argued that the whole damn thing was a trap. John shrugged this argument off.

Breg was in trouble because of him. He had to help if he could. He had only taken the time to retrieve the grey helm from his room before heading off. Grach followed in his raging friends wake, shaking his head in derision. This was a bad idea. The night air smelled strange; it smelled like death and disaster.

CALPHAN'S THOUGTS went along the same lines as those of the plant man. The air did smell foul in the warehouse; thanks to his strange allies. He could not see them, but the stench made their presence undeniable.

He waited and watched behind a bale of wool in the small warehouse. His gaze flickered momentarily to the scene in the center of the building; where he had previously met both groups of conspirators. He would not be able to use this building again for any clandestine meetings; it had been soiled beyond repair. He could not repress a shudder and looked away.

When he had informed the dark ones that Champion had apparently made a connection of some sort with his two servants, he was surprised by their reaction; joy and satisfaction. He had thought he might have to make up some pretense to have the servants disciplined, but Breg had done that for him; the fool had begun to talk about Champion to other servants in the embassy; Against Calphan's explicit instructions.

The rest had been simple; he had arranged to have Gret overhear his chastising Breg for spreading such rumors; and that Breg had to be punished. He had arranged for Gret to learn that Champion was staying with the Sisters of the Sublime; information courtesy of his smelly allies. How they came by their information he had no idea; but he would pay much to learn its source. To have Gret beaten and then left within a few steps of the temple was simplicity in itself; he had watched from the roof top of a nearby building as the broken mund was ushered into the confines of the great temple.

In his mind the use of Gret was cruel, yes; but necessary. The mund's injuries while they looked severe were well within the Sister's ability to heal; Calphan would then be the overwrought master whose small brained servant had gotten himself tangled up with a street gang of sorts; he would thank the Sisters profusely, even give a generous donation to have his servant returned to him. A useful servant should never be thrown away unless necessary.

When he had returned from the temple, the sight before him chilled his amphibian blood. After tonight, Breg would not be useful to anyone. Monstrous.

The dark ones had made good use of the time Calphan had been gone. They had been wise to wait until the spymaster was absent since he most likely would have tried to dissuade them from such a drastic course. Breg was gone; in his place was a bloody mess of a creature; a creature in constant pain.

The mund had been stripped and spread eagled on a large stone wheel. The wheel had been suspended from a chain that had been thrown over two of the rafters of the ceiling. Runes of a script unknown to Calphan dotted the surface of the stone. The servant's hands and feet had been welded to the wheel by some obscene art. His chest had been sliced open as if he were a piece of meat from a butcher shop. Pieces of rib bone and cartilage had been pulled back to reveal the organs beneath. Then, as if his body were some plaything, his lungs had been carefully removed from his body, and laid on either side of his shoulders. Somehow the lungs had remained still attached to the torso.

But, the most sickening aspect of his maiming was that somehow, the mund was still alive. His lungs still breathed, up and down, in and out. His heart still pumped blood. By some amazing, monstrously evil method, the dark ones had been able to prolong his pain even when death should have claimed his life. And that Breg was in pain was no doubt; his silent screams lit his face even now; the voice box had been removed to ensure that his cries alerted no one outside the warehouse. In a perverse way, Calphan had been impressed by the drastic measure; that he could try to justify what his eyes took in right now made his stomach churn.

His displeasure and disgust had been un-maskable when he had first been confronted with the vision before him. The dark ones, his allies, had given their hissing version of a laugh at his reaction. Quickly he had recovered himself and informed the three that they could expect the mage at any moment. As he turned to walk away, they spoke,

*"The mage will see this and despair. He will fall to his knees in fear. He may fight us, but he will be weakened by his own compassion."*

Turning back towards the voice, he saw one of the creatures running clawed fingers through Breg's hair; gently as if he were a favored pet. Looking into Breg's silent screaming face, it said, reminiscently,

*"We have not practiced our art in such a way for eons. We have much to remember; much to re-learn. You are an adept beginning. Very adept."*

Calphan turned away, unable to watch the tormenting of the mund. Even a mund was a living breathing creature. He moved into the shadows. Leaning against a bale of wool he attempted to collect himself; going through mind exercises to calm his thoughts.

*"Do you believe we have committed an error?"*

Calphan slightly jumped. Looking deeper into the darkness, he could see the vague outline of one of the dark ones. Shrugging off the interruption of his privacy, Calphan replied,

"Fear is one thing. Fury is another. I saw this mund burn his way through a horde of rabid mesk. You may cause him to make a mistake by this, through his anger, but I have little hope fear will be a result. Plus . . ."

His voice trailed off. Setting his lips in a hard line he stepped towards the dark figure. Craning his neck so he would be looking towards what he thought were its eyes, he whispered,

"Breg was my servant. My consent should have been sought."

The creature tilted its head to the side as if pondering his words. For a heartbeat, Calphan realized he might be on dangerous ground. These creatures were alien and unpredictable.

"*We offended you. The servant was your property. We overstepped ourselves. We apologize.*"

Calphan was slightly shocked. Courtesy on any scale was not what he expected. Nodding his head, he walked away trying to find some sort of privacy before the show started.

JOHN APPROACHED the open doors to the warehouse. He appraised the black maw of darkness for a moment. Waiting until Grach stepped up beside him, he glanced down at the shorter man. Grach calmly peered into the dark opening, the stone mace resting almost casually on his shoulder.

Reaching up, John peeled off the green guardsman mask. From the loop of his belt he untied the grey helm that Skurge had given him and placed it on his head. Unsoldering the ax, he was reassured by the feel of the smooth black wood in his hands. Giving Grach a nod, the pair entered the building.

If they had waited a moment more, they would have noticed a pack of dog like figures slinking onto the street in front of the warehouse. Silently, the seren pack waited. Maer almost trembled with excitement.

The warehouse was dark and appeared deserted. Appeared, that is. John and Grach slowly wound their way through bales of some kind. The strange combination of wet wool and something reptilian sent an almost putrid reek through the place. The total silence was disconcerting. No sounds of creaking boards; no mice scuttling in the corners. It was not just a lack of sound, but an absence of life. John shifted the ax in his hands slightly. Something waited for them.

Turning the corner of one of the larger bales, the pair stopped. They had found Breg. Or at least what was left of him. Nothing in his life had prepared him for the sight in front of him; John was surprised he did not cry or throw up; or both. Grach approached the stone wheel; his steps slow and steady. Breg seemed to sense their presence. He lifted his head and met John's eyes. Silently he tried to speak. A small trickle of blood bubbled down his chin.

John stepped forward. In a few strides he stood before the tortured man. Raising a hand, he gently gripped Breg's blood soaked fingers.

"It's ok, Breg. We are here. To set you free."

Breg continued to speak; his mouth moving soundlessly. He became a bit more agitated as he tried to communicate. Leaning forward, John asked softly,

"What is it Breg. I am here. I am listening."

Closing his eyes, Breg mouthed something. Leaning forward so he could see his lips closer, John nodded. The dying man breathed,

*Mund Mage*.

Gripping his bloody fingers tighter, John said,

"That's right, Breg. A mund mage. And I am going to make them pay. Make them all pay for this, Breg."

Unbelievably, Breg, laying there on a wheel of dead stone, gutted like a fish, with his life blood bleeding from his body, smiled; Breg smiled. A fierce smile. A smile not of a mund slave or a callow merchant's servant; but of a man who knew freedom was his. It was his.

Glancing over at Grach, John nodded. He stepped back, never taking his eyes from Breg's face as the stone mace crushed the back of Breg's skull; ending his torment.

John and Grach simply stared at the crime before them. Bregs broken body; the pain he suffered at the end. The pair stayed silent; a tribute to what a living creature had suffered at the end.

"What by the Forest is going on here?"

The voice reverberated through the warehouse. The pair turned toward the sound. There, lighted by a flame coming from her hand was a blue skinned woman dressed in a red robe. She looked to be a female version of Tyrell; check that, an older version; without the tattoos. On either side of her stood two other mages; one wearing a green robe and the other a blue; both were Ferrekei. Guarding the entrance appeared to be six or seven seren; they prowled in front of the entrance impatiently giving off quiet growls.

Shifting his ax to his unscarred hand, Champion called fire.

All three mages stopped in their tracks; shocked. Letting them stare at his firebrand hand for a moment longer, he motioned back towards the stone wheel.

"Did you have anything to do with this?"

Silence answered him. Asking this time a bit louder,

"Are you responsible for this?"

Again silence. The mage in the green robe leaned over and whispered something urgently to the blue skinned woman. Now he was getting annoyed.

"If you had anything to do with this, I need to know. NOW!"

Giving him a snort of derision, the woman responded,

"You are in no position to demand anything. I track you all the way across the forest cursed north and find you here in Hyberan, involved in some beastly blood sacrifice? Why I should . . ."

"Enough."

The interrupting voice belonged to a tall shadow.

"Enough, Mage Gazell. You are all in grave danger."

Stepping into the half light, a grey figure appeared. Immediately the seren made a defensive barrier around the three mages.

"A very real danger."

Stepping closer the figure came into view. Tall and lean, he, or she, was completely covered in a grey wrap material. The fine, shimmering, grey fabric covered everything except a pair of very long fingered, grey hands. Black on black eyes almost glowed in the darkness. With a sinuous grace, the grey man moved in between the two groups. Holding its hands out spread, he cried,

"Please, we must all leave now!"

Suddenly, a strong scent filled the air. Something reptilian; something not quite dead. A strange hissing noise sent a shiver down John's back bone.

"Hsss—ss-hsss. What a surprise. Four mages, their pets and a Keeper. A Keeper. A Keeper."

Out of the shadows behind the stone wheel appeared three black shrouded figures. Similar to the grey man in height and bearing, they exuded a sinister, alien feeling. As they passed Breg, one claw covered hand absently tousled his hair as though they shared a private joke. Stopping, the three faced them.

"A Keeper. A Keeper. Our Kin. Our Kin. We have felt your presence. Oh yesssss . . . . clever Keeper . . . clever."

Slowly, the three began to sway back and forth; in unison. John was taken back to the caves; when Tyrell and Calphan had described the dark figures who had attacked them. Black fire.

Stepping forward, the grey man, or Keeper as the black terrors called him, raised both hands. A dim, twilight glow surrounded him. Facing the three dark figures, he spoke,

"Kin we were. No longer. You are not welcome here. Be gone!"

*"Hsss-ssss . . . always kin, Keeper. Blood calls to blood. We are called by blood. Blood to blood. Fathers blood. Mothers blood."*

Slowly the three advanced. The grey man shifted his stance slightly, putting his feet farther apart. Suddenly, black fire raced towards him, billowing and deadly. A moment before it struck a grey wall of twilight surrounded him. Black fire washed against it like waves against a beach. Wave after wave flowed over the grey man; and he disappeared from sight. A moment later the fire stopped, and the grey man staggered back a few steps. White smoke curled from his hands; his breathing came in labored gasps. The three attackers kept swaying back and forth; an eerie hissing sound issuing forth.

A moment later the three robed mages stepped forth. Coming to stand beside the grey man, Gazell raised her flaming hand.

"Stop. This is Hyberan. You have violated the peace. Stop now, and you may live."

The three kept swaying, and ignored the irate mage. Instead they directed their menace at the grey man.

*"Your pet mages, Keeper? So brave. Have you made them so? Filled their hearts and minds with hope? With love? Did you tell them the secret? Our secret?"*

John stepped forward; Grach at his side. He hated listening to some conversation with its inside story; while he stood on the outside. He wanted the answer to one question; one. Motioning towards the stone wheel.

"Did you do that? Did you?"

Gazell tried to silence him but he ignored her.

As one, the three turned towards him. They seemed to see him for the first time. There was a pause.

"Ahhhhh . . . the fire mage. Human mage. Yessss, we remember you. You burned our creatures; burned the forest. So much anger; hot fury. Yessssss."

Unimpressed, John pressed on,

"Listen assholes. I don't care about your beef with his greyness over here. I have a good idea who, or what, he might be. Or these other three; by what I have seen on this world, all mages can burn for all I care."

The other three mages made choking sounds at this; he ignored them.

"All I want to know is who did that to my friend. Who butchered him like an animal. I have a good idea it was one of you three. Which one?"

The three stopped swaying. They tilted their heads simultaneously, as if in thought. The stand off continued for another moment; then fire. Black fire.

# Chapter Twenty

John was ready. He stepped forward and met fire with flame. Red flame met black. The two whirled around each other; neither giving ground. Sparks and flames sped upward at the collision; sending flaming destruction into the wooden beamed ceiling. Calling air; he buffeted one of the figures from its feet; flying headfirst, it struck the stone wheel with a sickening thud. With a cry of surprised rage, a black clawed hand raised up and John was engulfed in black flame; almost suffocating, he blinked his eyes through blackened smoke.

The other three mages had entered the fight and were faring better; the blue robed mage had thrown a bottle filled with liquid. The glass broke a few feet in front of the creatures, forming into a fluid wall of water, dowsing some of the black fire in a steaming mess. From near the dark ones, a strange figure made of dirt and roots had risen from the ground grabbing one of the creatures by the leg; John saw the earth mage, kneeling on the ground, his hands buried beneath the soil; red faced with exertion.

Gazell attacked with a fire of her own; though less powerful than John's it was effective; attacking the creatures in short bursts instead of matching them fire for fire; he could see burn marks on clawed finger and that she had managed to catch one of their robes on fire.

Loping through the flames, the seren pack skirted the fight, trying to find an opening.

Still trying to breath, John struggled to his feet. Looking around he tried to find Grach; the Molden was nowhere in sight. Coughing, he tried, gasping, to take a few clean breathes of air, but the foul black smoke sat in his lungs like a heavy weight. Soon, he felt light headed and weak; stars began to swim before his eyes, and slowly, he slouched to the ground.

Suddenly, John felt a strong hand pull him to his feet; another hand was laid on his chest and a soft warm glow flooded his body. A moment later, clean air breathed into his lungs; the hands held him as he recovered his balance. Lifting his head, he met a pair of black on black eyes; shadowed in grey.

"Human, you must attack while the other mages hold their attention. It is the only way!"

Nodding, getting groggily to his feet, John took stock of the situation. The water mage was down; black smoke curled from a fist sized hole in his chest. The other two mages were now matched up with the two remaining dark ones.

Earth was doing a bit better; his dirt and mud creation was holding its own for the moment, but the dark creature had produced an onyx colored blade and had begun hacking away like a lumber jack. Every time the blade touched the mage creation, dirt and roots dissolved; soon there would be nothing left.

Gazelle leaped around like a dancer; flame striking out like so many deadly fire flies; the dark one facing her was methodical; it batted the mage fire out of the air almost effortlessly and slowly began pushing the red robed woman into a corner. Soon, she would have nowhere to run and the dance would be over.

Concentrating, John knew he had to make this good. He felt slight tremors shaking down his arms. His energy level was low; taking on the black fire and then nearly suffocating to death had left him weak. He spared a brief glance over to the creature lying next to the wheel; no sign that it would be joining the fight. All around them, the building and its contents burned; bales of wool lit like bonfires had created painful obstacles. John knew that smoke was the real danger; soon everyone in the building would die from lack of air rather than each other.

He took a moment to catch his breath and decide where to offer aid. As he watched his decision was made for him; the woman in red had tried to leap over a burning bale and landed badly; the mage lay on the dirt floor with her ankle bent at an odd angle. Her dark opponent approached the burning bale, closing in on its now wounded prey. Calling air, John remembered the effort it had taken to throw the creature against the stone wheel; now he concentrated on the burning bale.

The creature strode slowly toward the wounded woman; who was now desperately trying to crawl away; blood and dirt marred her red robe. The dark one stood over the injured woman who had stopped crawling and simply glared at her executioner; obviously exhausted but defiant. Instead of finishing her off, the creature decided to spend a moment gloating. While it enjoyed its sick moment of victory, it had come to stand directly next to the burning bale.

*Bad idea*, John thought, and sent air rushing at the bale. As the forced wind hit the flaming wool, it teetered and fell; directly on to the dark one as it raised a deadly claw. As if it were made of oil, the thing lit up like a candle; flames engulfed its cloak and body, drenching it in burning light. A high pitched keening came from the living torch as it flopped to the ground; weakly trying to bat at the flames. In a matter of seconds the creature lay still as the fire consumed it.

John turned back to the earth mage. His dirt creation nowhere in sight, the mage dangled weakly from the grip of the last of the three terrors. Thick clawed fingers smoked as they squeezed around the hapless man's neck; the shrieks of pain quieted as his entire head seemed to lose solidity and melted off the body. With a sickening thud, the headless corpse landed in the dirt.

Shaking blood and grime from its hand, the creature turned toward the now charging seren pack. Which a wave of its hand, black fire engulfed the loyal creatures; growls turned to whines of pain and terror; the place filled with the smell of burnt fur.

Turning from the grisly inferno, the creature motioned for John to come forward. Hefting his ax in front of him, John's stance shifted as he prepared to move towards his opponent. Before he could take a step, the grey man appeared. Facing the dark creature, he raised a hand.

"Stop."

Suddenly, a grey glow filled the building; the fires slowed, and then stopped. In a moment, even the burning bales cooled. The dark creature stood still as if recognizing the grey man's feat of power.

Tilting its head in that bizarre manner, it spoke,

*"It is not your place to interfere, Keeper. You risk much."*

The grey man shook its head,

"Long have your kind slept. Much has changed. We no longer keep. We guard. We protect."

The dark one made a dismissive gesture.

*"Nothing changes. We are kin. Blood calls to blood."*

The grey man seemed to sag briefly for a moment; as if a great emotional weight suddenly were on his shoulders. Collecting himself, he straightened and met the creatures stare.

"We are kin no longer. We have chosen."

The dark one stepped back, as if struck by a physical blow.

*"You deny the blood? The Father's blood; the Mother's blood?"*

""We deny the Father's blood. We deny the destruction. We deny the corruption. We have chosen."

The grey man's answer seemed to rock the dark creature.

"Now go. Alone you cannot defeat me. I wish you no further harm."

The two figures stood for several moments and seemed to ponder the other. John got the impression that the dark creature was shocked to its core; emotionally devastated by the grey man's words. Or, whatever this thing passed off as emotions, in any event.

Suddenly, the dark creature flung its hands in the air, black fire enveloped its form, and just as quickly, it was gone. Nothing indicated it had even been present, except a dark patch of scorched earth.

For several moments, the grey man simply stared straight ahead; as if shaking himself awake; he turned and strode back towards one of the smoldering bales. John watched almost dispassionately as the red robed mage accepted help from the grey figure. Turning, John approached the stone wheel.

Grach's blow had struck the back of Breg's head, leaving his face undamaged. The man's face lay to one side; a cheek pressing against the cold of his dead shoulder. His eyes were wide open having kept the same expression when he had seen John; of hope. It almost broke John's heart to see it. Without knowing if it would work, he swung the great ax against the chain holding the wheel. The blade sliced through the metal with a crunch; the wheel landed with a thud still standing for a moment; then, slowly, it fell over. Looking up, John could see that the fire had burned holes in the ceiling, allowing pinpoints of stars and moonlight to shine on the mangled body of his friend.

Placing his weapon to the side, he knelt down and gently moved Breg's head so he could look up and view the darkened night, with the stars gleaming. With as much care as he could muster, John placed the man's damaged lungs back into his chest cavity. He then took off his green guards cloak and draped it over Breg; a simple act of decency that attempted to hide the horror of the final moments of the man's life. He bowed his head for a moment, no words, nothing profound came to his mind; he simply knelt silently.

Suddenly, John's head snapped around; Grach. Where was the plant man? Rising to his feet, he called.

"Grach! Grach!"

Where had he gone?

"Here my friend."

Turning, he saw the molden appear out of the smoky shadows. Before him, he roughly pushed a familiar figure.

"Look who I found skulking about. A long lost friend?"

John peered for a moment, recognizing the frog like figure standing before him.

"Calphan?"

The Mok merchant looked a little worse for wear. Burn marks scorched his cheeks, his clothing was ripped in places, and someone had given him a thumb sized bump above his left eye. Still, the merchant managed to comport himself enough to appear quietly non-pulsed by his current situation.

John stepped forward, and grabbed the Mok by the neck; yanking him to his tiptoes, he spat in the green face.

"Did you see Breg? Did you do that to him? Did you?"

Calphan's silence enraged him. With a cry, he threw the big frog across the dirt floor. With a heavy thud, the merchant's body hit one of the smoking wool bales; grunting in pain, his limp green body slid to the dirt floor. Grach stood back, watching his friend's fury; just watching.

Not satisfied, John approached the unconscious Mok and aimed a kick at his ribs. Flailing onto his back unconscious, Calphan laid still. John grunted in disgust at the merchant's shallow breathing.

"Enough."

A female voice rang out.

At that moment, the grey man and the red robed mage joined them. Leaning heavily on her grey companion, though her face was pale the mages blue eyes seemed to take everything in. John noticed that her ankle had been bound in a grey wrap. Seeing the red stain seeping through the material he winced in pain; remembering a number of ankle related injuries from his college football days. She was about to comment on something when Mr. Grey said,

"While the fires are out, this building is not secure. We must get to the safety of the street."

Shaking his head, Grach said,

"There is not much safety in the streets, strange one. There are fires all over the city; people are running in panic."

Pushing away from the grey man, the mage asked,

"What is he talking about?"

Shrugging, he motioned towards the unconscious Mok.

"We learned of plans by the Empire a number of days ago. We suspected that the Empress would try some internal attack on the Mages Council; an assassination attempt of some kind. We considered it a private matter between the Empire and Council. You know our position on such things."

While she nodded in understanding, the mage began to tremble. She took two hop like steps away from him and asked,

"What has happened?"

With a sigh, he closed black on black eyes, and tilted his head to the side, as if listening. After a few silent moments, the grey man answered,

"There was an attack on the Citadel. Many mages were killed; but it seems as if the intruders were repelled. The harbor is in chaos; an armada of Mok warships have disembarked a force which is now attacking the lower city. They have little chance of success against the city walls and defenses; it makes little sense; there is small chance of victory by the invaders."

John listened silently. Then asked,

"What changed?"

The grey man seemed a little unsettled by the question.

"What changed?" John asked again.

Running a shaking hand through her hair, Gazell said in an exasperated tone,

"What do you mean? What changed? We have been attacked by the Mok Empire! The Empress has ripped asunder a treaty that has kept the peace for three hundred years, yet . . ."

"Shut up."

Gazell stopped her tirade in mid sentence. Her mouth hung open. No one had spoken to her like that in . . . well . . . ever.

With a wave of his hand, John pointed at the grey man.

"What changed? Why did you aid us? You called this an internal matter. But not now, obviously. What changed?"

The grey man placed his hands in the folds of his cloak, refusing to answer.

Frowning, John walked towards the black figure lying next to the wheel. The creatures black garments had parted somewhat; John could see a black scaled arm exposed to the night air. Kneeling down, he pulled down the material covering the creatures face.

*Pretty*, he thought.

When the creature had hit the stone wheel during the battle, it must have struck head first. Most of the face was a crushed mess. What could be made out was altogether alien; reptilian. Black fangs protruded through full lips; a high arched forehead seemed to come to almost a point in the middle. In place of ears, three small holes were in evidence on each side of the head. Covering the face was a mass of black scales. Rising from his investigation, John looked at the grey figure watching him.

John pointed to the dead creature.

"This is what changed, isn't it? You did not expect these things."

Nodding, in concession, the grey man said,

"Yes. We did not predict their involvement."

"But you knew who I was, didn't you? You called me 'Human'. Your only the third to call me that since I arrived in this place."

The grey man had lapsed back into silence. Stepping forward, John stepped to within a few feet of him.

"You're an Orda, correct?"

Gazell tried to interrupt,

"Shut up!"

John's hand flamed. His scarred face flickered through the angry fire. He turned his gaze towards Gazell and said,

"I have a couple more pieces of this puzzle to put together. And His Royal Greyness here is going help me with those. As for you, I have no use for mages. You can either be quiet, or leave."

Hopping forward, Gazell placed herself right in front of the scarred man.

"I don't know where you come from, mund, but your training is sorely lacking! How dare you speak so to me! This city is under attack. We have to . . . wha?"

Slowly, Gazell felt herself being lifted off the ground. Grinding his teeth in concentration, John called air gently, not wishing to harm the annoying woman. When she rose high enough to meet his angry stare, he spoke softly, in a menacing whisper.

"I have seen what goes on in the citadel, woman. Thousands of Human Beings shackled in place; living through a waking nightmare. Not munds; Human Beings. Powering your rawstones. Their lives being eating away for your benefit; their bodies polluted and addicted. By my way of thinking, you are already guilty of horrible crimes; a solicitor of pain and abuse. So, shut your mouth or I will burn you to the ground. Understand?"

Gulping, the injured woman nodded. Satisfied, John turned back, gently lowering her to the floor. Out of the corner of his eye he saw Grach let the shocked woman lean on his shoulder. Her eyes wide with fear. Turning back, John asked,

"Now, you are Orda, correct?"

Silence for a moment. Then the grey head gave a slight nod.

"And you, or your kind, have been to my world, correct?"

Again, a belated affirmative.

"That's where you got the Meth; the White Tar isn't it?"

Again, a slight nod. John felt bile rise in his throat. Gulping down the rancid taste, he asked,

"Why?"

CALPHAN HAD been careless. He had stationed himself on one of the taller bales of wool to watch the ensuing battle. Things had started out much as the dark ones had anticipated; then, the Orda had shown up and things got very interesting. So engrossed was he in the battle, that he let his guard down; allowing the molden to get the drop on him.

It had been difficult for Calphan to let the mund handle him that way without immediate retaliation. But, he had quickly assessed the situation; he had no chance of escape being outnumbered in such a way. So, to avoid any further damage to himself, he feigned unconsciousness. And the ruse had worked perfectly; he had much to report to the Empress; though he understood little of it, and believed less. The mund was from another world? What nonsense. He had nearly chuckled at the mund's rough treatment of the High Mage. Served her right.

The Orda's revelation of the ineffectiveness of the attack did not surprise him. Success of the plan had rested on their dark allies' ability to quickly destroy the mund mage in the warehouse and then move to attack the cities defenses from within. Well, with two of their three allies dead, and the other fled, that was not likely to happen. Calphan had quickly estimated that even if Archen had managed to take out every mage target in the citadel that there were a little more than a hundred fully trained mages in and around the city. More than enough to blunt any attempted attack and subsequent occupation.

He simply had to wait until his fall back plan fell into place. Patience. Patience.

# CHAPTER TWENTY ONE

Gam cautiously peered out of the fire charred door. While he heard activity, it was not the mage clashing that had dominated the Citadel for the past several hours. Quietly closing the door, he turned back to his companions. Of the four guards who had accompanied Eldest Sister and Sister Kitla, only one survived; barely. The two sisters were working diligently on the man, trying to stop the bleeding. The girl, Tia, had stopped crying and was now holding the injured man's hand in both of hers.

*Damn, what a mess.*

If Gam lived for a hundred more years, he could not truly describe in any detail what happened. One minute, he and Tia are standing there next to their two mage guardians. Then, as Gam leaned over to say something slightly insulting to the mage closest to him, the poor man's head exploded. Blood and pieces of gore covered Gam's green uniform. The mage next to Tia acted immediately; sending a wave of mage fire against his assailants. Grabbing Tia in his arms, Gam bolted to the other side of the hall.

The four other guardsmen had formed a protective circle around the two sisters. Both of the women looked in horror filled shock at the scene before them. Mages, killing mages. It was something out of a nightmare.

The attacking mages all appeared to be Mok's. They had formed a square formation with a blue robed mage in the center. The group initially targeted the mages in the great hall. In a few minutes, the Mok's were the only living magic users in the large space. After a moment of quiet, as the dust settled over the shocked silence in the hall, the Mok's started in on the petitioners. In a matter of minutes, a panic induced mob was streaming towards the exit.

In the chaos, one of the guards slipped and was trampled to death. The group slowly began forcing their way through the press of the crowd. Seeing an opening, Gam raced for the relative safety of his fellow Guardsmen. Reaching them, he had handed Tia to Sister Kitla and had taken the dagger that one of the other guardsmen handed to him.

By the time they had made it to the relative safety of an old storage pantry of some kind, a second guard had been engulfed by mage fire, and another drowned by a wall of living water. The guard being attended by the Sisters had been nearly crushed by a piece of marble broken lose by an earth mage. Gam was amazed that any of them were alive.

He grimly watched as Eldest Sister slowly stopped her ministrations. Kitla reached over and closed the man's eyes, shaking her head. Tia gently raised the man's hand to her lips and kissed it; then slowly placed the unmoving fingers into his lap.

Stepping forward, Gam said quietly,

"Eldest. The fighting seems to have died down. If we are going to have a chance of reaching one of the barges, we should try now."

Nodding slowly, Eldest Sister rose. Placing her arms around Tia, she whispered something consoling into the girl's ear. Then, taking Tia in one hand, and Sister Kitla in the other, she nodded. Turning around, Gam opened the door slowly, and stepped into the hallway.

MOSHA WAS beside himself with fear. He had arrived at the library early in an attempt to gain access to the volumes on ancient scripts before his shift in the archives was to begin. Imagine his shock to be met by a crazed screaming mass of people pouring out of the Mages Hall; some of them injured by fire; many yelling that the mages had gone crazy and were killing people; others that the Mok's were attacking. Preposterous, all of it!

With no hope of swimming against the mass of crazed bodies, he had simply turned and had gone with the flow. Being a large man, it was difficult for members of the frightened mob to push him to the side. Mosha soon arrived, mostly undamaged, with the rest of the panicked citizenry to the outside barge landings. With a sigh of relief, the librarian saw scores of mages disembarking from one of the barges and rushing into the Citadel; not one of them was a Mok.

Turning, he viewed the city down below; from the citadel it was plain to see large green sided ships looming in the harbor. The huge vessels slowly and ponderously, were making their way to the wall of the lower city. Small plumes of fire could be seen coming from the ships and in return from the walls. This was madness!

"WHY?"

THE question echoed into the scorched remains of the warehouse. The Orda shifted a bit uncomfortably.

"Jonathan Champion. That is your name, yes?"

At his nod, the grey man continued,

"Jonathan Champion. Things are not always as they seem. Sacrifices need to be made; or all are doomed. All lost. Both worlds, lost."

John's face twisted in a grimace.

"I don't understand any of this. Sacrifices? Both worlds? All I know is what I have seen with my own eyes. And what they see is people, human beings, forced into using meth. Do you know how horrid that is? How twisted?"

At the Orda's non response, he asked,

"How long?"

Silence.

"How long have my people been used this way?"

Before an answer was forth coming, the earth trembled, sending everyone to their knees. A moment later, the warehouse was flooded with green skinned warriors; Mok's.

The Orda's reaction was immediate. Flinging his arms out, a grey twilight wall appeared, and several attackers were flung off their feet. John immediately turned to face the on rush; Grach now carried the injured mage in his arms to the safety of the Orda's magic.

It would have been utter foolishness to think that a dozen Mok warriors, no matter their skill, could hope to stand for long against two mages; even if one of the mages was a mund and the other injured. Nor was that the aim of the attack. The warriors were to keep the others distracted; off balance, until Calphan gave the signal.

Now was Calphan's chance. Leaping from his seeming unconscious state, he flung himself onto the big mund's back. With a cry of surprise, Champion went down in a heap as the Mok expertly paralyzed him with a strike to the neck. As the scarred man slumped to the ground at his feet Calphan pulled a rainbow colored stone from his shirt. Meeting the blue eyed glare of the female mage, her eyes widened at sight of the stone. With a cruel smile, Calphan clapped the stone in between his two hands. A short bright flash, and both man and Mok were gone.

GAZELL CONSIDERED the strange group in front of her; the story, once everyone gave their own chapter, was amazing. Tyrell sat on a chair, the protective Grach standing behind. To their left was the Eldest Sister and two of her fellow Sisters of the Sublime; one of them, Kitla, knew the mund mage intimately. Closely next to them stood a Green Guardsman and a delicate mund girl; Gam and Tia.

Across from them sat the fat librarian who fidgeted nervously, as he fingered a grey metal helm, his hand resting inside his rumpled shirt periodically; Gazell had not seen him for over ten years and his involvement had concerned her at first. Last, but definitely not least, sat the Orda.

The city had survived the attack with a minimal toll on its general populace. More deaths and injuries resulted from panic induced riots in the streets than to any Mok wielded weapon. Indeed, the heaviest losses were felt by the mages themselves. Eighty-three mages were killed; forty-five prior to the attack on the mage hall.

Archen and his coterie of traitors had spent the few hours before the attack on the Mages Hall tracking down fellow mages, one at a time and killing them; some in their private quarters. Of the fifty Mok mages in residence at the citadel, forty-three had participated in the conspiracy. Five were found dead in their beds; the two remaining were being held in custody. Nineteen of the traitors had been killed; the remaining, including High Mage Archen, were unaccounted for; for the time being.

Under mage supervision, companies of city guards and seren packs were searching every residence in the city; searching for anyone connected with the botched invasion. The search would take weeks as thousands of homes needed to be searched. Her eyes briefly traveled the faces in the room and rested on the Orda.

The grey man held an ax in his hands. Slowly, long grey fingers traced the rune like script on the grey blades. Grey skin contrasted with the dark black wooden shaft. His head bent over the weapon, it almost seemed as though the Orda were talking to it. Strange.

Clearing her throat, Gazell broke the silence.

"I think that we have all been rather misled."

All heads turned towards her; each face showed a different expression ranging from disdain, to defeat, to outright hostility; nothing friendly; nothing friendly at all.

"And who has been doing the misleading, honored one?"

When Tyrell spoke, while his voice was quietly respectful, his tone was filled with reproach. Before she could respond, she was interrupted,

"I did. We did. The Orda are to blame. To our everlasting shame." The grey man lifted his head from his musings.

"We are the Keepers. We turned our back on the kin. On the Fathers blood. We were charged. We carry the burden; a burden of two worlds."

"Charged with what? By whom?"

Gazell had forgotten the intelligence of the fat librarian. Ten years had not dulled the curious mind. The pudgy man leaned forward, waiting for an answer.

Chuckling softly, the Orda answered,

"Who else? By the Mages of course. We remember, even though they have forgotten."

# Chapter Twenty Two

John was floating in a strange place. He thought he was on a boat of some kind; a ship. Wooden walls surrounded him, and every now and then, he thought he could hear seagulls.

He tried to move, but his arms and legs were bound somehow. His mind was a foggy thing and it was impossible to wrap around any coherent thought. Every time his mind unclouded for a moment, someone leaned over him, a sharp pain in the arm, and he went back to floating. Sometimes he was fed; other times he went hungry. But he always floated; floated.

CALPHAN WAS not comfortable in the presence of the High Mage. Ever since the Armada had left the mages city, the small Mok had been a terror. His tyrannical attitude had even taken him so far as to openly question, in his words,

"What the hell was the Empress thinking?"

Now the two Mok silently stared at each other across the Boh-hat game board. Neither had made a move for several minutes, instead waiting for the other to blink or break the silence.

Blinking, finally, Archen slumped further into his chair. The cabin was plush by the standards of sea travel, but the small mage had complained endlessly about the cramped living conditions. Drumming his fingers on the arm of his chair, he broke the silence.

"Sixty seven."

At Calphan's questioning look, he continued.

"That's how many mages the Empire can count on. Sixty-Seven fully trained mages. Most of them water, at that."

Nodding, Calphan moved his green queen to a safer place on the board.

"It sounds like an impressive number, High Mage."

Snorting, Archen ignored the game board completely.

"Don't play me for a fool, spymaster. Even with the hurt we put on the Council, and we did hurt them, badly; however, we are still outnumbered three mages to one."

Glancing at the board, the mage moved his red horse away from the obvious trap. Settling back, he sipped from his glass. Calphan wrinkled his nose slightly; seaweed burbon was not to his taste.

"The Empress is confident in her plans. That she has not revealed the entirety of her plan does not allow us, her servants, to question it. Plus, it was not a total failure."

Green castle blocked red horse.

"You cannot be referring to that drug laced mund we have in the hull, can you? Worth the death of scores of mages? Of a treaty in tatters?"

Ahhh, thought the spymaster, the High Mage feels guilt in the death of so many of his fellow mages. It was understandable. As much as the rest of the world failed to understand the allegiance that each MoK felt towards the Empress, their ultimate brood mother, so too did the Empress forget the connection all mages had through their magic.

"Of course High Mage. You refer to the recent deaths of *Mok* mages of course?"

Shifting uncomfortably in his seat, the mage nodded his agreement.

In fact, the Empire was not in a weakened position; definitely not the strong outcome that the Empress had most likely expected, but not weakened. The Empire had been preparing for this war for three hundred years. Every year, the families of all the brood kin, great and small, had to provide the Empress with a special tithe; whether in materials, animals, munds, or both. This tithe had been handed over to the Chancellor of the Rod for the secret purpose of preparing for this very day; War.

The warehouses of the empire were bulging with rawstones to power their ships and weapons; food stuffs of all varieties and types stood ready to provide for the massive imperial force that would set out to take apart the shinning city; one magic brick at a time. This attack had just been a preemptive strike; a weakening blow to the mages to soften them up for the full out conquest that would follow.

Once the mages were removed, nothing would stop the northern expansion of the empire; nothing.

The timing was troubling. Calphan had the honor of actually being in the presence of Her Eternal Majesty on a number of occasions and listening, or eavesdropping, on important conversations among her most trusted ministers.

It was rumored among certain circles, that the Empress had projected that the Empire would be prepared to invade the north in five hundred years; that is as of the signing of the Treaty of Seven Fires. Five hundred years is nothing for an Empress who is immortal; indeed, some whispered that the treaty was not so much rammed down the Empire's throat but was proposed by the Empress herself.

So, many wondered at the recent invasion; wondered, not questioned. No one questioned the Empress; the Empire lived to serve her, not the other way around.

Calphan mentally threw that thought from his mind. Such thoughts could get a Mok killed; the Empress could sense her children's thoughts, it was rumored. Instead, the spymaster continued to play the board game with the little mage but his thoughts were on the mund.

His power had been impressive against the dark ones; and he had had the Ferrakei bitch nearly licking his boots.

He slowly savored that moment of fear he had seen in the blue woman's eyes. The Ferrekei people were a pest of a race. He would enjoy seeing them humbled and enslaved in his life time.

Yes, Champion was a feather in his cap; if they could find some way to use him, he would be a valuable asset to the Empress. In many ways the mund was impressive, regardless of his mage abilities. He was fearless and atypically proud for a mund. His pride allowed him to mentally think things through before he acted; instead of waiting for a master to decide for him.

On another note, it was taking an amazing amount of sedative to keep him under. The ship healer had worried out loud if there would be enough to last the trip back to Moksha. He would deal with that problem if it arose. Green warrior to red castle. The game was going well.

HE CONTUNUED to float. Almost listlessly. Sometimes he hallucinated. He imagined that he heard his loved ones voices; Rebecca's gentle scolding; Sam crying in the night. Other times it was Kitla or Tia; they were calling for him, screaming for his help. Still other times he heard Tyrell and Grach laughing. Sometimes he thought he joined in their laughter; he could not tell. With so many voices, it was hard to make out the one that was making the most sense.

"My Champion, tsk, tsk, why must you make such a mess of things?" he opened his eyes.

Sitting before him was Terra. Gone were the wooden walls; gone the nauseating floating, the pain in his arms. Reaching down, he found that his arms and legs were not bound. He sat instead, on a stone floor, in the cave where he had first met the crazy strange woman. The meeting place.

As usual, Terra was cooking something. Rising to his feet, John felt a little dizzy. Noticing this, Terra chuckled,

"Yes, the Mok is giving you some strong stuff. Come, sit next to Terra. We need to do something about that."

Walking over on unsteady legs, he slumped down next to the old woman. He watched as she slowly stirred a black pot over a small fire. The familiar smell of her hearty stew filled the air. An embarrassed growl escaped his stomach. Chuckling louder this time, Terra handed him a stone bowl, filled to the rim. Closing his eyes, he sipped the brew and felt its warm magic course through his body. Draining half of the stew, he opened his eyes and watched the strange woman work.

Her sure hands broke stocks of green leaves and ground them to a thin paste; then, from somewhere beneath her beggars cloak she produced a bag of spices. Carefully, she untied the string and poured a small portion of the sack into the pot; tossing in the paste, she again began to stir. He continued to slowly sip until the bowl was empty. Seeing his contented smile, she asked,

"Better, my Champion?"

"Yes, my lady, much better."

At that Terra laughed,

"I have been called many things, my Champion. Cook, lover, maiden, crone. But never a lady. Not until today." She laughed at her own weak humor. John smiled at her simple pleasure. Then, his smile faded. Seeing his face change, the old woman nodded,

"Yes, you have learned much in a short time, dear one. It is tough to swallow down in one gulp, is it not?"

"Very. Terra, the rawstones, they."

"Yes, dear one. I know." She had stopped tending the pot. Instead, she stared off into space, seeing nothing; as if remembering.

"You see, my Champion, we never considered that possibility. Never did we think the other races would use our children so; our grandchildren. Never in a thousand possibilities did we think that so much memory would be discarded; our sacrifice forgotten. So much pain; so much suffering. Never did we see this."

Tears slowly flowed down the old woman's browned cheeks. Reaching out, John brushed them gently away. Taking his hand she pressed her face into his palm and quietly wept. Feeling his own tears begin to flow, he asked in a cracked voice,

"You're a mage?"

Nodding, she lifted her face from his hand. From somewhere she produced a satin handkerchief. Soaking up her tears, she reached over and wiped off his tear damp hand.

"For all intents and purposes, I am a mage. I can share my knowledge with you and guide you at times. And trust me my Champion, I have not found a newly awakened mage who needs more guidance than you; and that is saying something."

The strange couple shared a laugh.

"I cannot share everything with you; I know you have questions that burn for answers. But I am under certain, limitations. Will you accept that for now? Please?"

Taking her shaking hand in his own, he said softly.

"What can I do?"

HIS EYES opened. As promised, Terra had allowed him to wake right before the next dose of sedative. She claimed it was a concoction used to deaden a mages magic while being treated for serious injuries or sickness; to protect the healer from any unconscious magical use. The Mok's had adapted it to keep him under wraps.

While he was as clear headed as he had been for some time, still he felt the effects of the sedative. Slowly, almost sluggishly, he called fire. Looking down at his bound scarred hand, he smiled as a small flame appeared.

Gently, slowly, he urged the flame to light on the bonds that held his arms. Leather straps, oiled to keep them supple, were looped around his wrists. The same leather bound his ankles. Each strap was attached to a metal ring welded to the floor; most likely used to lash down goods for transport.

Slowly, the flame worked on the oiled leather; small spirals of black smoke curled in the air. Terra had cautioned him to call fire slowly and he now understood her warning; the drug muddied his thoughts and it was taking all of his effort to contain the small flame. Sweat had begun to create small beads of moisture on his forehead; it was taxing.

Finally, after a few eternal minutes, the strap gave way. Grimacing, he took a moment to flex his fingers and get blood flowing back into his wrist and arm. Taking a slow breath, he began working on the other straps; though his head throbbed, he did not relent. He was not sure how much time he had before his jailer returned.

Ten minutes later he was free of the bonds; his body shook with the effort. He had not eaten properly in a number of days; add that to the sedative's side effects and his stomach was a rolling mess. He needed some water and something to eat desperately; but he had one more task he had to complete.

Sitting down in a corner, his nose wrinkled at his own stench; the Mok's had left him in his guardsman uniform and the smell told him he needed a bath. Seeing a nearby chamber pot showed that someone had been allowing him to address nature's necessities.

*At least they did not let me shit on myself. Thanks guys.*

Leaning his head against the creaking wooden hull, he closed his eyes; he mentally reviewed Terra's instructions:

*A veil of concealment is tricky, my Champion. It is more than simply calling fire and air; it is blending them together; weaving their threads like a seamstress. Usually it is performed by two mages; one fire, one air. A few times in our history has one mage controlled fire and air to the extent to create one single handedly. Remember, air and fire are linked; fire needs air to breath, to survive; through fire, Air becomes more destructive. Fire will resist the most. Now, try it, slowly.*

With her voice in the back of his memory, he slowly called air; then fire. In his scarred had, a flame appeared; concentrating, he slowly coaxed the flame into a long, fiery thread. In his other hand, he felt a small swirling of air; closing his eyes, he pictured air, and pushed the element into a long thin, thread. With his eyes still closed, he fixed in his mind the threading of the two; air on fire; fire on air.

Slowly he felt the two merge; meld. There was resistance from fire; it was not its nature to submit; air tried to be elusive; it resisted being tied to fire. But, it worked; the two threaded together. He opened his eyes to look down at his hands to see; nothing. The wooden floor of the ships stared back at him.

Moving his hand to the right, it appeared as if like magic. Which it was. He had created a small veil of concealment about a foot wide and two feet long. Smiling with excitement, he closed his eyes and called the two elements; fire and air became easier to manipulate into the weaving. Soon, he had a concealment veil that could cover his entire body.

He was shaking from the exertion and the lack of food. He was sure that his empty stomach would rebel soon. Nothing like a good dose of the dry heaves. He had one thing that needed to be done.

The next step was to attach it; Bind it. Terra had cautioned him:

*A concealment veil is a very useful thing; but in order to move about the Mok ship, it must move with you, my Champion. It must be attached to something; a cloak, a shirt. Most likely your guardsman uniform; lucky thing the Mok's didn't strip you bare.*

Yeah, but they took my gauntlets.

*Fucking thieves.*

The binding should not be that difficult; he lightly gripped his veil, it was a physical thing now; it had a strange wispy warm texture. Gripping the edge of his uniform sleeve, he tied the two together. Using threads from his uniform he was able to attach the veil. The veil now could be worn, albeit a bit awkwardly, by draping the unattached portion over his shoulders and head. Looking down, he saw that the length was a bit longer than he had at first anticipated and he would need to be careful that he did not trip as he walked. He was pleased to note that he could see through the veil.

After he had given a grunt of satisfaction with his clumsy results, his stomach decided to assert itself. It was not as though he was completely unprepared; it was just the timing. Because as he retched out his stomach contents, was the exact moment that the Mok Healer decided to check on his charge.

If his current situation wasn't so precarious, John would have taken a moment to appreciate the moment; the Mok healer getting a face full of puke as if appearing out of thin air. Instead, before the green man could raise a hand to wipe his face off, John drove a fist into the unsuspecting Mok's throat. With a gurgled gasp, the healer slowly slid to the floor. Silently thanking Gam for all of the hands on instruction in effective cheap shots, John dragged the healer out of the doorway. Glancing down to make sure he was covered by the veil, he stepped out into the hallway.

According to Terra all Mok ships were built along similar lines. The entire structure was built around the main artery of the whole operation; the stone room. It was here that the rawstones were used to power the heavy iron machine that propelled the vessel. The stone room was usually located in the center of the hull of the ship; very close to where John had been imprisoned.

Of course, this was the first time that John had been on a Mok Vessel and therefore, had no idea where to start. So, he made the dangerous decision to start looking on deck. Waiting until the ladders were clear, he quickly made the way up top.

John was impressed that there was so much room on the vessels deck. A huge open space allowed the Mok's freedom from bumping into each other. Like modern earth ships, the Mok's did not need to rely on wind power; indeed the vessel had no masts of any shape or form. Instead, in the middle of the deck was a set of very large, metal tube cannons. At least that is what they suspiciously looked like. It was impossible to get close to the things as there were Mok sailors constantly vigilant.

John saw that he was actually on the bottom level of the deck. The upper deck was reached by a set of stairs which were located at the aft of the vessel. On the upper deck there appeared to be sets of smaller cannon's and a large structure which was most likely command central for the ship; judging by the number of Mok's going in and out of the large double doors. Armed Mok warriors patrolled the upper deck, eyes watching everything, large blades were strapped to their backs; some held black colored cudgels as well.

This ship was crawling with frogs. Carefully, John began to search the lower deck.

CALPHAN FELT agitated; he would not admit to being worried; yet. He had checked on the mund prisoner earlier this morning and was satisfied that the man was still under heavy sedation. The armada was making good time; the danger of being caught by any force in pursuit was minimal; as long as they kept their current speed and course. No, he just felt a brief feeling of apprehension. A gut feeling that something was not quite right. Shaking his head, he decided to take a walk out on the deck to clear his thoughts.

CHAMPION HAD seen Calphan appear on deck from a side door. Acting on the spur of the moment, he quietly walked a wide path around the treacherous merchant and entered the door the Mok had recently exited. Closing the door behind him, John found himself in a small cabin. A bunk, a small writing desk and a built in cabinet with doors were the room's only furnishings. Walking toward the cabinet, he tried to open it. Locked; what a surprise. Calling on fire; John formed a small fiery shaft that he used to pierce the cabinets key hole; a few moments later, a satisfying crack from the cabinet, and the doors swung open. Lying next to a number of books and papers were his missing gauntlets. The feel of the metal was reassuring on his knuckles. Closing the cabinet doors, he quietly exited the cabin.

CALPHAN HAD spent nearly an hour out of his cabin. He had proceeded to the upper deck to give his regards to the captain. Then a leisurely walk around the upper and lower deck had allowed him to unwind.

By the time he had returned to his living quarters, he was relaxed and looking forward to a short rest before the evening meal; he was feeling so good that he might even look in on Archen and see if the surly mage was up for a game rematch. Coming to the door of his cabin, he stopped. Reaching his hand up to the top of the doorway, he pulled down a light brown thread. It was broken; almost neatly in half.

Out of habit, the spymaster had attached one end of the thread to the door and the other to the wood door frame. He used the sticky nectar of a Geish flower to attach the thread. It was a beginner's trick; used to see if a door had been opened. Many of Calphan's associates would have thought such a measure paranoid; after all, he was on a Mok ship surrounded by an armada. Of course, some of Calphan's most dangerous enemies had been Mok's, so he kept in practice with the thread alarm.

Quietly pulling out a wickedly curved dagger, he pushed the door open. At first glance, nothing was out of order. His bunk was made; the desk and chair were in place. Approaching the cabinet, he noticed that the metal on the lock had been somewhat charred. With a feeling of dire consequences filling his thoughts he opened the cabinet, even though he knew what he would find; or rather, what he would not find. He spent all of a second, looking at the charred remains of the cabinet lock before he lunged for the door.

JOHN SNORTED in disgust. He had spent nearly an hour looking over the ship trying to find what Terra had called the stone room; he finally discovered it one doorway down the long hallway from where he had been imprisoned.

Incapacitating the guard had been easy; a sucker punch from an invisible assailant is hard to defend. He had then cut the Mok's throat with the guards own blade; feeling a moment of guilt he pushed it aside; transferring all his concentration on the task before him. In the center of the stone room, was an odd metal device.

A circular wheel was perched on a pedestal; shooting from the wheel were seven metal tubes that disappeared into the walls of the room; making the device look like some sort of mechanized spider. Attached to the wheel were seven rawstones; each of varying colors. The device hummed with an eerie sound that made the floors shake. The stones seemed to vibrate and glow to the beat of the humming. Somehow this thing allowed the vessel to operate though John's earth bound mind had no idea how it functioned. As he studied the machine, he heard the memory of Terra's voice break through his musings.

*Don't get caught up in the Mok's ingenuity; they are as creative as their Empress allows. Instead concentrate on your task; find the stones; create the link.*

This was the basis around which Terra's plan had been formed. It was very likely that Hyberan had sent a force in pursuit; however, it was also very likely the Mok's would reach their territory before any force could catch up with the armada. So, the armada had to be slowed; or even stopped. Thus the stones; the link.

*"What are the stones, my Champion?"*

*"Meth?"*

*"Well, yes. Meth is a part. What is the other part? And don't be dense and say "Stone" either."*

*He had thought a moment.*

*"Life Force."*

"Yes. Yes, and what kind of life force? Human Life force. It is, may be, possible to link the stones on your vessel to those of the other ships in the armada. Link them, and then drain them of their life force."

"How? With what?"

"With this."

Ow. The bitch had poked him in the eye; his white eye. Apparently this dream/hallucination world allowed Terra to abuse him.

Chuckling, she said,

"Yes. This wonderful eye of yours. It allows you to see much if you would only use it. Among other things, fire is the element of seeing; of inner sight. The inner eye. Use it. You went through much pain to get it."

Closing his eyes, he took a deep breath. Slowly, he opened his white eye; keeping the other closed. Stepping towards the wheel, he leaned closer towards a red colored stone; looking deeply into its depths; watching the inner pulsing and flaring of the stones force, he waited.

Slowly, a small red line appeared reaching out from the stone; slowly it materialized, flickering slightly. At first it appeared that the line linked with the stone next to it; but then, a moment later, other lines began taking shape; lines from the other six stones; a matrix of flickering lines, over lapping and connected.

It was beautiful. Like a hidden world suddenly uncovered. The matrix of lines spread a pattern that seemed to go out of the room; out of the ship. If Terra's hypothesis was correct, these lines connected themselves to the other stones in the armada; or even other stones on the nearby shores.

What he needed to do was to drain the stones; to bleed them of the life force that allowed the ships to be powered. With a gentle touch, he called fire; softly, gently, he sent the element into the matrix; slowly, slowly. He needed the stones to burn their life force faster; and fire would do that. But fire was an unstable element at the best of times; it had to be precise; and controlled. Terra had told him to rein in the element; fire could not be freed in the matrix.

Slowly, he could feel the stones in the stone room weaken; their glowing faded; dulled noticeably. He hoped it was the same on the other ships. It was working. It was working.

THE GROUP moved down the hallway quickly; Calphan, High Mage Archen, and three Mok warriors. The warriors proceeded to the room where the mund was being confined. Stepping forward the warriors positioned themselves; one on either side of the door, the third facing it. At a nod, the door was kicked it. The spymaster quickly surveyed the room; the burned leather straps; the unconscious healer lying in a slumped pile in a corner. Motioning for one of the guards to attend the healer, he turned and led the group down the hall way. Similar searches were happening all over the ship. Calphan estimated that Champion had been free for almost two hours.

But what could he possibly hope to accomplish? Flight? Impossible with the ship moving at such a speed. Fight? Even with his impressive power Champion would at some point be out numbered and overtaken. What then? He stopped suddenly, making Archen curse as the mage ran into the spymasters back.

Sabotage. It was the only feasible option; Sabotage and delay. Delay for a rescue. Turning abruptly, Calphan headed towards the stone room. Sabotage.

JOHN WAS exhausted. The lack of food and the constant exertions from calling fire; even in such small amounts, was draining him. He only needed a few more minutes and the stones would be drained enough to stop the vessel; hopefully all the vessels. God he was tired.

Calphan burst into the stone room. Spread out on the floor, the body of a Mok warrior lay in a green pool of his own blood. Other than the dead guard, the room was empty. He ground his teeth in frustration. The spymaster had been sure that he was on the right trail. Why kill the guard and then leave the device in tact? Why?

Archen and the two warriors followed him into the room a short time later. The mage looked a bit baffled; and irritated. It was a bit disconcerting for the High Mage to be outsmarted by another mage; let alone a mund. He was about to give the spymaster a vicious opinion of his skills when something caught his eye.

"Look."

The mage pointed. Following his arm, Calphan looked at the device. The machine hummed along like it always did; fueling the ships engines.

"Look at the stones, you fools."

This time Calphan did notice it. The stones were dim; and flickering in a strange way. Walking forward, he was startled when he bumped into something; and even more startled when he heard a grunt out of the thin air. Putting out a trembling hand; his fingers met something solid; something that his eyes did not register.

"A concealment veil."

Giving the mage a questioning look, Archen repeated, "The mund must have a concealment veil."

The mage motioned the two warriors forward.

JOHN WAS losing himself. What he and Terra had not considered was the drain on his own life force. The matrix was so overwhelming, the drain of the stones so all encompassing, he was frozen in place; unable to remove himself from the matrix as the stones died out. While he felt his own life force ebbing slowly from his body, he could not feel despair. The matrix of life force he was witnessing, experiencing, was amazing. Each stone was akin to a piece of a human beings life; their fears, hopes, dreams, loves. All caught briefly in the stones. He was experiencing the lives of dozens of people; he knew their names, their favorite colors, their emotions. It was overwhelming, yet exhilarating. If given the choice between his ordinary life and leaving the wonders of the matrix, it would be a hard decision.

Walking forward, Archen reached his hand out; seeming to grab the very air, he wrenched the hand down. As if he had removed the hood of a cloak, there appeared the head of Champion. But just his head; floating there. The rest of his body was missing.

Calphan looked with slack jawed amazement as the High Mage gave another wrench of his hand and the tall mund came fully into view. Amazing. Even Archen seemed impressed.

The two warriors, who had momentarily been prepared to move forward, suddenly hung back; wary. The mund did not move a muscle upon his recent unveiling. Instead he stood transfixed; staring at the mechanism before him; with one eye closed. It was almost comical.

Archen would admit that this creature, this mund mage of all things, bothered him. He was a very orderly and conservative Mok. Everything in the world had its place; with the Empress and her children given the highest of pedestals of course.

But before him was a mund; a member of a magic less people. A people who for centuries, if not eons, were used much like chattel; beasts of burden. But here was this mund, this lug of an inferior breed, who was working some kind of mage magic, and Archen had no idea what it was.

He could feel something in the air; something that the mund was causing. Somehow the man was interfering with the workings of the rawstones; which should be impossible. It was not as if the mund were destroying or damaging the stones; that by itself was something that was understandable; explainable. What he seemed to be doing was beyond the High Mages experience. Something new; something foreign; something dangerous.

He watched as the spymaster stepped in front of the mund; and spoke.

"Champion. It is over. Give yourself up."

FROM A great distance, John heard a voice. He recognized it; not a friends voice, no. But he recognized it. He followed it; followed it out of the matrix. Away from the emotions, the life force, the spiritual ecstasy.

He felt himself somehow still connected to the lines, but he could breath. He could feel his own body; his hands. God he was tired; hungry; sick. But alive. Taking a deep breath, he opened his other eye to see a face in front of him. A recognized face. A green frog like face that sneered up at him.

Its over? Give himself up? Why? What was so important about this face? Not the face itself; no. Something other; some memory. He swayed a little, lifting his hands to his face; covering his eyes. He heard another voice, this one he did not recognize, say something; give an order. He felt his arms being secured behind his back. What was the memory? Why was it important?

And then there it was; in his mind. A stone wheel; a broken body; a dying man saying two breathless words. He remembered.

Opening his eyes, he regarded the triumphant smile of Calphan. Glaring down at the offensive toad, he said,

"Mund Mage."

Startled, the Mok looked up.

"What? Awake are you? You led us quite a chase. Remind me to relieve you of those pretty metal gloves. I must remand the healer to use more of the drug. You are surprisingly resourceful; for a mund."

He motioned to the guards who now had Champion secured.

John shook his head,

"No, that's what he called me. He called me a mund mage."

Making a distasteful expression, Calphan asked,

"Who? You are a freak, yes. An asset for the Empress, maybe. But a Mage? Who called you that? What fool said this?"

Time seemed to stop as John recalled Terra's last warnings to him.

*Now, my Champion, whatever you do, do not give in to your anger; especially when you are connected to the matrix. Control your anger; especially with fire. You don't want that element getting loose.*

Looking down on the spiteful green man, with Terra's words fading into the recesses of his mind, John said,

"Breg. Breg called me a mage."

John had the momentary satisfaction of seeing shame and then fear pass over the Mok's face. And then he called fire. He called it with wild abandon and furious intent. He could feel the elements joy at being free; felt its hunger as it spread uncontrolled down the lines; through the matrix, into the stones. For one heart beat, John looked into the matrix as flame engulfed the lines and smiled. Then, fire reigned.

# Chapter Twenty Three

Spuros could not remember being this happy; feeling this excitement in expectation. He looked over the remains of what seemed to be twenty ships; a small armada. Smoking hulls listed and wobbled in the slow lapping waters.

Hundreds of Mok corpses bobbed unmoving; their green blood changing the deep blue waters almost black. Some survivors clung to pieces of wood; their weak pleas going unnoticed for the time being. It was beautiful to the old corsair's eyes and ears.

War. That's what this meant. Word was the Mok Empire had attacked the Shinning City. By the remains of the armada, the mages must have taken exception to the invasion. War. Profit beyond his dreams if he did it right; smuggling, slavery, ransoms; all would be increasing exponentially if his guess was right.

It had been years since there had been a great war; long before Spuros' grandfather had become a captain. In those days the Corsairs had been a force unto themselves; all the great powers had to either deal with or placate them. Until the Treaty of Seven Fires. Until the mages and the Mok's agreed to root out and destroy the despoilers of the sea. Now the corsairs were a shadow of what they once were; a mockery of those great sea captains of old. Mostly thugs and thieves now; hiding in the dockyard shadows and scurrying out at night.

Nodding over to his First, the large Gurashi shouted out orders. Time to see the pickings; the beginning of a very large harvest. May it last a thousand years.

ELDEST SISTER hummed softly to herself. She lay back, playing with her hair and watching the large man work. They were in the quiet of her private quarters. She laid on her bed while the librarian had taken over the desk and chair.

Mosha had been devastated with the loss of Jonathan Champion. The Guardsman had told Mosha a story so extraordinary that the librarian's great intellect had been stunned; stunned by the mystery of it all. By the revelations that could be revealed. With the strange mund's loss, Mosha had almost grown morose with depression. For three days the librarian had wallowed in misery.

So, Eldest Sister had made a request of the Orda and High Mage Gazell; which had been granted. Now she watched with a sly smile as the librarian, now her personal representative from the library and mage council, leaned over the rune covered ax blade and helm. With the strange book now open, Mosha had been comparing the runes in an attempt to catalogue them. While he was engrossed in his work, she took stock of her large charge.

He needed to eat better. Vegetables from the temple gardens would do the trick. Also some routine exercise; walking at first and maybe swimming. She sighed as she let the pleasure of the intelligent man's presence wash over her.

Almost dreamily, she glanced down at what she had been reading. When Jonathan Champion had first arrived at the Great Temple and his unusual potential had been revealed, Eldest had immediately recalled the research of the brilliant, but strange, librarian. So, she had sought him out in an attempt to convince him to recall the ten year old work that she had commissioned. In the chaos of the failed invasion she had put the matter to the side.

Two days ago, Mosha had appeared and begged for her help to obtain access to the runes on the ax and helm that were currently in the charge of the Orda and the Counsel. She had made one request for helping him. Mosha's memory was amazing. It had taken him all of one night to write out the work from memory. A day later, the amazing man had provided it to her; complete with historical and library references. Amazing. Picking up the titled work, "The Mythical Race of Humans" she continued to read.

JOHN NO longer had any lasting sense of where he was or of the links between dreams and reality. The skin of his shoulders and arms had been blistered by the sun; his hands clenched the wood in a death grip he could no longer feel. Voices whispered in his mind, urging him to let go, to know peace. He ignored them.

Visions swam across his eyes; a two faced man who burned the whole world, a woman in a green dress with the face of a skull, black serpents rising up from the earth, grey cloaked figures huddled under a mountain.

Then he saw hundreds of people, humans, standing in a cavern, surrounding a strange old woman with bright blue eyes; one by one they approached the woman and slowly sank into her, their bodies melding. At last, the only one left in the cavern was the old woman, and she began to cry tears of fire.

The voices continued ceaselessly. One sounded like his uncle George, drunk and mean. Another was his mother, pleading with him to behave or he would get kicked out of Sunday school. He tried to answer her, but his lips were cracked, his tongue nothing but a dried stick in his mouth. Then came the voice of his little brother, who had died at the age of five.

"Be with me brother. It is so lonely here. Play with me."

He might have given in then, but the driftwood tilted and his bloodshot eyes opened. He saw a white skull on a black background floating over the waters. After a while he felt something touch him and opened his eyes. A powerful bald headed man with a black beard was floating alongside him. John tried to say something, but only tortured air came out.

"He's alive!"

He heard the man shout.

"Throw down a rope."

Then the man spoke to him.

"You can let go now. You are safe."

John clung on. No dream voices were going to lure him to his death.

The driftwood thumped against the side of a ship. John looked up at the bank of oars above him. Men were leaning out of the ports. A rope was tied around his waist, and he felt himself being lifted from the water.

"Let go of the wood," said his bearded rescuer.

Now John wanted to, but he could not. There was no feeling in his hands. The swimmer gently pried his fingers open. The rope tightened, and he was lifted from the sea and pulled over the deck rail, where he flopped to the timbers. He cried out as the raw sunburn on his back scraped against the wood, the cry tearing the dry tissue of his throat. A young man with bright red hair and grey eyes squatted down next to him.

"Fetch some water," grey eyes called over his shoulder.

John was helped into a sitting position, and a cup was held to his mouth. At first his parched throat was unable to swallow. Each time he tried he gagged.

"Slowly!" Advised the grey eyed man.

"Hold it in your mouth. Allow it to trickle down."

Swirling the liquid around his mouth, he tried again. A small amount of cool water flowed down his throat. He had never tasted anything so sweet and fulfilling.

Then he passed out.

# Special Note

If you are currently dealing with a meth addiction, or have a friend or loved one who is, and you just don't know where to start, please consider using or contacting the resources below.

http://www.whitehouse.gov/ondcp/meth-intro
http://meth-kills.org/resources.html
http://www.drugabuse.gov/drugs-abuse/methamphetamine

If you are interested in a literary work that does an amazing job of providing the history and background of the Meth problem in the United States please read Methland: The Death and Life of an American Small Town by Nick Redding. It is a well written work and the information it provides is as fascinating as it is shocking.

# ABOUT THE AUTHOR

J.E. Horn was born and raised in Alaska. He currently lives in the northern Chicago Suburbs with his wife and two children. When not writing, he is an attorney and full time baseball/golf/gymnastics/swimming dad for his kids. His cherished hope is that the Chicago Cubs will win the World Series in his lifetime.